Night Crawler Lake
An Unlikely Ghost Story

Kurt Mueller
Alaskan Veteran, Educator, and Author

PUBLICATION
CONSULTANTS
WE BELIEVE IN THE POWER OF AUTHORS

PO Box 221974 Anchorage, Alaska 99522-1974
books@publicationconsultants.com, www.publicationconsultants.com

ISBN Number: 978-1-63747-128-9
eBook ISBN Number: 978-1-63747-129-6

Library of Congress Number: 2022923684

Manufactured in the United States of America

Dedication

For Meg

Author's Note

Contents

Introduction

My name is Eric Luft, and I have a story to tell. I'm nearly 12 years old, and I'm going into the 7th grade this fall if I can get this almost impossible writing assignment done. Reverend Leverkuehn says I'm precocious. I believe he thinks I'm precocious because sometimes I use big words for an almost seventh grader. The truth is that I use big words because I like reading my dad's encyclopedia. The whole set is leather-bound. When I read it, it's like my dad's talking to me, but in a different way than when I imagine he's talking to me from his picture hanging on the wall in my bedroom.

Constable Benny has a different opinion about me than Reverend Leverkuehn. Constable Benny says that I'm technically a juvenile delinquent, because of what happened late last fall. I know he's right on that one little point, otherwise I wouldn't be sitting here in a

church on such a nice and sunny morning during Spring Vacation.
Well, unless it's a Sunday morning. Then I'd be in church probably
anyway. Constable Benny seems to like me well enough though, just
like Miss Flieschburger, Miss Lindquist and Mr. Red Cloud. They
like me, and so I don't *feel* like a juvenile delinquent, but I know
my behavior has been frustrating everybody, and I'm sorry about the
harm I've caused.

So here I am, sitting in Reverend Leverkuehn's library across the hall
from his office. He's got Mozart going on the record player in there,
because that's what he always does. I wish he'd play Elvis. I learned that
Mozart started composing when he was five years old. Heck, I didn't
even learn how to tie my own shoes until I was five.

I'm going to spend about an hour a day here, for I don't know how
many days, but at least through Spring Vacation, because I'm still on
the mend, and can't do any real chores. I'm writing everything down
about what happened. This could get very boring, but it could be worse.
There are books in here that look sort of interesting, and some of them
are bound in leather just about as good as my dad's encyclopedia set.
Plus, there's this cool picture hanging above one of the bookcases. It's a
woodcut by this German guy named Albrecht Durr, and it's called the
Four Horsemen. It has something to do with the Book of Revelations.
Well, let me get back to my own revelations.

The way I'm supposed to write this is to not get ahead of myself, and
to just write like I talk, as if I'm telling a story around the campfire. It's
Constable Benny, Reverend Leverkuehn, and Miss Flieschburger who
are asking me to do this. It's not like I absolutely must write this all
down, but Constable Benny is continuing to work on his final report
about what happened at Klammer Lake, and he wants more insight
from me. Reverend Leverkuehn is working on his own research paper
for theological and metaphysical reasons, and he is interested in the
voices that I used to hear in my head.

I'm willing to write about those voices, but it's not something I've
talked about to other adults very much, except my mom. It makes my
mom uncomfortable. Also, I really do want to get passed into the seventh grade, and of course this is where Miss Flieschburger comes in.

My deal is this; Constable Benny told me doing this would be for my own good. Plus, Reverend Leverkuehn and me have a signed contract which says I'll get a nickel for every typewritten page. So not only do I get to work off part of my probation here at the church, but by turning this writing assignment into my teacher I get passed to the seventh grade. And I get paid. It's not like I'm sitting here wasting my time.

However, I very much do not want to be here. It is so nice outside. I would much rather be making money walking around outdoors looking for empty pop bottles in the ditches around town. I cash those bottles in at Swenson's for two cents a bottle. Of course, I don't have the puff for walking around town as much as I used to, but they tell me I'm getting better because of the medication.

I can't take the credit for typing up this writing assignment. Mrs. Nackedy, the church's secretary and main bottle-washer will be doing the typing on a brand spanking-new IBM electric typewriter. She is going to use carbon paper so both Reverend Leverkuehn and Constable Benny have copies. Constable Benny says the copy turned into Miss Flieschburger may have parts of it blacked out.

Mrs. Nackedy's a widow, and I think Constable Benny and Mrs. Nackedy have some sort of contract between themselves as part of this writing assignment, too. They seem to spend a lot of time conferring in Reverend Leverkuehn's office while the good Reverend is out and about.

But before I start, I want to give a word of warning to Mrs. Nackedy and to Reverend Leverkuehn (and to Miss Flieschburger in case Constable Benny misses blacking out some of the parts of my story that has some naughty words). Sometimes my language gets salty. But I'm going to write just like I talk. I don't swear all that much, but sometimes I do. But I don't want Mrs. Nackedy to faint or something, and then have her think that I'm incorrigible. So instead of writing down the actual swear words me and my friends use, I'll write in #!%x like they do in the Sunday funny papers, like when some cartoon guy hits his thumb with a hammer. That way Mrs. Nackedy won't faint, and my probation officer won't call me incorrigible in his report.

I pick up most of my bad language from Dingo. Dingo is not his real name. His real name is Allen, but we all call him Dingo. I'll get to why we call him Dingo in due course, because I don't want to get ahead of myself. Dingo's Dad, as everyone knows, was in the Navy. One of the great pleasures of life is to be around when Dingo's pop bangs his thumb with a hammer, or drops a cement block on his foot, or gets the handle of a screwdriver bumped into his eye, like the time he was fixing a door hinge and we came busting through the door on the other side while playing tag.

This writing assignment of mine is supposed to be sort of hush-hush. I've been told to not talk about this very much to other kids, because of the sensitive nature of the investigation, and because of matters of confidentiality. I don't get the restriction, because my friends were all part of this. I'm not even supposed to discuss the fact I'm writing this with any of them. All they know is I'm working off part of my probation here at the church. I'm sure they'll be nosing around here sooner or later.

I know there are probably going to be other adults who read this besides Mrs. Nackedey, Reverend Leverkuehn, Miss Flieschburger and Constable Benny. I wish to apologize right off the bat and ahead of time not only to Mrs. Nackedey and to Reverend Leverkuehn for my language, but also to Mom, and to Miss Flieschburger, and Miss Lindquist, and Mrs. Wilcox, and to Mrs. Alighieri, and Mrs. Peterson, and to Mrs. Gustavsson, and to Grandma Lundgren. And just in case, to Mr. Red Cloud. I don't reckon I need to apologize to Constable Benny, because he's the one who told me to just write down my story like I was telling it around a campfire.

Sincerely,

Eric Luft

A Rite of Spring

Well, here I am again like yesterday. It's another nice sunny day and I'm stuck here in Reverend Leverkuehn's study. It's not a library, it's a study. It could be worse. I took a break yesterday and looked at one of his books, just for a little while. It's a book by Dante, with pictures in it like I've never seen before of demons and stuff. So, it could be worse.

When I came in to sit down, there were three typed pages sitting on the table, with a shiny dime and a dull nickel on top of them. I thought at first maybe it was some paperwork of Reverend Leverkuehn's. Then I realized it was my own writing. I was happy it looked so good, but then I got ticked off. I realized this little bit of change was my payment for yesterday. I was expecting more. Typed pages can really eat up pencil written pages. Now I know the true nature of the deal. Rats, rats, and more rats. But heck, I've started writing. I just wrote my first page today. It took me about a second. I wrote 'Part I'. Maybe I can get a nickel for that page. Ha! Well, nothing ventured, nothing gained. Today I'm just going to keep on going about as long as I did yesterday. Miss Flieschburger always says that the best way to start writing a story is to start writing it, so here I go.

I remember the first time I had any inkling about her. It was a memorable day which ended in a spooky night, at least for my sister. Aimee got really scared. Me, I just spooked myself a little bit that night. I don't really believe in ghosts, not even now. It was my own imagination all along. And it was my own imagination which caused us to have a very awful time indeed, and I have regrets to this very day. But I'm ahead of myself. Let me start with that day. I'm going to be very loquacious, because I'm getting paid to be!

Last year about this time we had a few days left of Spring Vacation, and there was nothing to do. Then Poopy pointed out it was high time for the Swamp Chicken Bike-Off. Now, Poopy isn't the sharpest tack in the box, but he often dares much, and we love him for it. So, without further deliberation we charged off to get our bikes, even though there was snow on the fields and in the culverts. The bike trails were still packed with snow. But things were starting to get melty you see, so it was time.

Poopy, by the way, is not his real name. His real name is Larry Alighieri. Yep, Larry has the same last name as Dante Alighieri, although back then Larry wouldn't have recognized Dante if Dante came up and bit Larry square in the butt. I've fixed things by showing Larry the part in Dante's Inferno where devils toot farts out of their own butts. Speaking of, there's a fine reason for Larry's nickname. Allow me to pontificate.

A few weeks prior to Spring Vacation we were having a quiet little farting contest in the back of Miss Lindquist's fourth and fifth grade classroom. In the back is where we all sat, but with Larry the farthest up, which put him at a serious disadvantage when our goofing off started in earnest. He got caught a lot.

Anyway, we were having this farting contest, but the rules were to keep it discreet, otherwise the girls sitting in our proximity would get annoyed to the point where they would rat us out. We were having a wonderful time, sneaking out a quiet one now and then, but most of the time just making small farting sounds with our hands and lips.

Larry turned back to us from his desk and whispered, "Hey boys, I got one for you." He reared up his right butt cheek and let fly with a truly Jovian blast, a two-parter. The first part, the Jovian blast part, was a deep and low octave growl. The second part was this high flute-like flutter that ended in an odd wet gurgling sound.

Larry's look of enthusiastic glee suddenly changed to one of surprised dismay. He had seriously blundered. He had been much louder than was appropriate, and as a result he was once again caught out. Miss Lindquist was looking right at him, and all the girls who were seated nearby were pointing at him. Acting quickly, Larry raised his hand and asked to go to the Nurse's office. Miss Lindquist readily agreed with his request. Larry got out of his desk and moved to the door with purpose but walking oddly like he was Charlie Chaplin. Also, I must note, when Larry stood up the air became very rank in the back of the classroom area.

Larry did not make it back to class that day, but when he came back the next day, he had himself a fine new nickname. As it stood, he became the third kid in our group to get any kind of nickname, up to that point in time. Larry became 'Poopy'. We still call him Poopy after all this time, and he always will be Poopy, Forever and Ever, Amen.

The first kid in our group to get a nickname was Allen Wilcox. He got his nickname in the second grade, before we really started hanging out together. Allen was sitting in a second grade reading circle, in these little blue chairs. They were reading a primer, something about Turkey Lurky and Ducky Lucky. Allen said something about how ducks aren't very lucky at all, and one of the other kids made a smart-mouth remark about Allen being a dumb farm kid. Allen flipped his lid, right then and there.

Allen threw his little blue chair at the other kid, giving the kid a big goose-egg right in the middle of his forehead. What got spread around the lunchroom and the recess yard was that Allen went 'dingy' during reading circle. Another telling had to do with Allen really 'dinging' another kid with a wooden chair. Somehow, as sometimes happens, older kids started calling Allen 'Dingo', and there you have it. That's how Dingo got his name – oh! Allen has been Dingo ever since, and will be For Ever and Ever, Amen. But I digress. I need to get on with my story.

As Poopy had pointed out, it was high time for the Swamp Chicken Bike-Off. So off we went to garages, basements, sheds and back porches to get our bikes. It took us a while to get back together, what with tires needing air and bolts needing tightening and so forth. However, we were hot to trot so it didn't take us too long to assemble. Our gathering point was at my house, which sits on a hill above the Swamp. Now, I guess it's not really a swamp. It's more of a big, irregular shaped pond, with cattails, muskrat houses, tall marsh grass, and trees along the east and west sides of the pond. The far end to the south is a marsh. And, while there are trees back there, it's still mushy ground, and that's why we call the whole thing the Swamp.

The afternoon air smelled like peeling birch bark and old bird nests. The day had started out sunny, with water running down the side of our driveway all the way down to the Gutzman driveway, where it pooled into a little pond in the middle of the road. Big fat dark clouds moved in, and a chilly breeze started up. Although water had started running, and the ice on the swamp was looking a bit dicey, it suddenly didn't really feel like spring. However Peachy said the ice looked rotten, which meant it was now indeed springtime.

It was a few years back that our glorious leader Peachy had the bright idea of riding our bikes down the hill and onto the ice as a Rite of Spring. At first, we didn't understand what Peachy was saying. I thought he was calling it a 'Riot of Spring'. I know this for sure, it has been a riot ever since. You see, at about this time of year the ice always looks kind of mushy and questionable, and we developed a stunt for this kind of ice.

Our stunt back then was to ride our bikes out as far onto the Swamp as we dared. The rule was he who goes out the farthest and makes it back without going through becomes the 'Grand Poo-Bah' for the rest of Spring Vacation. Poopy, as you may have guessed by now, had won the previous year, and he lusted for another shot at glory. The Beetle, or as we just call him, Beetle, was the most timorous this time out. His parents had told him that if he got into any more trouble with us, he would be grounded for a week, or he would have to stay away from us for a week, his choice.

While Poopy was still bragging about how far he was going to go out this year, Peachy dropped his coat and took off like a shot. He tore off down the hill, following what was left of our old sled trail. His was truly a demonstration of exceptional bike riding skill. He hit the ice, slid a bit sideways, reared up off his seat with his butt in the air, and kept on going.

Peachy got way, way out there. He rested his boot on one of the muskrat houses, looked at us with that big ****-eating grin of his, and yelled, "Come on then, you chickens!" He followed this with, "Buck, buck, *buck-cock*-buck!"

Beetle went next, his face kind of all scrunched up. He was not smiling when he took off. Beetle pretty much lost control of his bike about two thirds of the way down the hill in a spectacular sort of way. He slid sideways, hit the ice, landed on his side, and broke through. He squealed as he went in. It was right offshore in only about a foot of water, but it was a hoot. I laughed so hard I nearly wet my pants. Dingo was right next to me, and he was laughing hard, too. Then Dingo dropped his coat and pushed off while we were both still laughing.

It's always me and Dingo. We don't say it out loud, but we're always vying for who is really 'El Segundo' of our crew. This tests me, because Dingo is good at nearly everything, you name it. He took off just fast enough to keep up momentum, breaking with his boots on the sled trail as he went down. He then steered off the sled trail and onto the Swamp well away from where Beetle had made his hole in the ice.

Dingo peddled along slow and easy, all the while with the pond making these cracking sounds, with cracks appearing here and there at random. Dingo eased a little past Peachy and stopped. He then turned to Peachy and said, "I think I won, let's get out of here!"

"*Not so fast Dingo,*" I thought to myself. I saw a possible route that I could use to get out there, away from the hole that was welling with water. The water was spreading farther and farther out on the Swamp. I slung my coat away from the others, because I knew better than to leave my stuff near their stuff. I left on my hat and gloves.

As I took off down the hill Poopy also decided to launch, and so it became a race between the two of us down the hill. This was not a good thing. Poopy was almost out of control going down the sledding trail, because it had got icy. He bumped me, sending me towards the hole. I overcorrected and ran into him just as we hit the pond. Poopy yelped, slid sideways, and went down and through the ice. I looked over my shoulder at him and started laughing hard. That was a mistake. I went into a slide.

I somehow stayed upright and got back to going forward, but a big honking crack in the ice followed my back tire as if the crack had a mind of its own. In fact, as the crack chased me it seemed to shout "*Crack, Crack, and Crack!*"

I looked back, lost my balance, and went down and through the ice. I wasn't that close to where Peachy and Dingo were standing, but close enough, I guess. They had both been yelling and gesturing "Slow down!" and "Stop!" For all their yelling, they only lasted a few seconds and then the ice gave out under them. Not that I was paying too much attention to any of them at that moment. I had my own problems.

I had let go of my bike and was up to my chest in ice-cold, swampy water. My boots were planted in the sticky goo of the bottom, and I could feel a handlebar against my right leg. This was an awful situation. Plus, the wind was getting down-right cold. I plunged down, grabbed hold of my bike, and then making loud huffing sounds started for shore. After a few lunging steps forward something down there in the murky water tangled up with my left foot. It felt like a bunch of branches or sticks. I managed to work my foot free, but whatever it was down there nearly pulled my boot off. Dingo yelled something at me in an angry voice. Dingo at the time was by far the best swear artist in our group. As I've pointed out, his dad is retired Navy.

So, there he was behind me, swearing up a blue streak. I looked back to make sure things were ok (as ok as they could be) and saw both Peachy and Dingo struggling along. Dingo obviously had his bike in grip, pushing it along under water. Peachy was a little better off, as he had managed to perch his bike on a muskrat house as he went in. Once he had gained his footing, Peachy had put his bike on his head, like a guy on safari.

I set my face back forwards and started slogging to shore. I had to lift my bike from time to time because of the muck down below. I would lift my bike and then sort of shake it underwater. Then I would push, then I would lift, and then I would push some more.

After what seemed like a very long time, I got close enough to shore to know that I was going to make it out of the Swamp with my bike. Poopy waded in to help me, because he was wet already, I guess. The two of us lugged my bike out. I was all but done in. I was cold to the bone, I was shaking so bad my teeth were chattering, and I had cold muck in both boots. Poopy waded back in and headed towards Peachy and Dingo.

"*Darn it,*" I thought to myself. I knew I had to go back in too, so I did. I heard splish-splashing behind me; it was Beetle. He had been sitting on the bank crying. He was still crying, but he was in the water following me and Poopy. We got to Dingo and Peachy and pulled them and their bikes out of the Swamp. Because we had all gone into the water, nobody won. Poopy retained his title from the previous year on a technicality.

We all looked like we had been through the wringer, and this wasn't for the first time. I'm not saying we had all gone into the Swamp before. Not all at once, anyway. No, this was a first. I'm just saying there had been previous assorted incidents when we had all gone home looking like crap, like we had been hauled behind a hay wagon or garbage truck or something. The Beetle's parents, by that time, were just about done with us as a group. Especially Beetle's mom.

The Beetle was sobbing so hard he looked like he was convulsing. "I'm never going to get to hang out with you guys, ever again." He gulped.

"Jiminy Crickets, shut up!" said Dingo.

"Stop crying, Beetle, it's not manly," advised Peachy, and that got Beetle to stop.

"Guys, I gotta be home in forty minutes. I'm done for. It's all over," said The Beetle mournfully.

But I had an idea. Desperate times call for desperate measures. Because my sister and Mom were off shopping, I thought we might be able to pull off my scheme. I explained as we went. I told them we would go to my place through the basement door. We would strip down, dump our stuff in the basement deep sink, give it all a quick rinse, then dump the whole mess into the dryer. I finished up by saying, "If we move fast, this will work, guys!" They were all in full support of the plan.

I must say we moved crisply. We were highly motivated. We stripped down, piled our stuff into the deep sink, and turned on the hot water.

We all jumped about as we did so. Peachy took over at that point, as always. "Not the coats. They're not that wet. Hang em by the furnace," he advised.

Everyone's coats got hung up except for mine, because they weren't all that wet. My coat got good and wet. Poopy had stood over my coat after he had gone into the drink. I threw my coat near the floor drain. Water and mud were starting to pool up around the deep sink. Peachy got to work and found old newspapers he then used to soak up the pooling mess underneath the deep sink. Next, he showed us how to twist-out and wring-out the shirts and pants, with a boy grabbing each end of the garment and twisting it out over the floor drain. I had to move my now sopping wet coat again. I threw it into the deep sink along with my gloves and hat. We each of us twisted out our own skivvies and socks. Dingo was quick to point out that Poopy's underwear had 'skid marks' in them. The poor guy is never, ever going to lose his nickname.

We had a brief debate about if we even wanted Poopy's drawers in the dryer with our stuff. After giving the matter due deliberation, we decided that his underwear would go into the deep sink. Poopy grinned as he dropped his boxers into the sink, because my coat, hat and gloves were all in there. I gave up trying to defend my things. I just let it all alone. We got everything that was going into the dryer into the dryer, and I cranked it up to high and pushed the button. Then we all started hopping about, because we were cold and buck-naked. Peachy looked at me and said, "This ain't gonna work, do something, Eric."

I jumped over to the laundry basket and pulled out two bed sheets that were in the dirty clothes basket. I tossed them towards the guys. Peachy and Dingo snagged them first. They wrapped themselves up like a couple of Roman senators. I ran upstairs to my room. I pulled out my ratty old purple bathrobe, a frayed old yellow sweatshirt, and last year's pair of swim trunks for Poopy and Beetle. For myself I got out my 'just about done for' blue jeans (the ones with the knees out and the butt almost out) and my old grey t-shirt, the one with the hole below the left armpit. I ran back downstairs and tossed Poopy the bathrobe (Poopy tends towards chubbiness, and even back then he never would have got into my swim trunks). Beetle got the sweatshirt and trunks.

"Jeez." said Peachy, "Do me and Dingo have to sit around down here looking like a couple of Greeks? Don't you have anything else?"

"Well, I've only got my school clothes for Monday, that's kind of it," I told them.

The truth is, I didn't have much, and they all knew it. Peachy didn't press the point. Instead, he smiled and pointed at the dryer, which was now thumping along with our wet clothes. "She go-a bump-a, bump-a, and a chunk-a, chunk-a! Bump-a, and a chunk-a!" said a leering Peachy. Dingo grinned and said that the dryer sounded like his parents in their bedroom on Saturday night. Poopy started making these little 'eee-ah-eee' sounds in synch with the dryer. We laughed so hard that tears ran down our cheeks and snot blew out our noses.

Dingo blew his nose in his sheet. Poopy looked around for a moment and then blew his nose in Peachy's sheet. Peachy took offense and punched Poopy a good one in the shoulder, then went over to the deep sink for a quick rinse. His dignity restored, Peachy wandered off through the basement, casting about for something, which I guess he found in the form of a dusty pack of cards up on the shelf with what was left of the year's preserves, and right next to the pickled pig's feet. Of all of us, I'm the only kid with preserves in the basement; canning jars with pickled carrots, green beans and cucumbers. I wondered how long those cards had been up there. They were dusty.

Anyway, Peachy overturned an empty card-board box and placed it underneath the bare bulb with the pull chain hanging down from the ceiling next to the furnace. Poopy, although at times slow, got what Peachy was up to quickly enough. Poopy got the two almost useless lawn chairs from next to the deep sink and set them around the box. Peachy simultaneously set a steel bucket and an old paint can around the box. I went around to the other side of the furnace and produced my sister's old blue pony rocking chair and set it down across from the lawn chairs.

So as not to be saddled with the rocking chair I grabbed the bucket as my seat, because Poopy and Peachy had already claimed the lawn chairs. Beetle got the paint can. Dingo, who had been eyeing the dryer, which was now really thump, thump, thumping along, was a bit slow on the draw. As a result, Dingo got the blue pony rocking chair, but to his credit he made the best of it. We played 'Follow the Queen', and every time Dingo passed some good and rotten cards to Poopy, he whinnied like a pony and set to rocking the little blue rocking chair. It was fun.

In a while the dryer buzzer went off and we got our clothes. They were just a bit damp, and they smelled kind of weird. Peachy said that no one would notice, as his mom always says that boys our age smell bad most of the time anyway. Peachy then gave out careful instructions on how to sneak into one's home, with one's coat off, get to one's room, and then be 'Home Free'. I only half listened because I was already 'Home Free'. Peachy's main concern was for The Beetle, as he is not as naturally sneaky like the rest of us.

My friends all trundled outside and got ready to push off for home. Being down in the basement we hadn't noticed how dark the day had become. It was only about a quarter to six, but it was dark. I mean *dark*. A big hummer of a storm was coming, we guessed. Peachy, Dingo, Poopy and The Beetle organized themselves. It was decided that Peachy would escort Dingo to his farm, because Peachy's bike light still worked, and Dingo's now didn't. Then Peachy would turn around and ride back to his place. This was typical Peachy. See, Peachy didn't want Dingo to get nailed out on the old highway by some drunken Swede. Or, even worse, to get knocked flying by Old Man Durr's International Harvester farm truck, the one with the shotgun rack in the back window. Once Old Man Durr hit a dog on the road, and he just kept right on going.

The Beetle would ride with Poopy into town like they would have anyway, and Beetle's bike light still worked. I guess Beetle's bike light didn't go underwater when he crashed. This was a good thing, for a couple of reasons. First, Beetle wouldn't have to explain to his parents why his bike light wasn't working. Second, Beetle's farm is on the other side of town, where the tar ends and the gravel starts, and we didn't want him getting squished by a drunken Swede, or maybe even a drunken Norwegian, either. With Peachy in the lead and Beetle in the rear they headed off. I ran upstairs from the basement and watched them from the living room window.

They peddled off into the gloom, Peachy and The Beetle's lights bobbing along in the dark. Their little lights split off, with Dingo and Peachy heading to Dingo's farm, and Beetle and Poopy heading across the old highway towards the better part of town where the sidewalk starts.

The Booger Lady

At this rate I'm going to be here forever. It's taken me days to get this far. Reverend Leverkuehn is playing something by Mozart called *Don Giovani*. I don't understand a word of it. But I must admit that the music puts me into a kind of trance, and I start writing away. My fingers are starting to get a little callused. And the money is reliable. It's not catch as catch can like with pop bottles. So, on with the story!

A few moments after the guys left wearing their still somewhat damp and swampy smelling cloths Mom's car came pulling into the driveway, headlights on. I acted normal as Mom and Sis carried in the groceries through the back door of the kitchen. The first words out of Mom's mouth were "You boys been behaving yourselves?"

I told her yes. Aimee gave me one of those looks of hers, with her lips all pursed tight. Aimee is a pain in my butt at times. I helped put things away, and then I went to the living room to catch the weather on channel six. I know, you're thinking, "*Yeah, right, ten (but almost eleven) years old and watching the news.*" But, you see, I did want to watch the weather, because I have a growing regard for Breezy, who is the channel six weathergirl.

Breezy comes out in a skirt short enough to see her knees, wearing high heels, and she walks across this big map of Minnesota. It's very cool. She points down to different parts of the state where there are cloud symbols and sunshine symbols, and along with the symbols you get a good view of her heels and her legs. Every now and then when she says that there's going to be winds out of the east or southwest or wherever, there's this wind sound and her skirt blows up a little. Sometimes fake leaves or fake snowflakes blow across the map around her high heels. Whoever thought of this way to present Minnesota weather should get a medal.

Breezy told us what we already knew. A big and ugly spring storm was on the way. She said to stay off the roads if you could avoid it. This worried me so much I didn't really notice whether there was a blowing skirt or not, because Beetle lives the farthest out. I was worried about Mom going to work, too.

I called Dingo who lives next farthest out. He was home, no problems. He also said it was like nighttime at his place. I gave it a little while and then called The Beetle's house. His mom answered the phone. She just plain doesn't like me. She started out being very brusque with me. I explained what with the bad weather coming in, I was just concerned about Godfrey (That's Beetle's real name). She let me talk with The Beetle, who let me know he was 'home free'.

The idiot should know by now you never talk code within earshot of our elders, and most definitely not on that party line of theirs that anyone can listen in on. But he got away with it just the same, because his mom had walked off. I hung up and came to the table for supper. We had meatloaf. It was the good kind, with crumbled up crackers and one egg in it, with ketchup on the top the way I like it. All was well with the world.

After dinner Mom stated she was going to work, storm or no storm. I protested. She pointed out that the Old Kountry Kettle was only three miles away and it was right next to the truck stop on the highway overpass. She finished her retort by informing me the money for a meatloaf dinner came from her job. She kissed Aimee on the head and told me to hold down the fort. As Mom drove off, I caught Aimee's worried expression. I told Aimee that the OKK was only three miles away like Mom said, and not to worry. And of course, there really were no worries, storm or no storm. All kinds of people pull off at the overpass to fuel up and chow down. Mom would be fine.

I let Aimee pick whatever dumb, dorky program she wanted to watch on TV, which is usually the *Mickey Mouse Club*. I will admit sometimes *The Wonderful World of Disney* is OK, but not necessarily *The Mickey Mouse Club*. Anyway, a few nights earlier we had both watched a Saint Patrick's Day special which I did find interesting. On the Saint Patrick's Day episode there was this one part with a howling banshee. The banshee part scared Aimee good and proper. But what was on now was the same old boring stuff, so I curled up in the old easy chair by the bookcase and picked out an encyclopedia.

Before he died my dad was an encyclopedia salesman, and we got a leather-bound set of encyclopedias, with a bookcase included. Like I've already said, when I read from these encyclopedias, it's like my dad is talking to me. As I read from these wonderful books, I hear his voice in my mind. This simply does not happen with other books. The encyclopedias comfort me. There I sat, calm and safe and warm in my favorite chair with my favorite books. I read and heard Dad's voice tell me about banshees and omens. Outside, the wind picked up, and it started to snow hard.

That night was a real howler, like Breezy the weather girl said it was going to be. Tree branches bumped against the roof, and the windows shook. In the middle of the night Aimee just walked right into my bedroom, without knocking or anything. My light was off, and I'd been trying to sleep, but with no success. She just walked right in, which is not like her at all. Even stranger, she closed my bedroom door tight behind her. She had her arms wrapped around herself as she stood there at my bedside. "Eric, I'm so frightened," she said. I turned on the light. Tears were running down Aimee's face and dripping off her chin. There was snot, too. The wind had gone from howling to shrieking.

"It's just a blizzard, Aimee," I told her. "Come on, you're a Minnesota girl."

"It's not the blizzard, Eric," she said. "It's her. It's the *Booger Lady*! She's scratching at my window again."

Wow. I'm here to tell you, this was the first time I'd ever heard about this so-called 'Booger Lady', and when Aimee said what she said goose flesh broke out on my arms and all the way down my back.

"I'm not going back in there Eric. I can't," she said in a quavering voice.

Well, I was spooked now, too. I was spooked enough to let Aimee crawl into bed with me.

"I'll leave the light on, and we'll be as snug as two bugs in a rug," I told her.

That's how it was. I left the light on, and Aimee pressed tight into my shoulder while the wind shrieked and howled outside. I'll be honest. It was good to have company during that storm. At about 2:00 a.m. the wind stopped, and shortly after that I heard our car drive up. A few minutes later Mom opened my bedroom door. "What's this?" she asked.

Aimee was fast asleep. I told Mom about Aimee's nightmare, or whatever it was, and suggested that Aimee finish the night in Mom's bed. "Well, I'm whipped, Eric. You carry her in," Mom said.

I did just that. I carried Aimee into Mom's room, and I even tucked her in. I went back to my own bed and cranked up my imagination. See, I can do this thing where I can sometimes conjure up things with my imagination. I can see and hear things. But sometimes I see things and hear things without even doing anything. It just happens. Reverend Leverkuehn told me I have intuition and imagination. I don't think so. If I had any good intuition I wouldn't get into so much trouble. Anyway, I imagined Aimee's Booger Lady as something like the banshee.

Even though the wind wasn't blowing anymore I managed to scare myself, so I turned my imagination off and eventually fell to sleep. Then I had the nightmare. That's what I called it to myself at the time, and I still do. I mean, one minute I'm looking at the Booger Lady's face in my second story bedroom window, and the next minute I'm suddenly wide awake, sitting bolt upright in bed, and it's nine in the morning.

My heart was pounding. I thought the whole thing was goofy, because it wasn't dark anymore. It was daylight, not night. But just a moment ago it had been night, and she had been looking in my window. But daylight is daylight, and this was a special kind of daylight. The light was almost blinding white, and it was pumping in through my window. I got up and looked out. The landscape outside my window was like somewhere on another planet, or maybe Canada. It had stopped snowing, but boy howdy was there a lot of snow on the ground.

The pine trees were wearing shrouds of snow, and there were drifts of snow against the church across the road.

As I thought about how it looked like a dream outside, I used the way it looked to help put the nightmare out of my mind. I really had to work on it. I kept thinking about that disembodied face in my window. She hadn't any eyes, just black shadows where her eyes should have been. Her hair was waving around her head. Her mouth kept opening and closing, but the only sound was the moaning and groaning of the wind. I finally shook it off. The day outside looked just too splendid.

Suicide Hill

I pulled on my purple bathrobe and went down to the kitchen. I looked through the kitchen window down at the Swamp. The snow had pretty much covered up where we had all gone through the ice. This was very cool, and a very good thing indeed. Aimee trudged into the kitchen, wanting breakfast. I poured us both bowls of frosted flakes (They're Great!) and we set to it. There was a knock on the kitchen door and Aimee nearly jumped right out of her nightgown. I jumped a bit too, but not as bad as Aimee.

It was Poopy, wearing that goofy grin of his. His black watch-cap was pushed back on his head with his hair standing up in the front like it always does. His ears stick out, and his eyes are big and wide, making him always look like he's just been surprised by something. Dingo says that he looks like a taxicab coming around the corner with its doors open. Poopy let himself in, looked Aimee over, and said, "What, did I startle you, toots?"

Aimee shook her spoon at him, and then acted like she was going to use her spoon like a catapult. But why waste a delicacy like frosted flakes on Poopy? After a split second of consideration, my sister decided to continue to chow down on her breakfast.

Poopy was all geared up, and I do mean geared up. Watch-cap, scarf, his big winter coat (not the one that had gone into the Swamp yesterday), snap-up rubber boots and chopper mitts. "Let's go Eric! Come on, man! The others are gonna meet us over at Suicide Hill in a little while. Come on. This is great! Let's go! Look at all this snow out here!"

Letting Poopy's sense of urgency energize me, I went charging off. My problem was that I really didn't have that much to wear. I only had my good school clothes for Monday, my jeans with no knees (and almost no butt) and the pair of jeans in the basement. Well, the pair in the basement was dry, so they got put on. A good dose of snow would probably rub the swamp-stink out of them anyway, I reckoned.

I put on my gray t-shirt and the sweatshirt that The Beetle had worn yesterday. Whoops! I realized that I had left my coat, hat and gloves in the deep sink. I hung my hat and coat on a nail behind the furnace, where I expected them to dry. That area back of the furnace is a not so noticeable place. I put my gloves on top of the dryer. I then ran upstairs to the upstairs closet and pulled out my flannel lined blue jean jacket, which would have to do.

I got out a scarf, an ear brassiere, my chopper mittens, and the pair of buckle up rubber boots I had worn yesterday. The boots had a buckle shot on both sides, and they were still wet inside from yesterday. I fiddled with them in the kitchen, trying to wipe them out with the dish towel, because I was in a hurry. "Come on," said Poopy. "We're gonna try out that toboggan that Hanna's brother found in the Hoot Owl Barn!" You see, Hanna and Molly were the kind of friends back then who shared stuff all the time, including dresses, baseball mitts and now an old toboggan.

"You *smell* funny." Aimee said to me as we headed out the door.

"You smell like a fart." Poopy commented back to my sister with his characteristic grin.

My sister grinned back at him. Then she looked at me and said, "Be careful."

This was an odd and uncharacteristic thing for my own sister to say to me. Poopy looked at me in a questioning way, and I just shrugged and kept moving on. Off we went to meet the others at Suicide Hill.

We trudged through the snow as fast as we could go. It helped that we weren't pulling sleds.

We call it Suicide Hill because of the big snow bumps we always build halfway down the hill, and because of the old, barbed wire fence at the bottom of the hill. The fence marks part of the property line of Dingo's farm. There used to be a gate in the fence, right dead center at the bottom of the hill, but the gate is long gone. All a kid needs to do is steer their sled though the opening, and then cruise to a stop in the old pasture beyond. Off to the right side of the pasture on the other side of the fence is a steep drop-off into Black Goose Creek. We used to love this place.

Although there are legends about kids running into the barbed wire, to tell the truth, this is a hard thing to do. I mean, you must be a real dork to hit that fence if you're riding a sled. In fact, there are a few places along the fence where the bottom strand of wire is high enough so that kids can ride their sled right under the fence, but they've got to be lying down, rather than sitting up. I only know of two kids who have run into the wire: Beetle and Poopy. It wasn't entirely their fault.

There had been a real whopper of a blizzard in December right after Christmas, and it damaged a billboard sign out on the highway. It was a Pepsi billboard sign with this big tin Pepsi bottle cap as part of the sign. The wind blew the bottle cap right off the billboard. The gusts must have been so strong that it sailed the bottle cap into the woods, just like a giant Pluto Platter.

We found it while looking for Peachy's dog Bernard (who is not a Saint Bernard). As a matter of fact, that's what we call Peachy's dog, as in "Has anyone seen Bernard Who Is Not a Saint Bernard?" We were all of us very concerned about Bernard, because he normally doesn't run off. Molly was about ready to have a cow if we didn't find Bernard, and that's the only reason she came along. Peachy mumbled something about how annoying kid sisters are, but Molly just gave him her famous stare, and then off we went.

Anyway, we found Bernard Who Is Not a Saint Bernard because a guy over at Fred's gas station told us he had seen a big black lab that looked like Bernard in the woods near the new freeway. Two miles on a county road in the winter isn't any fun, and that's how far Peachy's house is from the freeway, but we started hiking it anyway.

As things worked out, before we got to the highway, we found Bernard. He came trotting out of the woods with something in his mouth, which turned out to be a black knit hat. It looked almost the same as Poopy's. I claimed it right off the bat. I had been making do with an ear brazier since losing my other hat. I didn't put it on, though, because it had dog slobber on it, and I also figured that it might have cooties. I stuffed it in my coat pocket. Then we noticed that Peachy had followed Bernard's tracks back into the woods. It was there we found the giant bottle cap. Peachy was the first to realize its potential. "I think we could use this as a flying saucer down Suicide Hill!" he exclaimed.

The rest is history, like they say. We trudged back to Peachy's and got his big sled, then most of us went back (except for Molly) and retrieved the bottle cap and lugged it all the way over to my place. Every time a car or truck came along, we pulled off the road and into the snow, as we were sneaky enough not to want to attract a lot of attention.

Once we got to my house, we debated taking it down my hill as a test run, but decided not to, owing to us wanting to keep our find from prying eyes. Instead, we hid it against one side of my house under a wheelbarrow and a tarp. The guys left, and I was kind of worn out, but I rinsed out my new-found knit cap and hung it up on the little nail in the wall behind the furnace to dry. I hung it up because I thought that if I put it into the dryer it would shrink down to something resembling a doll's hat. After dinner I went to bed and slept like a rock.

The next day we got the giant bottle cap over to Suicide Hill. Since Molly had been with us when we found it, she insisted on coming along. She brought Bernard, too. The bottle cap was big enough to seat three, so we played Paper Rock Scissors, to see who the lucky three would be. Poopy, The Beetle, and Dingo won the first (and last) ride down. We lined them up so that the bottle cap would hit the big snow bump that we had built halfway down the hill, so, we hoped, the boys would really go flying. I gave Beetle my leather chopper mittens because Beetle had gloves on that day, and the tin edges of the bottle cap looked kind of dicey.

Well, with a lot of hooting and hollering we gave the boys a shove, and down they went like a shot. Then, my goodness, did that big bottle cap ever start spinning. That thing was the best flying saucer I've ever seen! It went sailing down Suicide Hill, hit our bump, and up into the air they went. When they came down, they bounced hard, and Dingo was ejected out. Dingo was lucky. The bottle cap, spinning in circles as it was, and with no steering mechanism to speak of, slung Poopy and the Beetle right into the barbed wire fence a good deal to the left of the gate opening.

Poopy piled into Beetle, who took the brunt of the fence, as the long, thin white scar above his left eyebrow attests to. This was the very first time Beetle was grounded because of us. He was banished from our company for a few weeks, until he healed. Beetle's *Mom* and dad called the Sheriff's Department. Some Pepsi guys hauled the bottle cap away, and we got to meet Constable Benny for the very first time.

I figured Constable Benny at that time as a sort of stand in for a real sheriff's deputy, because most of the time the guy just wore jeans and old work shirts. On the day he met us however, he had on his constable shirt. He talked with all of us, and he wanted to know if we had seen anything else along the highway. We all told him that we never made it out to the highway, and that was that. I neglected to tell him about the black knit hat that Bernard had found.

That whole bottle cap business with Constable Benny had been back at the start of January. Now we were all once again on Suicide Hill, on what turned out to be the last good sledding day of a winter fast turning into spring. We had this fine old toboggan to take on a good fast run down good old Suicide Hill. What could go wrong?

Peachy and Molly had got there ahead of us. Molly said she was there out of morbid curiosity. We didn't necessarily like having Molly hanging around, because we always had to mind our manners. Otherwise, Peachy would get ticked off. But, from time to time, she would inevitably insist on tagging along. She had helped Peachy pull the old toboggan through the deep snow to Suicide Hill.

Bernard Who Is Not A Saint Bernard showed up next. His tongue was out, and snow was on his snout. He was giving us that great big dog grin of his and diving in and out of the snow. He was obviously happy to be with us, and not out of morbid curiosity. Then we saw The Beetle's red ski cap bobbing along through the trees. We hollered and yelled for him to hurry up. Bernard Who Is Not A Saint Bernard charged off to greet him.

We got the toboggan lined up perfectly so it would hit the snow bump straight on. After our misadventure with the bottle cap, we had shifted the snow bump to the right. For some reason, when kids hit our repositioned bump, it tended to send their sleds off to the left, making it easier to hit the gate opening. We were sure that the toboggan would react just like a sled when it hit our bump.

We all climbed aboard, except for Molly and the dog. Molly was having none of it. She had brought her little pink flying saucer along on the toboggan, and she was going down on that, after pushing us off. We got on in the sitting position rather than the kneeling position because we didn't know any better. Dingo sat in the back with barely enough room to sit. We scrunched forward, wrapping our legs around each other. Our sitting method was kind of a mistake.

We grabbed onto the rope holds running down both sides of the toboggan and whooping and yelling told Molly to give us a shove. She did good, falling forward while making this 'ufta' sound as she went face first into the snow. Off we went. We accelerated quite rapidly. Dingo way in the back was laughing his fool head off. Peachy in front was whooping. Poopy was right behind me and he was sort of screaming. Beetle in front of me wasn't making a sound. He was hanging on for dear life. I recall yelling something like, "Hey, we're going fast! Hang on!" These were words of true wisdom.

We hit the bump and were suddenly transported into a loftier realm. I was shocked about how high in the air we were. The laughing and whooping changed to 'Whoa' and 'Ooh' and 'Eeee'. Poopy's screams went up a pitch. I was expecting a 'broken bones' kind of landing, but instead we landed with a whoosh and kept right on going. I have never gone so fast in anything without doors and wheels. And we were not heading for the gate opening. Oh no.

We were heading straight for a twisty nasty looking part of the fence. We hit a bump or maybe a buried rock, and Dingo bounced off. He went whirling through the snow like some sort of human egg-beater. Poopy's legs were squeezed tight around me. Peachy yelled "Duck down!" and we hunched down as low as we could. I closed my eyes.

We went right under the fence, and it made this twanging and rattling noise. There was also this odd sort of high-pitched ripping sound. The toboggan kept right on going and dumped us over the gully into Black Goose Creek. This is not to say we went into the creek itself, as we all tumbled out into the deep snow before the toboggan hit the creek. Afterwards we started referring to the old toboggan as 'The Dive Bomber', or just 'The Bomber'.

Dingo was the first one to get to us, and he just sat on the edge of the gully laughing. I had snow down my back and neck, and in my face. Poopy was somehow ahead of me, and he had these great big fluffy white things coming out of his back. It was his coat stuffing. Peachy's coat was oozing out the same kind of puffy stuff, only grey. I started laughing so hard my eyes and nose started running, but then I thought to check my own back. My very fine flannel-lined blue jean jacket had been slit open like a sunfish on a cleaning board. The Beetle's jacket was ripped open too, between his shoulders and down for about six inches. He was also missing his glasses and his red ski hat. Molly appeared above the drop, next to Dingo. She kept saying "Oh, my God, oh, my God."

We all helped Beetle find his glasses, while trying to calm him down. He was sure he was at the end of his rope; he would be banned for life from hanging out with us. Dingo said that he could fix everything. Peachy gave Dingo a funny look, but Dingo seemed pretty cock-sure of himself. Peachy said, "OK, we're in your hands." We followed Dingo over to his place, dragging the toboggan behind us.

Peachy and The Beetle got into a discussion about Newtonian Physics, and how maybe the length and speed of the toboggan, along with our weight on it, made it fly off in the wrong direction after hitting the bump. I couldn't follow much of what they were saying. What I do know is that we often seem to find ourselves right in the middle of dramatic applications of Newtonian Physics.

Dingo's place is a working farm with livestock, unlike The Beetle's place, which is mostly just a crop farm, although they do have chickens. Peachy's place really isn't a farm at all. It's just six acres, but they do have a tractor shed with a small garden tractor parked inside, and they also keep a few chickens. Dingo said there was nobody around his farm now, as Gunter, the hired hand, had just quit. That meant that we had the whole Wilcox farm to ourselves.

Dingo took us over to the workshop building next to the barn and cranked up the gas heater. Before anyone even had a chance to think about it Poopy claimed dibs on the radio. This is often very annoying. Poopy, you see, likes polka. With the polka music blasting out of a New Ulm radio station, we got busy. Peachy got out the coffee pot along with three ceramic mugs. I got the hot plate going and found the last of the hot chocolate mix in the same bench drawer as the instant coffee.

As there were only three mugs and six of us, we had to share. Molly shared with me, because according to her, I probably had the least awful cooties of anyone, including her own brother. Nevertheless, we were careful not to use the same 'lip place' on our shared mug. Bernard Who Is Not A Saint Bernard got an empty coffee can filled with water, and he seemed happy enough about that. Also, Molly looked cute that day; she had a hot chocolate mustache.

After getting comfortable we set to work on our ripped coats. Before doing that however, we swore Molly to secrecy, telling her to not blab her mouth off about stuff. After swearing Molly to a cross your eyes and cross your heart secrecy pledge, we got curious about what Dingo had up his sleeve.

What Dingo thought of was kind of ingenious. He got duct tape, and spray paint. He matched the paint surprisingly close to the colors of our coats. Then we set up an assembly line. We very carefully cut and sprayed the tape. Dingo, in charge of the last step, taped up the rips in each coat.

The polka music seemed to help the process, as we were all bobbing our heads in time with the polka music. Poopy pointed out that even Bernard Who Is Not A Saint Bernard was using his tail to thump along in time, or so it seemed. We gave both Poopy and Bernard Who Is Not A Saint Bernard the benefit of the doubt.

Beetle's coat got done first. "This won't work!" declared Beetle. "You can still tell if you even look half-close enough."

"You gotta sneak in." advised Dingo, who went on to instruct us to walk into our respective homes natural enough, and just hang our coats in our respective closets, or on our respective coat racks, with the back facing away. "The winter's almost over", Dingo went on to say. "You guys might get away with it!"

Well, we almost all did. In any event, the day had been a wonderful diversion. I didn't have to think about seeing (or dreaming about seeing) the Booger Lady looking in my bedroom window. She had been looking in my window with the snow-filled wind blowing her hair in swirls around her face, and her mouth silently opening and closing, opening and closing. The apparition's opening and closing mouth was by far the creepiest part. Nope, I didn't have to think about the darn dream all day.

When I got home, I ran into a regular **** storm. I'm sorry. I'm using a swear-word here. Mom was really bent out of shape. She had taken the rest of the bed sheets down for washing, and after washing them had of course put them all into the dryer. They came out kind of smelly, grey and streaky looking. Mom had inspected the dryer, and then found and examined my winter coat. She put two and two together. She was waiting for me when I came in the door, and then she discovered my ripped jacket. Things went from bad to worse. I was grounded from Sunday through Friday, and I was given extra chores from 'now until forever' as Mom put it. Then too, I had concerns about the coming night. We had left-over meatloaf for an early supper. Left-over meatloaf is not as good as fresh meatloaf. After supper I decided to check the television weather forecast.

Breezy the Weather Girl doesn't work weekends, so I watched this dork of a guy do the weather. He's the same guy who does the sports. He always has a can of some local yokel beer on his sports show desk, and he always gives a commercial about how good the nasty stuff is while doing the sports. I'll take Breezy any day. Anyway, the guy said that we were done with the snow, and that things would be warming up. Aimee seemed very chipper, which struck me as odd. I pulled her off to the side and said, "Aren't you worried about tonight?"

Aimee looked at me as if I was goofy and said, "No, why should I be worried? She only comes around at night when it's snowing, and it's done snowing." Since it was Aimee who had tuned me in to the Booger Lady, and since Aimee was now so unconcerned, I relaxed a bit. Aimee was right about it not snowing. Aimee was also right about the Booger Lady not showing up that night to haunt my dreams. "*So far, so good*," I thought to myself.

Ninja Bob

The next day Mom slept in like she does every Sunday. I kind of slept in too, because I had pulled my curtains shut before turning my light out, so my room was darker than normal Sunday morning. It didn't matter then, sleeping in I mean. We weren't a churchy family back then. Church was to come later, for me and Aimee, anyway.

Mom eventually got up and put together my chore list. I asked her if I got credit for making me and Aimee breakfast (which I always did, anyway) and she said "nope." I had to do the dishes. I had to clean out the dryer drum with towels and bleach. I had to do laundry. I shoveled the sidewalk and the driveway, in late morning sleet. It was sloppy cold work. I got my first (and I hope my last) sewing lesson, and then stitched up my jean jacket. All the while Mom sat in the kitchen smoking at the kitchen table and talking on the phone, like she does every Sunday.

Later in the afternoon I got a break from chores. As I was grounded, there was just Aimee to talk to, so I asked her what was going on with this Booger Lady stuff. Aimee told me that she had been dealing with the Booger Lady for the last few months, starting in January. Aimee said she only came when it snowed. She also said that Friday night was the first time that she had seen the Booger Lady in her bedroom window.

Aimee went on to explain that before that it had just been scratching sounds at her window when it snowed, and that she had just pulled the blankets over her head until she fell asleep. I asked her about her window when she heard the scratching the very first time. She said that it was pitch black outside and she hadn't seen anything. There was just the scratching. Friday night was the first time she had seen the Booger Lady. Then Aimee changed her story a little, saying that it wasn't really a recognizable face or anything, just a kind of moving and shifting dark shape with a glowing spot.

Then I asked her what I thought was a darn good question: What makes her the Booger Lady? Aimee said that she wasn't sure how the name popped into her head. She said that the first time, she thought it was just a tree branch, and that in her imagination it reminded her of an old lady scratching at a door. After a few more times, she started thinking of the scratching sound as 'The Booger Lady.' Then Aimee leaned over and very seriously told me that she had gone outside and looked at her bedroom window, and there weren't any tree branches even close. She said I could check for myself. I decided to do so.

I went out the front door to conduct an inspection. Aimee was right. There were no tree branches even close to her window. There was a tree limb that almost touched the front porch roof, but that was still a good distance from Aimee's window. Mom caught up with me as I came back in and gave me one last task before supper; to sweep out the basement. This included dusting off the shelves down there. And, while I was at it, I was told to bring up a jar of cauliflower preserves. While I was down in the basement Ninja Bob yowled to be let in.

I think that Ninja Bob was first sighted out at Dingo's place, but I'm not sure. Dingo told me that this big cat had been slinking around the chicken coop one night when Dingo's Dad saw him. Dingo's Dad, (Chief Wilcox that is) thought he was a bobcat or something, because of his size. Mr. Wilcox went after him with Dingo's 22 caliber rifle but missed. A few nights later Mr. Wilcox tried again and missed again. Dingo's Dad remarked that whether it was a bobcat or not, it moved like a ninja. What I think the mystery creature turned out to be was this big old beat up brown tomcat, with a head almost as big as a dog's head, and strange tufted ears.

After deciding that Dingo's place wasn't very hospitable, Ninja Bob sort of adopted me. He first showed up near the beginning of January at about the same time as the giant Pepsi bottle cap episode. When he showed up, he was a mess. Mom allowed him to be in the basement at first, but not upstairs. I did what I could to patch him up. The first night I barely heard him. I opened the basement door and there he was, sitting on the ratty old doormat. Because of all the snow on him I didn't notice his eye at first. He came in and just flopped down, panting. I had never seen such a big cat in my whole life. It was kind of scary.

I wasn't sure what to do. I winged it. I took the doormat from outside, shook it off, and put it next to the furnace. Then I picked up Ninja Bob and laid him down on the doormat. That was when I noticed his eye. It was all gunky with pus and goo. He didn't smell very good, either. I went upstairs and got the hydrogen peroxide. I poured it right on his eye. He growled at me but didn't move. That stuff just foamed out of his eye. I wiped it off with a towel out of the laundry basket, and a bunch of gunk came off all over the towel.

I went back upstairs and got two small plastic bowls. I put water in one, and what was left of chicken soup in the other. No one wanted the soup because it had been in the fridge a bit long. I took the bowls downstairs, and then threw together a litter box. It wasn't much, just an empty peach box lined with newspaper. I took the bucket and went across the street and two doors over and raided the Timmerman sand box. That was about it. When I got back to the basement, I noticed that the black knit hat that Bernard had retrieved from near the highway was on the mat, and that Ninja Bob was curled up on it. The hat had dropped off the little nail and onto the floor before, and this must have happened again. The cat must have moved it onto the mat, I reckoned. I thought about putting a towel over him, but Ninja Bob had curled up into an almost total circle, so I let him be.

In the morning when I checked on him his food bowl was licked dry. He was on his side, but he looked up at me and meowed. I poured hydrogen peroxide on his eye again, and it foamed up like the first time, but he didn't growl this time. Instead, when I wiped away the place where his eye had been, he started purring. That was all back in January.

By the start of February Ninja Bob had settled in. His care and feeding became part of my routine.

So anyway, I refilled Ninja Bob's water bowl, and poured out some dry cat chow for him that I stole from Swenson's when Katrina Hooch wasn't looking (I'm sorry). Then I went up for my own supper. It was ox tail soup, and OKK dinner rolls that Mom had brought back from work. Oh yes, and pickled cauliflower. After we finished supper, I felt like going down to the basement and checking on Ninja Bob for no special reason.

Ninja Bob was fine, fast asleep on the old doormat next to the furnace with his big head on my hat, like my hat was his pillow. Looking at him sleeping there all snug and curled up reminded me of just how tired I was. Then I remembered my bike, and how the lights on Poopy and Dingo's bikes hadn't worked after going into the drink. I pulled my bike in from outside and checked on what looked like was a ruined bike light. I opened it up and hoped the frozen sludge inside would drain out. I pulled out the batteries and set them on the shelf next to the furnace. I trudged back upstairs, said goodnight to everyone, went to bed. I woke up in the middle of the night because I had a dream about Ninja Bob. I went down to the basement to check on him. He was there, just sleeping away. I went back upstairs and got confused, because my bed was all made up, nice and neat.

Why would I make it up if I was going back to bed? And I sure didn't remember making it up in the first place. But I felt tired, so I got back into bed and slept like a log. I almost overslept the next morning because I had closed the curtains like I had the night before. That, and the fact that I tried very hard to get back a dream I was having about Ninja Bob using my hat for a pillow.

Peachy Blows It

It was great to be back in school, what with my being grounded and all. Like I said, I almost overslept, but not quite. I had time enough to make my bed real fast. Then I bounded down the stairs and made Aimee and me breakfast (They're Great!), packed our lunches, let Ninja Bob out, and then ran out the kitchen door. I did arrive a wee bit late to school and got marked tardy by Miss Lindquist. This was no big deal. What was a big deal was that Miss Lindquist had an awful trick up her calico sleeve; she had set up a new seating arrangement for our classroom.

I was moved way over by the window, behind Boy Scout Kurt (Hanna's brother) one of the nicest, best-behaved boys in our class, if not in the entire school. It was just me and Boy Scout Kurt in that last row by the window, because of the reading table. The next row to my right was all girls except at the head of the row where Dingo had been placed. Poopy was left where he was, near the front on the other side of the room. The Beetle and Peachy were left near the back. I could see the twisted logic of Miss Lindquist's tactics. Both The Beatle and Peachy are A-B students. Me and Dingo are more in the C-D range, with Dingo more a C student and me more of a D kind of guy. Poopy seemed to get quite a few A's and B's for effort. But there was this other teacher that came in and helped him a few times a week.

There I was, sequestered off in the corner of the room almost all by myself, and grounded for a week to boot. It's just when things look darkest that a sudden ray of light peeks out. For me it was the discovery of very interesting material in the handsome collection of National Geographic magazines in the big bookcase under the window. From where I was sitting, I could reach right out and grab one.

About halfway through the morning we were supposed to be working on a geography assignment about Europe. I was doodling in my binder as usual, and Miss Lindquist suggested (in a kind of grumpy tone) I might simply pull out one of the National Geographic magazines that had something in it about a European country. I did just that and discovered a few mildly fascinating things about Eastern Europe. I also discovered something considerably more interesting about New Guinea. In the article there were pictures of women with bare boobs. I kept very still, and very quiet, and became very studious right up until milk break time. Everybody gets a milk break at Black Goose Falls Elementary.

We all lined up and went down the hall to the milk machine. I always get chocolate. I smiled but didn't talk much. I knew that if I let on to my discovery that my friends would screw it all up. I'm no fool. As a result, they talked over and around me. Although I was somewhere deep in my own reverie, I realized that Peachy was up to something. While in line Peachy said that Miss Lindquist would soon pay for her act of perfidy. Peachy was angry about the new classroom seating plan. Whatever Peachy was up to was fine with me. Let Peachy take the heat for a while, I reckoned.

After the milk break it was math time. Oh, how I hate math. Oh, how I hate fractions. However, I did some work, and tried to understand more about fractions, because I was now motivated to keep my place by the window. Boy Scout Kurt, the kid in front of me, helped me for a bit. It was almost time for lunch when Peachy's master stroke was revealed.

There is a water fountain in the classroom up front near the door. Unbeknownst to any of us, Peachy had cunningly placed a white piece of chewing gum into the upturned faucet part of the fountain. Miss Lindquist bent over to take a sip from the fountain and caught a nice face full of squirting water. It almost knocked her glasses off. Peachy looked up in mock surprise. Poopy was clueless. The Beetle was truly shocked. Dingo had been looking away and was unsure of what had just happened. I saw the whole thing and was busy pinching myself black and blue underneath my desk. I didn't want to get blamed for this. It was time for lunch, so Miss Lindquist just wiped off her glasses and took us down to the lunchroom. On the way to lunch, she quietly but clearly said we would discuss this incident after lunch. Grace under pressure, that's our Miss Lindquist.

What with us being scattered around the classroom, the lunchroom, recess and gym were the only places left during school where we could converge. We therefore moved quickly to our favorite table. Basketball Head, the noon duty, was in a high state of alert. We call her Basketball Head because her head is perfectly round, like a basketball. She was watching us like a hawk because we all came in laughing. My theory is that because we were laughing hard already when we came in, that that was what caused the next incident. Or it at least primed the pump, so to speak.

We were all sitting there, across from each other, laughing. Goulash was on the menu that day, along with a roll, carrot sticks, and peach halves in their own natural juice. Tommy (that's Peachy's real name) had popped a peach half into his mouth along with a sip of milk, holding it all in the roof of his mouth with his tongue, the better to slowly suck off the sweet goodness. Poopy was staring at his goulash in a speculative sort of way. Dingo asked Poopy if he was really going to eat that glop, to which Poopy exclaimed that he was hungry enough to eat the butt-end out of a rag doll through a picket fence.

Tommy, at that instant, with his mouth-full of a peach half and milk, made this odd sort of snorting sound. And then, an almost miracle of Newtonian Physics occurred. Tommy snorted the peach-half lodged in the roof of his mouth up and through his right and left sinuses (or septum?) thereby quartering the peach-half on the way through (See, I kind of *do* know fractions!) Suddenly Tommy was sitting there with these peach quarters wiggling and jiggling out of his nose; roughly one quarter per nostril. Milk was also coming out of his nose, along with natural peach juices and snot, too.

Tommy was at a tough decision point. He could either suck the wriggling stuff in or blow the wriggling stuff out. Either way, his dignity was badly impugned. I think what he did next was reflexive. He blew out the dangling peach chunks and various fluids onto his goulash. Pandemonium ensued. Basketball Head wasted no time, swooping down and grabbing Tommy by his right ear as he was still sounding. She grabbed him so hard that his glasses were knocked off into the goulash/milk/peach/snot mix in his tray. He was then summarily drug down to the office by his ear, gooey glasses in hand. We didn't see him for the rest of the day. It was an odd sort of cosmic justice, I think, if you believe in cosmic justice. For my part, I'm not so sure about cosmic justice.

Cosmic justice suggests an invisible web that somehow connects everything in the universe. It's either that, or everything is just about random chaos and playing the odds. But then again, you've got stuff like gravity and Newtonian Physics, which suggests some kind of order. I'm just not so sure. I went to bed thinking about cosmic justice.

My bed was nice and made up, just like I had left it in the morning. After I got into my bed, I thought again about how it had been made up last night, in the middle of the night, when I had checked on Ninja Bob. I thought about the bed, then thought about how Tommy had got into trouble, then fell fast asleep. Ninja Bob stayed out all night but showed up the next morning.

Desperate Measures

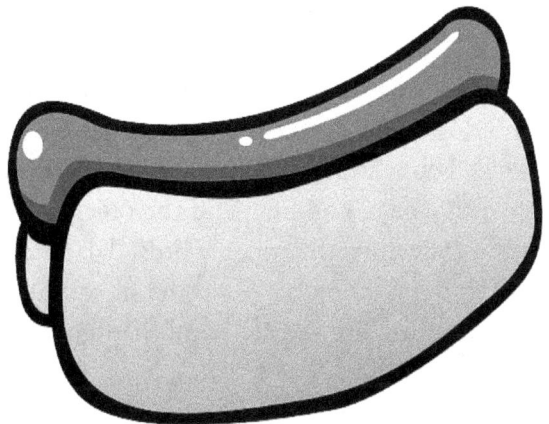

When Tommy came back to school the next day, he was much subdued. He wouldn't even talk to us, other than to say 'Hi'. The scuttlebutt in the morning milk line was some kid had told Miss Lindquist that it was Tommy who had put the gum in the drinking fountain. It wasn't one of us guys who ratted him out, to be sure, but a fourth/fifth grade classroom has many eyes. Somebody must have seen him do it and then squealed like a little pig. At lunch Tommy didn't even sit with us, instead sitting with a bunch of kids he knew from 4H, including Boy Scout Kurt and Hanna. This was a concern, because we needed our leader back amongst us. However, I rose to the occasion, for the time being. Desperate times call for desperate measures, I always used to say.

Basketball Head was keeping a very close eye on us. Lunch was hotdogs, celery sticks and chocolate pudding. Like always, I had a peanut butter and jelly sandwich, because I'm usually a brown bagger. I talked Poopy out of his hotdog, just the hotdog, not the bun. I hid the hotdog under my bag, and when Basketball Head looked over, I was very obviously enjoying my peanut butter and jelly sandwich. Then I asked The Beetle to break off one tip of his hotdog and give it to Poopy. I told Poopy to put the hotdog end in his bun, and to make sure it was sticking out. I made sure The Beetle and Dingo had at least one hotdog end poking out of their hotdog buns. The setup was complete. It was now time for phase two.

I told everyone to very obviously enjoy their hotdogs when Basketball Head walked by. She did, and as expected, she glared over at us. We chowed down for her benefit, Poopy, Beetle and Dingo very obviously enjoying their hotdogs. She moved on, giving her back to us. Quick as lightning, I took Poopy's hotdog from under my brown paper bag, rolled it in Poopy's chocolate pudding, and then flicked it over my right shoulder on a low trajectory. In other words, I launched the classic 'chocolate -pudding weenie bomb'. A chorus of squeals erupted from the lunch table behind us. My weenie bomb had gone right down the back of a kid's shirt collar.

We all turned to look as the kid, Frank Fingerholz by name (oh the irony, the rich, rich irony) pulled the weenie bomb out from the back of his collar. He was angry, and so was Basketball Head. She buzzed over to us and demanded to know who threw the hotdog. Quickly looking around to the next table over from us I spotted Phillip the Pig. Phillip was our local bully until he moved away (but then he moved back again), and I hate his guts. He had chocolate under his chinny-chin-chin, no hotdog on his tray, and a empty half-eaten hotdog bun. I pointed at Phillip. Basketball Head pounced on him (bounced on him?) just as the bell rang, and we made our escape. This act would quickly come back to haunt me, as if I needed any more haunting.

We still had the issue of Tommy's avoidance, so we had a huddle during recess. Tommy held forth, telling us that because of us he was semi-grounded for the rest of the week, and that he was supposed to avoid most of our company for a while. He could still go over to Beetle's, because they were in the same church youth group. They're cousins, too, I might add.

I never used to go over to Beetle's. Well, almost never. I'm pretty much not welcome. I've only been over to Beetle's a couple of times, kind of snuck in by Beetle while his parents were out. In Beetle's living room there's a picture of Major Charles Adams, a distant ancestor of Beetle's, who got shot up along with most of the rest of the 1st Minnesota Regiment during the second day of the Battle of Gettysburg. Beetle told me that on the third day of the battle what was left of the Regiment captured a Virginia outfit's battle flag, right during Pickett's Charge. Not surprisingly, only a few of those 1st Minnesota guys made it back to Minnesota.

Anyway, to get back to where I was, Dingo took exception with Tommy blaming us for his restrictions, pointing out that it was Tommy who put the gum in the fountain, and that it was Tommy who had blown a peach out his nose. Tommy countered it was Poopy's fault for making him laugh so hard, thus drawing attention to himself. Poopy countered that it was Dingo who had taught him the phrase about being hungry enough to eat a rag-doll's butt. Then Poopy turned towards Tommy and said, "Don't get on your high horse, peachy nose!"

Oh, how we laughed. Then Beetle looked at Tommy and said, "Peachy Peterson. Yep, it fits." Tommy gave Beetle a withering look. What I'm saying is, that if looks could maim, The Beetle would have left the playground in a wicker basket. But truth to tell, it was that very look on Tommy's face that sealed the deal. Both me and Dingo jumped on the bandwagon right fast.

"Don't get so upset, Peachy," said Dingo.

"Yeah, Peachy," I added.

From that day on Tommy Peterson became Peachy Peterson, For Ever and Ever, Amen. The whistle blew and we had to go in. Miss Lindquist had been watching us from the door, and we all instinctively knew to cool our jets in her classroom for the rest of the day. It wasn't until gym that we were able to have our second huddle.

Peachy kept it short and sweet; with both him and me grounded (well, him semi-grounded) until the weekend, we simply had to avoid making a commotion for a while. As a matter of fact, it was time to be on our best behavior. Peachy called it 'courtly' behavior'. We all spit-shook on it, and then we split up. Miss Lindquist had herself a quiet afternoon. You could tell she was a bit puzzled, but watchful and in a state of high alert.

Walking home from school I spotted Piggy lurking along the edge of Anderson's Woods. I don't like fights. I don't like bleeding. I don't like bloody noses, busted lips and black eyes. I considered my options. I would be on my bike by tomorrow, as the roads were good enough again for bikes. But what was I to do now? I could hear oncoming traffic behind me; two farm trucks. I picked up my pace and timed it just right to cross over to the other side of the road just ahead of and in front of the trucks. Then I just kept on jogging. I had distanced Piggy before he could effectively react. I don't like fights, and Piggy doesn't like to run. I made it home fine. My chore list was on the kitchen table. Mom had gone to work early, so it was up to me to make supper. I made mac and cheese.

About Ghosts

After we were done with supper, I went down to check on Ninja Bob, and give him a little mac and cheese. He had used his litter box, so I took care of that. He asked to be let out, so out he went. I knew I probably wouldn't see him for a day or two, but I was OK with that. Aimee wanted to watch her precious Mickey Mouse Club, so I curled up with the encyclopedia. I normally just pick one out at random and see where it takes me. But that night I decided to research the topic of ghosts.

Through Dad's soft and sonorous encyclopedia voice I read about how cultures throughout history have exhibited a belief in ghosts. I read about how ghosts haunted people who had something to do with their unhappy circumstance, or who in some ways were associated with them. I read about how tribes in New Guinea believe that the dream world is where the living and the departed mix company. I read about how in the Bible the ghost of Samuel appeared to King Saul. In short, by looking up the topic of ghosts I managed to scare myself right down to my toes. I must have tranced out for a time, because suddenly it was late. Aimee was in her nightgown, just standing there in the living room and staring at me. Ninja Bob picked that moment to start yowling to be let in down at the basement door.

Now normally, I'm a brave guy. Or maybe I not brave, just reckless. I take risks. But I had just read about this stuff, and there had been the business with my sister about the Booger Lady, and I hadn't got around to changing out the burned-out light bulb in the basement stairway. You could flick on the switch, and nothing happened. You had to go all the way down into the basement and pull the light cord on the overhead bulb hanging near the furnace. *Rats and more rats*, I didn't want to go down there.

Aimee was no help. She ran back into the kitchen and called from the kitchen that the stupid cat wanted in. I told her to please let him in through the kitchen door. Aimee called and called, but Ninja Bob just kept yowling from down by the basement door. Stupid cat! Finally, Aimee said that I should just go down and let the stupid thing in, because it was my cat.

I went into the kitchen. Aimee was sitting at the table with a coloring book, as if to say she was having none of it. I had just seen her run into the kitchen. When had she found time to get a coloring book? And when had she changed into her nightgown? When had she started coloring in her coloring book? A picture was half colored in. I was confused. Ninja Bob yowled again.

"Let him in, Eric," said Aimee.

"Come on down with me," I said.

"What's the matter, are you a fraidy-cat?" she saucily replied.

"OK, the Booger Lady's gone, but it's your fault that I'm a little jumpy. You come down with me, OK?" I implored.

Aimee was delighted. She took great pleasure in pointing out that she was now nine years of age, and therefore only one year behind me. Now really, it had been her birthday last month, and I would be eleven in a few weeks. Her big 'Oh Wow' gift had been a Brownie Camera. She had already used up both rolls of film. She is such a pain. No matter, I certainly felt like indulging her, given the circumstances. I told her how much I appreciated having a sister who was almost as old as me, and down into the basement we went.

With the kitchen light on and the basement door wide open, you could pretty much see all the way down the steps. Beyond the steps was stygian darkness. The furnace cut on, which was reassuring. We went down, with Aimee holding my hand behind me. My theory was that since it was dark at the bottom of the stairs, I would close my eyes once I hit bottom, and thus make my way to the pull cord by the furnace. What you can't see can't hurt you. My theory worked well, up to a point. Aimee, still holding my hand as she followed behind said, "It's right there, don't you see it?" I reached out my hand, found the cord, pulled on the light and opened my eyes. Aimee screamed. She was all over me, clutching me frantically, and screaming.

"Eric, look! Look behind the furnace, behind the furnace!"

"It's only my coat Aimee. It's only my coat!"

"You did that on purpose! You're a big jerk."

"No, I didn't do anything on purpose, Aimee. I really was a fraidy-cat, just like you said."

She calmed down, because she knew that I was being sincere. Ninja Bob yowled again and scratched at the door. Aimee almost jumped right out of her skin and went back into a panic, with her face all scrunched up.

"It's her!" she screamed, clutching my arm.

"Nonsense, that's just Ninja Bob," I stated with authority.

"Don't open the door!" cried Aimee. "That's just how she scratches at the window!"

Aimee's eyes were as big and wide open as the headlights on a Volkswagen. She was really, really scared.

"It's not snowing Aimee. It's not even raining right now," I said. "It's Ninja Bob, and I'm letting him in."

I kind of roughly pulled her off me and went to the door. I really didn't look out the door's window. I just focused on the doorknob, turning the little knob lock and opening the door.

Ninja Bob came trotting in, soaking wet. There was a slight rustling sound just outside the door, like a paper bag or piece of newspaper being swirled about by the breeze. I didn't bother to look, nor did I care to. I simply shut the door and reset the lock.

Ninja Bob plopped himself down on his mat and started licking himself.

"Eric, let's go," implored Aimee.

Then I noticed my hat wasn't on the doormat by the furnace, where I thought I had seen it last. I looked around for just a moment, but Aimee wanted to go upstairs, so up we went. Besides, I didn't really need that winter hat anymore. It was spring, and time for my baseball cap. I left the light on down there in the basement. I was sure Ninja Bob wouldn't mind the light.

Aimee had calmed down, so we went to bed. Lying in bed a little light went on in my head. Aimee had said the scratching on the door was just like how the Booger Lady scratched at her bedroom window. Eureka! That's a Latin word by the way. It means a light went on in my head. In a flash I reckoned it was all about Ninja Bob. You see, Aimee's bedroom window is right over the front porch roof. Ninja Bob had probably got up there on those snowy cold nights and tried to get in, I reckoned. I rolled over in bed and fell fast asleep.

The Gallant Ones

The next day I was in good spirits. I had only a few more days left of being grounded, which meant only a few more days of courtly behavior to seal the deal and be free once more. This put me in a fair frame of mind. I could get through this ordeal. After all, I had my *National Geographic* magazines. Dingo, on the other hand, was about ready to bust. He would turn around in his seat to look imploringly at Peachy, and Peachy would just shake his head. Poopy however seemed as contented as a clam. It didn't take much to occupy Poopy, and his special teacher had given him a drawing activity to go along with his Social Studies project. The Beetle, I think, enjoyed courtly behavior, as he was really leaning into his classwork.

Dingo finally came up with something mildly amusing, and even better, something mildly subversive. It was mangled French. See, Miss Lindquist had been taking French classes up at Mankato State over the summer. She liked to throw a French word or phase out to our class now and then. You could almost see the wheels whirling in Dingo's head. At just the right moment, and within the appropriate context (for the actual French phase) Dingo turned in his seat towards Peachy and said, "Suck, re-blew!"

This was a masterstroke. Mangled French was born. It was Peachy next, making exaggerated groin thrusts in the milk line while saying "Wee-wee"!

Next it was Poopy, of all people, who stated with enthusiastic glee, "I make with zee Toot Sweet!" With that he let out a particularly sly and ghastly fart.

I swear to you, that kid must sprinkle garlic on his Wheaties in the morning. In a flash of inspiration, I turned to them all and said, "Bone Sway!" I think that was pretty good, for the spur of the moment, if I do say so myself.

We were somewhat focused for the next few days, staying courtly while at the same time amusing ourselves with mangled French. As a matter of fact, courtly behavior and mangled French seemed to go well together. Everyone knows French knights have the very best manners. However, I just about messed everything up on Friday.

I had used the last few days to make several thrilling discoveries in the *National Geographic*. The article *Everyday Life in Ancient Times* had become my new favorite. Although there weren't actual photographs of women's boobs, as time travel has not yet been invented, there were very beautifully drawn full color pictures of ancient ladies with their boobs out. But then, on Friday, during Social Studies just before lunch, I hit the Mother Lode. I discovered American Samoa.

I was staring down at the most thrilling and unbelievable picture I had ever seen. It showed a classroom, much like ours. There was a blackboard, desks, and an American Flag hanging near the door. And all the girls were sitting at their desks with no tops on, and their boobs out! That's when Miss Lindquist snuck up on me, coming up from behind. I just stared at her with my mouth open. The lunch bell rang, and she said, speaking over my hunched over shoulders "Have a good lunch." to the class, like she normally does (except like on the squirting water fountain day). But she stood where I couldn't get up and she said, "Let's have a talk, Eric."

Oh Jeez, I was so embarrassed and humiliated. I had been caught out for the knave I was, rather than the courtly knight that I was pretending to be. I felt my cheeks flushing, and my eyes filled up with tears. The thing about tears is that sometimes they can really help a situation. The look on Miss Lindquist's face changed. She got that 'Mom' look in her eyes. She sat down in the desk across from mine.

She said, "Look Eric, I know it's natural for a boy your age to discover that he's interested in how young people naturally change as they get older. You are all going to be talking about this as a class next year. I'm going to call your mother to let her know we've had this little chat, but you're not in trouble. I am however, going to remove this magazine, as I don't want it to become a distraction to either you or the other boys. OK?" she asked.

"OK" I croaked.

"OK then, Eric, you can go to lunch."

I got my lunch from inside my desk, and I got out of there fast, you bet! I was so relieved. American Samoa had been lost, but New Guinea was saved. The guys had kept a place open for me at the lunch table, and they all wanted to know what had happened.

I told them that Miss Lindquist had caught me goofing off instead of doing my work, which was kind of the truth. Both Peachy and Dingo were looking at me very closely. Dingo for sure wasn't fully buying it. Dingo can see right through me. He's kind of spooky that way. I think it's because we are so much alike. Not that we look alike, although people say we do, even though he's a toe-head. It's just that we think alike, a lot.

"So, are you in trouble, or not?" Dingo asked.

"I'm not in trouble," I said, looking him in the eye.

He bought that, sensing that at least that part was the truth.

Next, while we were out at recess Peachy coordinated Saturday's adventure during a game of tag. We would have a 'round up' at about ten in the morning. A round up is when we converge somewhere on our bikes. In the morning Beatle, Poopy and Dingo were to converge at

Peachy's place, and then they were to all ride on over to my house. From there Peachy was going to take us to a 'classified' location. I was almost giddy with anticipation. The bell rang and we were herded back into the building. All we had to do was hold it together for one last afternoon. If we could just do that, the horrors of grounding would be over for me and Peachy as of tonight, and we would be free at last.

We hung in there, doing exactly as we were told. Eventually the last period of the day came around. Friday afternoons was our Music session with Black Goose Falls Elementary School's Music teacher, Miss Walker. Everyone had had to sing a song in front of the whole class, and the five of us had resisted this to the bitter end, hoping against hope that maybe Spring Vacation would make this uncomfortable idea just magically go away. At first there was a glimmer of hope, because Miss Walker led the class in some very lame rounds. But then hope vanished.

"OK, let's finish up with those solo song presentations that we haven't heard yet," she said. The Beetle raised his hand, but she didn't call on him, wanting to get the true cowards out of the way first. "Eric, why don't you come up and give us your song, please," said Miss Walker through one of her most pleasant smiles.

Although I didn't want to do it, I was ready. Because I liked the song so much, I had memorized the words to *One Eyed, One Horned, Flying Purple People Eater*. I sang in tune and got most of the words right. I got applause. I got a 'B', because although not encouraged, contemporary rock and roll music was allowed.

Miss Walker continued to ignore Beetle. Next up was Poopy. He gave an entirely serviceable rendition of *Oh Suzanna*. Miss Walker complimented him for keeping the contradictions of the song straight. Poopy beamed. Next up was Peachy, who sang something he called *Trash Cans Away!* This song, which I don't know if he found it somewhere, or if he made it up, was sung to the tune of *Anchors Away!* Peachy told us the next day that he didn't get a very good grade.

We were getting down to the wire, with only minutes of class to go. Next up was Dingo. He sang *I've Been Working on The Railroad*. When he started in, I saw Miss Walker roll her eyes. Miss Lindquist smiled at Miss Walker and made this little 'It's OK' movement with her hand.

Then it was Regina Schlagel's turn. She was by far the prettiest girl in class. She had been absent, and so she was worked in amongst us true laggards. Regina got up and sang *You Ain't Nothin but a Hound Dog*. She gave it real bumping and grinding, real body language while she sang it, and that's for sure. While she was singing, she kept looking in Peachy's direction. Peachy seemed oblivious, but The Beetle was grinning from ear to ear.

At last, with only a couple of minutes left of class, it was time for The Beetle. Miss Walker reminded him that we only had a few minutes left and to make it quick. The Beetle got up in front of the class and belted out *The Battle Hymn of The Republic*. After the first verse, both Miss Walker and Miss Lindquist started clapping, and so did some of the kids. But Beetle rolled on into the second verse, his voice getting stronger and more passionate as he went. When he got to the part about dying to make men free, his hands were out, palms towards us.

Poopy looked like he was in a state of rapture. He suddenly joined in on the chorus. The place went nuts. Everyone in class (except for the teacher ladies) sang the last chorus in full throat. Even the school bell system helped with the splendor of the moment by going off on the very last note of the song. Glory, Glory Hallelujah!

Miss Walker tried to say something, but we were already charging the door. I saw Miss Lindquist give Miss Walker another one of those 'It's OK' hand gestures as I beat feet. I was in such a rush you see, because I wanted to get well ahead of Phillip the Pig, and his class across the hallway from us was spilling kids into the main hall in a regular stampede.

I had to weave and dodge my way down the hall because I had been one of the last ones to get out of the room, owing to my new location by the window. As I scooted past Beetle, I noticed that Regina was walking down the hall with him and telling him how much she enjoyed his song. As I ran, I heard him tell her how much he had really enjoyed her song. They were both grinning at each other. I mulled over (as I ran for my life) what a crazy, mixed up place my class had turned into. I made it out the door and kept on chugging.

I jumped on my bike and only then took a quick look back. Phillip the Pig was just clearing the door. He looked about, found me, and then we locked gazes. Too bad for him, my back tire was already kicking up gravel. I gave him a nice little 'bye-bye' wave and got going.

It was a sunny afternoon, but the air was still cool. Because of the rain over the last few days, the road was clear with only a few water-filled potholes. I stuck my arms out and did the 'Look ma, no hands!' trick out of sheer exuberance. Peachy pulled up alongside me grinning, also doing the trick. The Beetle caught up behind us only long enough to holler out "See you tomorrow!" and then turn off towards Main Street.

Dingo rode up alongside me and Peachy, grinned, and took the short-cut towards his place, while also doing the trick. Dingo is one trick-riding devil. Someday I'm sure he'll have a job in the circus. We kept going, every now and then having to grab our handlebars to keep from crashing over. We heard Poopy come huffing and puffing up behind us. He shouted out "See you guys tomorrow!" then he turned his bike around and headed towards his house, one block behind the fun part of Main Street. Poopy had both hands firmly on his handlebars. Poopy refuses to do the 'Look ma, no hands!' trick due to an unfortunate accident the year before. The accident involved Poopy doing the trick, and a mailbox. For a while we called Poopy 'The Mailman', but it didn't stick.

Peachy turned off into the driveway of his place, where Bernard ran up to meet him. Peachy waved to me and Bernard grinned at me, while wagging his tail. I stopped doing the bike trick, and just took my sweet time. I guess I was just enjoying my 'ungrounded' status. I decided to turn around and ride through town after making sure that the coast was clear, and that Piggy was long gone. I rode all the way down one side of Main Street, then past the grain elevators, and then across the railroad tracks. I could see Beetle way, way up ahead, well on his way to his farm.

I turned around, went back through town on the other side of Main Street (the 'un-fun' side, with the post office, the bank, the hardware store, the law office, the barber shop and the grocery store) and then back across the old highway. No one was outside at Peachy's, so I headed for home. I was so much looking forward to tomorrow. Mom was waiting for me in the kitchen.

"I got a call from Miss Lindquist this afternoon, Eric."

Gulp.

"What's going on, Eric?"

"It's nothing Mom. I was just looking at a *National Geographic* when I should have been doing my work."

"Well, it's a bit more than that," she said. "You're starting to become interested in girls, and that's OK. But we should talk."

Gulp.

"Mom, I get it. I know about the Birds and Bees."

"Eric, it's more than just the biology, it's how to treat girls. It's about being a decent young man."

Gulp.

At about that uncomfortable point of our conversation Aimee and her dorky friend Mary Holmberg came charging through the kitchen door, all chatter and giggles. "We'll talk later, Eric." *Woof-Ta!* I figured I'd dodged that bullet, at least for the time being. I determined to stay very busy until Mom left.

A Sleepwalker

After making my escape from the dreaded birds and bees talk, I checked on Ninja Bob, who very much wanted out. I let him out and got my chore list done before supper. I stayed very busy on purpose. I most sincerely did not want to have that talk with Mom. After supper, (which was beanie-weenie and the last of the preserved pickles) Mom went to work. She told me to hold down the fort. I gave her a salute as she pulled out of the driveway, and she smiled. This was a good thing. Mary had gone home, *Lassie* was on TV, and Lassie was saving some little girl's kitten. All was well with the world. I settled myself into the easy chair by the bookcase and dug into human reproduction in the encyclopedia. My Dad's soothing voice led me through the at times boring, and at times stimulating, universe of human reproductive biology, quirks and all. But when I got to the boring bits Dad's voice shifted into a droning monotone, so I closed the book.

Aimee stayed up a little longer than usual, but it was Friday night, so that was OK. Most of what was now on TV didn't interest her, so she sat in the kitchen coloring. I shelved the encyclopedia (the subject was mostly dry and boring, to tell the truth) and watched *Gunsmoke* instead. Dingo says that Miss Kitty and Chester make out in the hayloft. I have never seen anything, ever, to substantiate such a far-fetched notion. But Dingo has a deep and abiding interest with haylofts ever since he spied his stepsister in a state of disrobement with some high school hot-rod guy up in their very own barn's hayloft. My goodness, but that hayloft is a storied place!

Dingo's stepsister moved out a few years ago, and she's going to Mankato State to become a teacher. I wouldn't mind having her for *my* teacher. Ooo la-la, as they say in France.

Bedtime rolled around and I realized I was bone-tired, although I sort of wanted to stay up late, because it was after all, Friday night. But I was tired.

I went down to the basement, all brave as brass, because I just marched right down to the pull chain without a qualm. I opened the basement door and called out for Ninja Bob. He didn't answer or come running, so I just looked around. Even though there wasn't a full moon anymore, there was still plenty of moonlight. I didn't see hide nor hair of him, so I reckoned I'd call it a night. Ninja Bob had proven repeatedly that he could take care of himself. I brushed my teeth, and after checking in on Aimee, I hit the sack. It was around midnight that I heard my door open. I could see the silhouette shape of my sister in her nightgown standing in the doorway.

"You OK, Aimee?" I asked.

She didn't say anything, so I turned on my bedside lamp. It was Aimee, alright. She was just standing there in the half-shadow of the doorway, and it looked like her eyes were closed.

"Aimee, you OK?" I asked again.

She just stood there. Then she said "Leave us *alone*. He's *my* cat!"

I got out of bed and went over to her. I'd never seen sleep walking before. This was a first. I had heard that you weren't supposed to wake somebody up who was sleepwalking because you might give them a heart attack or something. I just real gently turned her around and said, "Let's get you back to bed." I guided her back to her own bed, made sure the covers were back far enough, and then told her real gently to get into bed. She did just that, no fuss, no muss.

I sat next to her in the 'sick chair' for a while. The sick chair is a small easy chair that Mom pulls into our room so she can sit with us when we're sick. Aimee had been the last one sick with the flu, so the chair was still in her room. I just sat there until I was sure she was really and truly going to stay in her bed. I decided that there was no use in worrying Mom about this in the morning. I also decided to ask Aimee in the morning about if she remembered any dreams. And finally, I decided I'd read up on the topic of sleepwalking. I thought maybe Aimee had something to do with my bed being all made up in the middle of the night. The thought gave me the shivers.

Hobo Joe

I woke up feeling pretty good. I didn't even hear Mom come in from her night shift at the OKK, so I must have slept hard. I pulled open my window curtains to get a look outside. It was all gray outside, overcast but not rainy. I heard noises in the kitchen. I knew Mom wouldn't be up yet, so it had to be Aimee. It made for a good time to ask her about last night, in a casual sort of way.

"Morning Aimee," I said.

"Morning," she replied, not looking up. She was pouring milk on her cornflakes.

"How'd you sleep last night?" I asked.

She looked up at me absently and said "Uh, OK."

"Did you have any interesting dreams?"

"Uh, no," she replied, still tending to her corn flakes.

Well, that was that I thought to myself. Last night was much ado about nothing.

"You gonna be hanging out with your weirdo friends today?" inquired Aimee.

"Yep, and my chores are done, and I'm not grounded," I replied smugly.

"I know that," she said, spooning up her cereal.

I made my own bowl, leaving just enough milk for Mom's coffee for when she got up. I finished, rinsed the stuff in the sink, and looked out the kitchen door window. I could see them all coming my way. I grabbed my jacket with its very fine stitch marks down the back, and my treasured Minnesota Twins baseball cap, waved goodbye to Aimee, and headed out the door.

Down by the railroad tracks is one of the places we're not supposed to hang around. We're supposed to stay away from the tracks, period. That said, the old trestle bridge near the Tree of Death is one of our most favorite spots. It's a favorite spot that we only savor on a very few rare occasions. During the summer when it gets really hot the creosote oozes out of the trestle support beams, and you can smell it before you even get there. Last time we were down there in the fall, just as the leaves were turning, we saw Hobo Joe. We judiciously decided to find a different location to fool around in and let him be. I don't think he even saw us. He was not there on this fine day, nor was there any sign of him. Thank God. He is a filthy and foul creature.

The first time we met him was two summers ago, right after we finished the fourth grade. We went down to the trestle bridge and discovered a campfire. It was out, but it was recent. We poked around the fire pit, not finding much except a couple of burned-out cans that you couldn't even tell what had been in them. Then Beetle yelled, "Look at this!"

There was a cracked molar tooth laying on a flat rock. Why would anyone crack a molar, and where did it come from? We were studying this mystery when he suddenly came up from further down the embankment. How we didn't see him down there, I don't know. It's like he just appeared. "What the hell you little dirty piggies doing?" was his greeting. We took off, scrabbling back up the embankment to our bikes. "That's right, go run off little boys, 'cause if I catch you, I'll twirl you around, pull your pants down, and treat you like a little girl. Then, I'll eat you all up!" he said while smacking his lips.

We got to the top of the embankment and looked down at him. He continued to spout filthy language. He was missing teeth, and the teeth he did have were black and crooked. He seemed to be dressed in black, but it just may have been soot and dirt. I don't know. You could get a slight whiff of him too. A camp fiery smell mixed with what I think of as the smell of dirty laundry.

Peachy reached down and grabbed a rock. He slung it towards Hobo Joe, who danced aside quick as you please. He made a hissing sound, then picked up a somewhat bigger rock and threw it back hard at Peachy. It was a close miss. We got the heck out of there. Ever since then we've referred to him as Hobo Joe. We haven't any of us told the adults about this, but now I am. Back then we didn't want to get in trouble for hanging around the area of the trestle bridge and the railroad tracks. The Tree of Death is just a little way down from the bridge.

The Tree of Death was the location of Peachy's big Saturday surprise. He had found a replacement rope while scouting for stuff around the Aldrich place. Mostly everything of value had been taken out of the house, the barn and the out-buildings over there, and the fields were sold over to old man Faust and Mr. Anderson, I guess. A kid can still find interesting stuff out around empty or abandoned places, like the old toboggan, and a fine good old rope.

Peachy had tied in a couple of good big knots near the bottom end of the rope, and then shinnied up the Tree of Death and tied the other end to the overhanging branch where our original rope had been. We all figured the railroad guys had removed our original rope, maybe sometime last summer.

The whole reason we had gone to the tree last fall was to replace our missing rope. We had figured that Hobo Joe was only a summer guest. We figured wrong. But at least he wasn't around on this fine day, and as I've said, there was no sign of him either. But we were kind of wary. Peachy had done a good job, securing the rope away from the direction of the train so that it couldn't be seen by the engineer. We heard the train coming and hid ourselves. I love trains.

She came chugging along, a nice slow freight train with nothing but boxcars. I've always thought that slow trains are much less dangerous than fast trains. We patiently waited for the engine to pass. Once it was good and past us, we all got up. Peachy shinnied up the Tree, readied himself with rope in hand, and then kicked off. His swing and tap were perfect. His right foot just barely tapped the side of a box car. He swung back to hand-hold number one on the Tree with flawless control. Peachy's got a future in the circus if he wants one, along with Dingo.

Dingo was next, and he did just as good, putting the pressure on me. I guess I grabbed the rope a little too low, because I kicked my boxcar with the entire flat of my shoe, and that spun me back towards the Tree a little faster than I would have liked. I kind of scrabbled for my handhold, and nearly missed it. I also banged up my right knee. We still had plenty of train left, so Poopy was up next.

Poopy made the same mistake that I had, but worse. He kicked away too hard, missed handhold number two, and dropped before the rope could swing him back out towards the train. He tumbled part way down the embankment and then had to scramble his way back up. By the time Poopy got back up, The Beetle was ready to swing.

We all yelled for The Beetle to hurry up, because we wanted to get out of there before the caboose came around the corner. The Beetle looked down at us and grinned. Then he puffed up his cheeks and blew out, kind of making a buzzing sound with his lips. The Beetle kicked off, and at first it looked pretty good. And then, not so good. I don't know if he did it on purpose, or if he just didn't get it, but instead of just tapping his boxcar he gave it a very solid kick. As a result, The Beetle twirled on the end of that rope like a kind of crazy, toe-headed yo-yo.

Whether by intuition or design, Peachy had climbed part way up and was holding on to hand-hold number three. He snagged the Beetle as he came twisting in and they both tumbled down the embankment. The caboose came into view, and you could see this guy hanging out the window, and you could tell that he was yelling. Of course, we couldn't hear a word that he was yelling at us, but his mouth was opening and closing quite fast, and his arm was waving up and down very hard. The guy looked like Casey Jones might have looked if a bumble bee flew into his ear. What I mean is, the guy was angry.

Peachy and The Beetle came puffing up the embankment and we got out of there pronto. We didn't think the caboose guy had seen The Beetle swing on the rope, but he darn sure saw Peachy and The Beetle on the embankment. So, now we were on a high alert look-out for Constable Benny. We had developed a reasonably fair idea of Constable Benny's routine. I suppose he was hired to take up some of the slack for off-duty deputies. We used to call him 'Benny Belly', but we don't call him that anymore. Anyway, because he worked on weekends now and then, on weekends now and then he was the bane of our existence. We knew he might be coming around soon, so we thought it best to find a place where we could lay low for a while. West Anderson's Woods came to mind.

We didn't go there by way of county road, because we're not stupid. We took a route behind the grain elevators along the service road, and then cut into West Anderson's woods. We were kind of hoping that the rain had melted off the snow in the riding trail through West Anderson's Woods like it had on the roads and streets around town. No such luck. After a few yards in, the trail was still full of snow. We were about ready to turn back out when we saw Benny Belly's old International Harvester truck drive by.

Constable Benny had on his constable's shirt, and that met trouble. He was driving along at a slow pace, and that met more trouble. We could only assume he was looking for us. The Beetle decided to apply common sense to the situation.

"I'm going home, guys," he said.

"Me too," said Poopy.

"Wait, guys," said Peachy. "That train conductor saw me and Beetle run up the embankment. We gotta swap caps."

We swapped baseball caps and then without saying another word we all split up and headed home. I got home and pulled my bike up to the basement door. Ninja Bob was down by the weeds along the swamp, and he came bounding over when I opened the door. Just as I put my bike up the phone started ringing. I ran up the stairs and picked it up just in time with a cheery "Hello?"

"This is Constable Benny – am I speaking with Mrs. Luft?"

"No," I said. "This is her son, Eric."

"I see," said Constable Benny. "When will your mom be home, Eric?"

"I'm not sure, sir. Her and my sister are gone shopping. I'm just here watching the fort," I said, trying oh so hard to sound casual. There was a pause.

"Can I leave her a message?" I asked.

"Yes son," replied Constable Benny. "Let her know that there's been a report of boys playing down by the tracks west of town, and we want her to be on the lookout for such dangerous behavior. And let her know that I'll be watching really close."

"Yes sir," I answered. Constable Benny hung up.

I immediately called Peachy. I was well pleased that he picked up the darn phone. I rolled it past him real fast. He said he'd call The Beetle. I called Poopy. It took me a while to coach Poopy along, but I got the job done. Then I called Dingo. We all laid low for the rest of the day. We all had to do chores according to Peachy's orders, but in a generally nice and easygoing sort of way. Not like we were trying to cover anything up. It had started raining again, so it wasn't a big deal staying home for the rest of the day. I thought that it was only by the grace of God that none of the adults had noticed our roundup. But I will admit that we learned to be sneakier when we decided to get into more mischief.

In checking with each other later that afternoon, The Beetle said he had caught Constable Benny's call. Both his mom and dad had been out, and he had told Benny Belly that it took him a little long to get to the phone because he was outside sweeping the walkway. *Nice job, Beetle,* I thought to myself. Only me and the Beetle had been called. What concerned me was that Benny Belly had called my house and The Beetle's house. Was good Constable Benny starting to put two and two together?

Well, it had been Peachy and The Beetle on the embankment when the caboose came into view. I don't look anything like Peachy, but I had swapped my baseball cap for his. I was pretty sure the guy in the caboose didn't know any of us, so maybe Constable Benny was just guessing. Or maybe Constable Benny had caught a glimpse of me wearing Peachy's stupid 4-H cap. My guard was up. I hid Peachy's cap under my mattress, along with my comic books.

Mom and Aimee got home, and I helped them put away the groceries. Mom looked around and noticed that I had done more work around the place.

"Well, thanks for doing the dishes and putting them away, Eric. Did you vacuum too?"

"Yeah, Mom," I said, "It's been raining all afternoon."

"Any calls, Eric?"

"Yeah Mom, Constable Benny called and said to watch out for kids playing down by the tracks. I told him I'd pass it on."

Mom gave me one of her narrowed eye looks. "Well," you and your friends stay away from those tracks, understand?"

"*Ja, ja Mutti*," I muttered.

"Sometimes tramps camp out in those woods down there, Eric. I don't want you going down there. Do you understand?" Aimee's eyes got wide when Mom said that.

"Yes Mom," I said again with all sincerity. That ended our discussion. Case closed.

It was still raining out, but Ninja Bob yowled to be let out. Both Mom and Aimee gave me the 'look' so I let him out. I remember being so hungry and ready to eat. We had fried chicken, mashed potatoes and green beans for supper. As I go on writing all this down, you'll notice that we ate fried chicken a lot back then. We've shifted more to pizza lately. But back then the OKK always had left-over fried chicken. Anyway, it continued to rain outside, and Mom had to get to work. I told her I'd make sure the house didn't burn down, and she smiled and gave me a hug. Aimee watched *Lassie* on TV again. And once again, Lassie was saving some little girl's kitten. Hadn't that episode just been on? How goofy was that?

The rain really picked up and thinking about the kitten made me think about Ninja Bob out there in the rain. "*Well, he wanted to be let out"*, I thought to myself. I cracked open the encyclopedia and dug into the subject of sleepwalking.

Dad's mellow voice in the encyclopedia said that sleepwalking is also called somnambulism, and that it's when a sleeper leaves their bed and engages in an activity that fulfills a wish. He also said that the sleeper might be re-enacting a past event. This really made no sense to me at all, considering what I remembered her saying while she was sleepwalking. As if to make some sort of point, Ninja Bob yowled to be let in. "Let your big stupid ugly old cat in." said Aimee absently while watching Lassie's latest rescue (again).

Ninja Bob was yowling to be let in from the basement door. I had let him out from the kitchen door. I tried calling him up, but he just kept yowling from down by the basement door. I went down and let Ninja Bob in. He was soaking wet, and very hungry. I went to the pickle shelf to get the last of the cat food, and when I went back to replenish his food bowl I noticed, lo and behold, my black knit hat was back on the doormat by the furnace. Ninja Bob must have dug it out of wherever he had stashed it and put it back on the doormat without me noticing when I got his cat chow. I reached down and touched the hat and noticed it was wet. I thought he must have sat on it or something. I decided then and there to let Ninja Bob have the darn hat. Anyway, only dorks wear winter hats in the spring. Ninja Bob really chowed down.

It was a good thing all the rain was washing the snow out of the culverts because I'd be able to start collecting pop bottles again to cash in at Swenson's Groceries for cat food. He was almost out of food, and I was almost out of money. With the snow gone there was no snow shoveling work, and it wasn't lawn mowing time yet. I went back upstairs, and Aimee went to bed. I stayed up and watched *The Ghost of Frankenstein* on Shock Theater. It's not as good as *The Son of Frankenstein*, but it's ok.

After the movie got over it was almost midnight. I brushed my teeth and checked on Aimee. She was fast asleep. Maybe she really wanted to be friends with Ninja Bob somewhere deep in her sub-conscience. Maybe that was her unfulfilled wish that made her sleepwalk. I decided I'd ask her about it in the morning, without letting on to her about her sleepwalking. I crawled into bed and was soon fast asleep. Nothing happened that night except for the odd business of my black knit hat showing back up in the basement.

In the morning when I woke up, I just lay in bed and thought things through. I told myself that all the spooky stuff with Aimee was well over with. All I had to do was to settle the hash with her and Ninja Bob, including hopefully catching Ninja Bob scratching at her window, to put an end to the whole spooky business once and for all.

The day looked sunny. I had plenty of time, because Peachy, The Beetle, and Dingo wouldn't be getting done with church until the early afternoon. A lot of times Poopy gets done earlier, because he's a Catholic. Maybe I'd give him a call, I thought to myself. I got dressed. Aimee was up, Mom was still sleeping in.

"Morning, Aimee," says I.

"Morning, Eric," says she. Look, we got raisin bran!" said Aimee, as if raisin bran cereal was a big deal.

"That sounds good to me." I replied, realizing that it did sound kind of good, as it was something else besides sugar-frosted flakes. Then I moved on to more important matters.

"Hey, Aimee, I've never really asked you before; would you like to help me take care of Ninja Bob?"

"No Eric," she replied. "Not unless you get his eye fixed. If you get his eye fixed, then I will help you take care of him."

This flummoxed me. "But he's *missing* an eye. That can't be fixed," I pointed out.

"It looks gross," she said. "Mom says the vet could do something."

I had to mull that one over. I could barely afford cat food, much less a medical procedure by a vet. After a couple of hours spent cruising around, the day looked like it was going to be a bust. It was nice enough out, but nobody was home yet. They were all probably enjoying church potlucks at their respective churches, as that seems to be what Black Goose Falls churches are famous for. I biked past Peachy's place to see if maybe Bernard Who Is Not a Saint Bernard was on the front porch. He wasn't, which meant my pal was probably locked up inside. A lot of times, if there's nobody around and he's hanging out on his front porch, he'll go into the woods with me.

I decided to look around the Aldrich place. I figured if Peachy had been over there then, I might as well have a look. I took the gravel road that goes to the Beetle's place but then turned off towards Anderson's Woods. I kept going past the woods until I could see the Aldrich place up ahead, then I peddled up the lane just as bold as brass. There was a **SOLD** sign on the fence post. Peachy was right, the place was cleaned out. Someone had even taken the storm windows off the old farmhouse. They were stacked up and leaning along one side of the house.

Because it was broad daylight, I felt leery of going into the house, even though it was so obviously empty. I rode my bike over to the tractor shed and dismounted. I could see into the shed, and there was absolutely nothing in there. I walked behind the shed and hit pay-dirt. There was an orange crate chock o' block full of empty pop bottles. I picked up the crate. It was too heavy. I pulled off my jacket, tied the sleeves together, and turned my jacket into a sort of bag. Into my jacket-bag went the bottles.

I took my swag over to my bike with the intent of just getting on and riding off. But then I decided to peek into the barn. The barn door was wide open. I walked up to the barn, and just as I got to the door, I caught a whiff of a fiery-smoky, dirty laundry smell. I figured Hobo Joe was lurking somewhere close. I turned right around, got to my bike, picked up my jacket full of bottles and balanced it on my handlebars. I kicked off and got the hell out of there. I didn't look back. I just concentrated on balancing the bottle loaded jacket with one hand and steering my bike with the other. I sounded like some sort of tambourine going down the dirt lane.

Being oh so very careful, I made it off the lane and onto the gravel road, and finally onto tar by turning off on Parker Street. It took me longer to get to Swenson's, but it was easier going on tar with the kind of load I was packing. As I went by Emmanuel Lutheran, I saw Phillip the Pig. He was between two guys, one who I recognized as his dad. Phillip was crying. I hate to see a fifth-grade boy cry, even a bully like Phillip. It's unmanly.

Phillip was saying "No, I don't want to go! No, I won't go!" and the two men practically lifted him into the car.

I felt bad for him a little bit. I felt bad for framing him about the weenie bomb too, a little bit. I decided if I had the chance on Monday, I'd try to mend fences with him. Phillip being Phillip meant that it probably wouldn't work, but I'd try, anyway. Phillip didn't always used to be a jerk. He was OK when we were little kids. In the last few years, he started to pick on kids, with me included. His mom and dad used to own the Chatting and Chewing Café on Main Street. It was no big deal back then, just a little place on the other side of the movie theater, the last place before the sidewalk ends at the railroad tracks and the grain elevators. Poopy used to call the place the Chootie-Chew, maybe because of all the trains that go by. Anyway, that's what we all called it, too.

In my opinion, the food was never really very good there, just burgers, fries, hot dogs, milkshakes, and pop. The burgers always were better at Lucky Lurky's, on the old highway. For a real sit-down type of meal most everybody in town still goes over to Jenny's Diner across from the bank. At least, that's what I've heard. I don't get in the Diner much. I did go to the Chooty-Chew every now and then.

The local patrons of the Chooty-Chew used to be mainly teenagers with nothing to do, and little money to spend. But anyway, before they put in the new freeway there were always a few cars parked in front of the Chooty-Chew. I suppose they were people just passing through. Then Phillip and his family left, and the Chooty-Chew grew a new **For Rent** sign in the window. That made it look so very dreary, and it had already been looking dreary for some time. When things started to go bad for the place Phillip started to get mean as a snake. I looked back at him as I peddled along, just for a second, and he was crying like a baby.

Katrina Hooch

I continued down the street, past the dairy, and then crossed over to Swenson's Grocery, jingling and clinking all the way. I almost tipped my bike over while parking it by the bench outside the store. I set my jacket full of bottles down on the bench so that I could put myself together before peeking into the store window. I was sweating, and my shirt had come un-tucked. After putting myself in order, I peeked in to see if Katrina was there, like she sometimes was on Sunday afternoons. The store was closed but the lights were on, and that was a good sign.

Katrina Hooch was in there, putting goods on the shelves, like I hoped she'd be. Katrina worked at Swenson's part time on week-ends. Her bike wasn't in the bike parking space where she sometimes parks, but on nice days she liked to walk. She saw me peering in and cracked the door open.

"Whoa, Eric," she said smiling at me. Looks like you've got quite a haul!"

"Yes, indeed I do ma'am." I said grinning up at her.

"We're closed, Eric, but you're sweating like a pig. Let's sneak you in, count those bottles, and send you on your way."

While she was counting I looked around. There wasn't much to look at, the same old stuff except that the community bulletin board had been updated. The picture of a run-away girl from New Ulm (she hadn't looked like a girl to me, more like a young woman) had been replaced by a Lion's Club flyer. That was it. Katrina counted out twenty pop bottles. That was forty cents! I'm not complaining, mind you. I am making some real good change writing all this down. But forty cents!

Katrina *binged* open the cash register and plunked down a dime on a nickel on top of a quarter.

"There you go sport," she said smiling. Then she reached into the candy jar by the register and pulled out a jaw breaker. "And this is on the house."

I grinned at her and she grinned at me. Then I skipped down the row where the cat and dog food is before Katrina could say anything and snagged the cheapest box of dry cat food that I could find, for twenty-five cents. I plunked the quarter down and then made a careful and graceful exit, unlike the time I knocked over the little apple barrel right next to the counter.

On the day that that happened I thought I was going to die from embarrassment. I had been looking at Katrina, rather than where I was going. I knocked the barrel over and apples went bouncing and rolling everywhere. Katrina rushed from behind the counter and dropped to her knees next to me and helped me pick up the apples. I learned a great truth on the day I knocked over the apple barrel. I learned that the sound a pretty girl makes when she's chuckling is one of the most beautiful sounds in the world.

I got home in time for Creature Feature on channel eleven. See, somebody at the TV station set up monster movies like this: you have *Shock Theater* on Saturday nights, and *Creature Feature* on Sunday afternoons. As everyone knows, *Shock Theater* is the vampires, werewolves, and mummies kind of stuff, while *Creature Feature* is the science fiction kind of stuff. The movie *Invaders from Mars* was on, and that's one of my favorites.

We had spaghetti and meat balls for supper. During supper Mom remarked that I didn't stay out too long during the afternoon. It was one of those remarks disguised as a question. I told her everyone had been at church, so I had gone looking for pop bottles, and that I found a bunch over at the Aldrich place. She didn't seem interested, and she moved on to talking to Aimee about helping with my birthday cake. Aimee was very much interested in that. I let them prattle on and finished up. Without being asked to, I did the dishes. Ninja Bob wanted out, so down I went and let him out. It was nice enough outside, so I wasn't concerned too much about letting him back in. I would be mindful of any strange scratching sounds in the night; however, I so wanted to catch him in the act of scratching at Aimee's window.

I was tired enough to go to bed early, so I wished everyone a very good night and turned in. I thought about the day as I waited to fall asleep. I decided to hit the Post Office on Monday after school and take care of my business with some of the money I had made plus the little I had left. That got me to thinking about the Aldrich place and that smoky, funky smell in the barn. It was probably just nasty stuff, like a bag of garbage that had been left behind in there. I dreamed that night, but I knew I was dreaming, so it wasn't a nightmare. A nightmare is something you can't seem to get out of. This was just a bad dream.

In my dream it was night, and for some reason I was hanging around the old trestle bridge down by the Tree of Death. Hobo Joe was under the bridge, and he had a small fire going. He was crouched over the fire, and he was cooking a chunk of meat on a stick. Grease was dripping off the meat, and when it hit the fire it would flare up and light up Hobo Joe's face. Suddenly I was standing right next to him. The fire flared up and he looked at me, smiling.

The flaring firelight made his face look orange and red, all in swirling smoke and shadows. Not only that, but Hobo Joe had a mouth full of teeth, and they were all very white, and all very pointy. I turned and tried to run up the embankment, but I kept falling to my knees, and then had trouble getting up. I wanted out of the dream, so I woke myself up. I decided that my dream was just a sort of a warning type of dream, and I reckoned I would take the hint.

A Black and Shining Thing

Monday was a very boring school day. I did my morning chores, and then looked around for Ninja Bob. He was nowhere around. "*Well, he'll be good and hungry tonight,*" I thought to myself. I did find out that Poopy's folks had taken the family to visit relatives in Mankato, and the potluck at Emanuel Lutheran had lasted longer than usual because everyone was saying goodbye to Phillip's family. So that explained why Poopy, or Dingo didn't get back at their normal times on Sunday.

Because Dingo's a Lutheran, he normally got home right after Poopy. As things worked out, Peachy's family spent the afternoon with Beetle's family over at Beetle's house. They had all gone to church, and because the Petersons and Gustavssons are all Methodists, Peachy, Molly and Beetle were always the last ones to get home on Sunday. Of course, now I'm in the mix, too.

I remember thinking on that Monday morning how much I wanted to hang out with them all next weekend, because we weren't having so much fun together during the week. The adults were seeing to that. Miss Lindquist continued with her punitive seating arrangement, and Monday just dragged on and on. For lunch however, Peachy provided us with a wonderful and clever diversion.

On days when they are going out to do some sort of concert or program, the choir kids like to all sit at the same tables. I suppose they do this to show off their white choir shirts. That fine day the choir was gearing up to sing at the Black Goose Falls Senior Center after lunch.

When we were released for lunch Peachy was off like a shot. He got into n the lunchroom ahead of everyone else, and very slyly smeared yellow mustard along the edge of one side of one of the tables where the choir kids normally sit. That he managed to do this without being noticed by the lunch ladies or Basketball Head is a testament to his stealth and cunning.

The choir kids came in and they all made a beeline for their favorite table, and got seated quick, all giggly and excited. Peachy tipped us off to watch, but to watch, not obvious, but sneaky. All at once the choir kids on one side of their table realized that they had yellow stripes across their tummies. They got very upset, and Basketball Head had a conniption fit. It was very hard to keep from laughing right off, but we held on until everyone else was laughing, then we joined in. We were suspect, of course, but nobody could prove anything. There were accusations during recess which added to the fun. But all good things must come to an end, including recess. The whistle blew and we had to go back inside.

The afternoon dragged on, just like the morning, but at least it turned into a sunny afternoon by the time school let out. We all had our bikes, so we headed for Anderson's Woods to check out the bike trail. Now I'm not talking about the tar bike path that runs along the road that goes by Anderson's Woods. The town put in the bike path for us kids when the new elementary school was put in out close to the old highway. Nope, I'm talking about the trail that loops through West Anderson's Woods. That's the horse trail I've already mentioned, but we consider it a bike trail. It's full of excellent curves, both uphill and downhill. There, you get to catch some truly exciting curves either coming or going.

We turned off the bike path into the easternmost trail entry into the woods. The snow had mostly left the woods, but the trail was very muddy, sloppy and not worth the trouble. We only got as far as Dead Man's Curve. This is hallowed ground. It is the very place where The

Beetle got his nickname, along with the noteworthy red scar that runs up his belly. We stopped there, and relived the afternoon that Beetle got his name. Beetle is the second kid in our group to get a nickname that stuck. He got his nickname after Dingo, and before Poopy, Peachy, and me.

It was last summer, and we were in the woods to check things out after a real ripsnorter of a thunderstorm. There were fallen trees here and there, but it was Dead Man's Curve that had the greatest new enhancement. The curve itself is a sharp turn at the bottom of a twisty and turn-filled downhill run near the eastern outlet of the trail back onto the bike path. A big, splintered tree limb had fallen part way into the turn, jagged end out. What could be a more thrilling challenge?

We found that we could just get around the jagged end of the limb, so we peddled through the curve and went up the hill so we could give the trail a proper run. We lined up with Peachy in the lead, then Dingo, then me, then Poopy, and then scrawny little (but game for the run) Godfrey. Godfrey is Beetle's real name. With Godfrey in the rear, we pushed ahead. Peachy made a yodeling cry and off he went. Dingo turned, grinned at me, and pushed off. Then it was my turn.

I can say that for myself I used a little more technique while standing on my brakes than I normally do. However, I still came down fast enough to keep my honor, and to also scare myself nearly bonkers. Poopy was the next guy to come rattling down the trail. He overcorrected just a little too much. He missed the tree limb, made part of the curve, hit a root and plowed into a bush. We were just able to clear the tears of laughter from our eyes in time to view the full scope of Beetle's stupendously amazing and death-defying crash.

Godfrey was just barreling down the trail. His glasses were reflecting glittering sparks of sunlight, and little moths and big butterflies dodged out of his way. He sped through those slanting rays of afternoon sun in something approaching a state of rapture, clearly caught up in the grandness of the moment. Poopy, who had untangled himself from the bushes yelled out, "You better *slow down*, Godfrey!"

Godfrey just let out a laugh. And as he laughed, a great big fat black beetle flew right into his wide open and laughing mouth.

You couldn't see his eyes because his glasses were firing off those flashes of sunlight and all, but Godfrey's mouth went into this big 'O'. Suddenly gulping something half-down like that must have been very distracting. It was like he steered right for the splintered limb instead of trying to make the curve. He didn't hit the splintered part, which was a good thing. He could have impaled himself. But he sure did hit the thickest part of the limb and got flung right over the handlebars of his bike.

Now, to be sure, up to this moment, the only time that I had ever seen a guy go flying through space was in one or two *Three Stooges* movies. But if I'm lying, I'm dying. Godfrey went flying through that sun spangled summer air like Superman himself. His arms were stretched straight out in front of him and everything, just like Superman. He flew right through the bush that had tangled up Poopy, and then did this incredible summersault, landing on his back with a thud. We weren't laughing at this point because we were all of us deeply and suddenly concerned.

We all ran over to him, and he was kicking the ground with his feet and pounding the ground with his fists. He made croaking sounds, flipped over, pushed himself up on his elbows, opened his mouth wide, and looked like he was going to throw up. Then, out of his mouth flew that big, black, glistening beetle. I guess the beetle had lodged in Godfrey's throat. I think that big old beetle was probably as unhappy with the situation as Godfrey was. It must have been wriggling and kicking down there without being too badly damaged, because it buzzed as it flew off. Godfrey sat up and took in a deep shuddering breath. Then he grabbed his stomach and said "Ouch!"

His t-shirt was ripped and bloody, but we couldn't see what was going on, so we pulled his t-shirt up. He had this big gash from just above his belly button to just below his rib cage. We think it must have been the center bolt on his handlebars, because he did sail over them very closely. Peachy guided Godfrey home and took the blame for the accident. Both Godfrey and Peachy bravely took their punishments and shielded the rest of us. Godfrey had to have stitches. We looked at them the next day, and they were very cool. In retelling the story, one of the funniest parts for us was when he croaked out, "beetle!" He also confirmed for us the beetle was indeed kicking up a storm in his throat. How cool is that? Anyway, it was the day following this most spectacular of all crashes that Godfrey got his nickname of The Beetle, Forever and Ever, Amen.

Cats and Crows

After retelling the highly entertaining and legendary story of how Beetle got his name, and having a good laugh over it, The Beetle, blushingly stated that he had to be getting home, so off he went. We all split up, which was fine with me because I had business at the Post Office. I cut down Frost Street and came out on Main Street on the corner where Otto's Tavern is located. I hate Otto's Tavern.

A few years after Dad died, I was riding my little kid's bike past Otto's Tavern. The door was open because it was a warm day. It always looks dark in there, and it always smells like stale beer. I slowed down because they were talking about my dad's accident in there. His car hit a telephone pole on a little county road on the Iowa border. Some ***hole in Otto's Tavern said that my dad was spread across two states. The men in there, whoever they were, *laughed*. I will never set foot in that piss-hole of a place.

However, I had much more elevated concerns. I needed to get to the Post Office. I peddled on across the street and over to the Post Office and parked my bike in the bike rack. You can tell you're in a civilized part of the world when you can park your bike in a bike rack. I went in and waited in line for my turn at the teller cage. The old guy in front of me talked on and on, a regular twenty questions kind of old guy. I just waited and looked around. There was a fresh new recruiting poster. This one was of a crew cut and extremely fit and tan looking marine climbing straight up a very thick, high rope. The poster stated, 'THE MARINE CORPS BUILDS MEN'. The poster was down-right intimidating. I think I'll take a pass on the Marine Corps when I get older.

At last, it was my turn, and I went up to the guy behind the cage. He recognized me and I recognized him, but we neither of us know each other's names. I put a nickel and five pennies on the counter and said, "The usual." He had already got out my US Savings Stamp, so it was a quick transaction. That's how transactions at a Post Office *should* be.

I put the stamp in my shirt pocket, not my jeans pocket. I had learned about that the hard way. Then I got myself home but taking my time because it was nice and sunny out. Aimee asked why I had taken so long, and I told her it was none of her business. She is *such* a pain. Mom didn't think I had been inordinately late, so I stuck out my tongue at Aimee and then concentrated on the beanie-weenie we had for supper. After we got done with supper, I made sure to go upstairs to my room, pulled out my Savings Bond Stamp book from its secret place, and stuck in that stamp. I reckoned in a little while the book would be full, and I'd exchange it at the bank for a Savings Bond. One day I know I will be able to buy a hot-rod, and then be able to have a girlfriend just like Katrina Hooch. All that I must do is just to keep plugging along and keep the faith.

I didn't feel like reading the encyclopedia that night, so I watched TV instead while half-listening for Ninja Bob. I prefer more mature stuff, as I've mentioned, and so I watched Cid Caesar. There was this one great cigarette commercial, where this dancing box of cigarettes came out while Cid Caesar was telling a joke. He complemented the dancing box on her (it's?) legs. It must have been a she, because it (she?)

had on nylons and high heels. I remember thinking that that dancing pack of cigarettes had legs like Katrina Hooch.

After checking again for Ninja Bob, I went to bed early enough for a school night and fell fast asleep. I woke up in the middle of the night because I heard Aimee talking in her bedroom. I wondered if *mom* had got home early, so I got up. Aimee's light was off in her room, so I opened her bedroom door. She was lying there in the dark and saying something, but I couldn't make it out. Whatever she was saying was all babble. This wasn't sleepwalking, this was just talking in her sleep, and I decided I had better wake her up. I turned on her bedside lamp and gave her a gentle shake. Aimee's eyes popped wide open. She quickly looked all around her bedroom, and then she finally looked at me.

"You were talking in your sleep, Aimee. You must have been dreaming," I said.

"Yeah, I was having a dream about a little cat that climbed a tree," she replied. "Then, it flew into the air and went higher and higher. Then a whole swarm of crows came flying towards the little cat when you woke me up!"

I felt a little twinge of unease growing in my mind when suddenly there was a scratching sound at the bedroom window.

"It's her!" Aimee screamed, clutching my arm so hard she left claw marks.

"Hold on!" I said angrily, pulling out of her grip (hence the scratches *and* the claw marks).

With all the confidence in the world I strode over to her window, thumbed open the latch, and raised the window wide open. In jumped Ninja Bob, as if he had spent his whole life jumping in second floor bedroom windows.

"Aimee, look! It's been the cat all along! Look!"

Aimee looked, and her expression of terror turned into one of deep consideration. She sat straight up in bed and gave Ninja Bob a very narrow gaze indeed.

"I think you're right Eric," she said, but I don't wanna sleep alone tonight."

I didn't want to press the point. Besides, I was feeling triumphant. "OK, let's go," I sighed.

We got to my room and Aimee climbed into bed. Ninja Bob jumped onto the bed too and stretched out across the whole bottom.

"Oh no, no you don't Ninja Bob, you're going down to the basement," I said.

"Please don't go," begged Aimee.

She said it in a way that I understood. She really meant it. Well, that kind of fit into my plans to get her more comfortable with Ninja Bob, so I just played along. I got in bed and switched off the light. When I did that, Ninja Bob started purring. He was loud. I tapped him with my foot under the blanket, and when I did, he let out this very odd sounding meow-purr. Aimee giggled, so I did it again, and Ninja Bob gave us an even louder meow-purr. We both laughed. Aimee snuggled into the hollow of my shoulder and then fell asleep. It's funny, but between Aimee's snoring and Ninja Bob's purring I got sort of *carried* off to sleep. There is no other way I can describe it.

Haunted Places

I woke up the next morning with no Aimee and no Ninja Bob. I heard clinking and clanking in the kitchen, so I got up, got dressed, and got going. Aimee was dressed for school and had poured out cereal in a bowl for me. She was downright chipper.

"Where's the cat?" I asked.

"He's in the basement. He ran down there so he could go to the biffy. If he sleeps upstairs, we better leave bedroom doors open so he can do that. And I fed him too," Aimee chattered on. "I talked to Mom, and she says as long as I brush Ninja Bob and help take care of him, he can stay upstairs sometimes. But we really need to get his eye fixed. Will you promise me we can get his eye fixed?"

"Yes," I said absently. "We'll get his eye fixed. I'm going to school. See you there."

I congratulated myself on doing such a fine job with my sister, Ninja Bob, everything. Of course, I didn't have a clue about how I would get Ninja Bob's eye taken care of. That morning I found school to be very boring. Worse yet, lunchtime held a horrible surprise. We had seen Basketball Head talking with Miss Lindquist in the milk line, and while talking both peered in our direction from time to time. We all felt a bit of unease, so we behaved ourselves ever so appropriately. It was all for naught. We got into the lunchroom, and we were each one of us confronted with assigned seating *in the lunchroom.* The horror.

The afternoon was even worse than the morning, but after school we consoled ourselves with the fact that at least we weren't grounded. We decided because the trail through Anderson's Woods was still unusable, we should check out the path through Firefly Field and all the way past the Hoot Owl Barn. It was sort of on the way to Dingo's place anyway.

The Hoot Owl Barn is a haunted place, just like the Crossroads at Hanging Tree. My sense of the place was that something sad and melancholy happened there, either in the house or the barn. There isn't anything left of the house except the foundation. I guessed the place burned down. The Hoot Owl Barn is where Hanna's brother found the toboggan that nearly decapitated most of us. It had been stuffed up in the rafters where it looked like it was just some planking.

Nobody goes into the Hoot Owl Barn at night, but on summer evenings, right at dusk, we do sometimes sit away back from the Hoot Owl Barn so that we can watch Firefly Field. Firefly Field on summer nights is very cool. I don't mean cool as in temperature, although it is cooler at night. I mean the place is cool in a quiet and muted spectacle of nature kind of way. Around the end of June fireflies come out all over that field. When we're camping, we'll sneak over there after dark with blankets tied to our handlebars and just watch the show. Bats come out and they swoop and dive after the fireflies. This we take in all under the wheeling stars, with toads, crickets and hoot owls playing a croaking, chirping and hooting musical accompaniment. As a bonus, sometimes there are shooting stars. Sometimes there are a lot of shooting stars, especially in August.

When we got to Firefly Field the path was passable because it's not really in the woods, and the sun was able to get to it. We took it all the way past Hoot Owl Barn to where the trail lets out at the crossroads at Hanging Tree. This is a truly haunted place. There are a couple of stories about the tree.

One story is about a hundred years ago during the Red Cloud Uprising two Sioux warriors were hung there. Another story is during the same uprising, two German farmers were hung up on the Tree and shot full of arrows by the Sioux. A lot of times there are one or two crows perched on the Tree. I don't know for sure about either of those two stories, and we haven't found anyone who knows anything for sure. I mean really, can an oak tree even live for a hundred years? I don't know, and I haven't looked it up yet. But I do know about Mrs. Johansson.

A few years back, Mrs. Johansson was running the manure spreader through the field prior to putting in that year's sweet corn. All the locals kept telling the Johanssons that the field should only be planted with feed corn, not sweet corn. The Johanssons, being from Iowa, didn't listen. Mrs. Johansson had a case of beer along with her to keep her company. At some point during the process, she fell over backwards into the manure spreader, and the manure spreader just kept on running. The Johansson farm was sold to one of the Lundgrens following this gruesome accident. Now only feed corn is planted in that field.

Dingo doesn't like being around the crossroads at Hanging Tree after the sun goes down. I don't blame him. It wasn't at all dark yet, but it was pushing towards supper time and The Beetle had to get home, and he had the longest way to go. Everybody else had to get going, too. I got home and pushed through the kitchen door just in time for supper. Instead of pestering me about getting home on time for supper, the first words out of Aimee's mouth were "So when are we getting the cat's eye fixed?"

"What's this?" Mom asked.

Thinking fast, or rather, thinking too fast, I said "Well Mom, I was thinking that Ninja Bob needed to go to the vet and get his shots, so that he's legal. And oh, yeah, so he stays healthy."

"I see," Mom replied. "And who is going to pay for this, may I ask?"

"Uh, well, I was thinking this could be my birthday present," I blurted out. "That's a done deal," Mom said without further ado. I'll make an appointment with the vet for after school tomorrow. That's your birthday present."

"What about his *eye*?" wheedled Aimee.

"Shut up, Aimee." I said crossly.

"That's no way to talk to your sister, Eric," admonished Mom.

Aimee stuck out her tongue. Not wanting to mess things up, I kept my temper. I apologized in a very dignified manner. Then I said, "Aimee, I'm working on it."

There you have it. Between my own darn cat, my own darn sister, and my own darn mouth, I had managed to royally screw up my birthday. But I knew at least I'd still be getting birthday cake. I moped around, let Ninja Bob out, and then took a nap in my bedroom. Aimee asked if everything was alright through the door, and I told her I was fine. I told her everything was hunky-dory. I dozed off and then got woke up with a tap on my door. I got up and opened my door, and there was Aimee with Ninja Bob standing next to her. She must have let him back in. "He wants to sleep with you," said Aimee.

Sure enough, Ninja Bob trotted right in and jumped on my bed. As before, he selected the spot at the foot of the bed to go sleepy bye. This change in behavior meant that I now had to sleep with my bedroom door open.

I was in a funk all the next day. I hardly said anything to anyone. I just let the day go by. At recess Dingo asked me what was going on, so I told him. I told him my birthday present was going to be getting Ninja Bob fixed up with shots, and that I would probably end up paying to get his nasty old eye sewed up. Dingo looked at me like I was nuts.

"Why are you doing this for that nasty old cat?" he asked.

"I don't know," was all I could tell him.

I walked away from Dingo and moved off by myself on the playground. Unpleasant tasks need to get done and over with. After school let out, I got myself right home. I went to the basement, got out my old, old red wagon, and got a box from under the stairs. Ninja Bob followed me down, probably expecting supper. He had a surprise coming. I picked up my big old cat and dropped him right into the box. He yowled. I used duct tape to tape up the box. Ninja Bob started batting at the top of the box. Tough cookies.

I trundled my red wagon loaded with a yowling cat in a cardboard box down Main Street. This was a drill. This was an exercise in attempting to maintain my dignity during inauspicious and unhappy circumstances. Ninja Bob had started to *eat through* the box. I am not kidding. It was awful. It was embarrassing. People on the street stopped and stared at me. I walked along as fast as I could, almost trotting, but I had to stop for the light on the corner. I finally made it to the vet's office. *Doctor of Veterinarian Medicine,* that's what the words on the window say. The vet nurse lady at the desk asked about my business, and I told her I had an appointment, name of Luft. Ninja Bob yowled and yowled.

"Can we hurry up, please? I asked.

"Oh yes," the nurse said. "Have a seat. You're here a little early."

"What have we here, Sally?" asked the vet, hurrying out amid the uproar.

"It's the Luft cat, for shots," the vet nurse said.

"Let's have a look at him," said the vet.

"Sir, could you please give me an estimate on how much it would cost to sew his eye shut, or at least make it so it isn't so gross looking?" I asked.

"I'll see what I can do, son," said Dr. R.H. Hobson, Dr. of Veterinarian Medicine. Then he stripped off the duct tape and peered into the box.

"Sweet Mary and Joseph", exclaimed Dr. R.H. Hobson. "Because he's here, I can take care of his eye wound now. It'll cost less than making a second appointment," good Dr. Hobson went

"Yes, please," I said, without getting a quote.

"Come back to the clinic in about an hour. I should be done with your very large and unhappy cat before closing time, provided I can wrestle him down for the procedure."

"Yes sir," I said.

I wanted out of there, so I took off. I couldn't stand to hear Ninja Bob yowling anymore. He wasn't yowling just then, but I didn't want to be around if he started back up. With time to kill, I decided to go visit Dad. It'd been a while.

The Black Goose Falls Cemetery is a few blocks from downtown, but on a nice day I like to get there by walking first down Silk-Stocking Street, with its big wide sidewalks, big old trees, and big old houses. Down past Silk-Stocking Street is where I cut over to the cemetery. I walked over and through the gate, and down the curving path underneath the trees. Once the path gets to where there aren't any shade trees anymore, then I'm where my dad is. There's no stone at his grave, just a veteran's marker. As far as I'm concerned, that's just as good as a stone.

I told him how things were going, and what I was up to. I didn't say these things out loud of course, just in my mind. The hoot owls were hooting in the trees, even though it was still daylight out. I've noticed that they do that in the cemetery. The owls at the cemetery sound like the same owls at Firefly Field.

I said goodbye to Dad and went back to the vet to collect Ninja Bob. He was brought out all floppy and groggy, but at least he wasn't yowling. He had a very dashing looking black bandage over his eye. He looked piratical. I placed him in the box, and the vet handed me the bill.

"I think you've got yourself a Norwegian Forest Cat," said Dr. Hobson, looking at me in a questioning way.

"Well, he just showed up one night, that's all I know," I replied.

Dr. Hobson told me that Norwegian Forest Cats were sort of rare for this part of Minnesota, and that the cat may have an owner who was worried about it.

"It's probably then some Norwegian," I said. "I've heard the woods around here are full of Norwegians."

Dr. Hobson smiled, and then suggested that I put up a lost and found notice on the bulletin board in his office. I felt miserable, but I took pen to paper and made a lost and found notice.

I guess Dr. Hobson saw how miserable I was, and while I was writing he changed my bill behind the reception desk before giving it to me. I didn't want to look at the bill, so I stuffed it in my pocket. The vet gave me a small packet to take home, which I put in the box next to Ninja Bob.

"Have a good day, son," said Dr. Hobson.

"Yes sir. Thankyou sir," I said.

Then I got out of there. That was my birthday. But as things turned out, I still ended up having sort of a birthday party, a few days later. The day after getting Ninja Bob fixed up, I paid off the vet. I did it by cashing in my savings bond stamp book at the bank. I hate debt. As far as I'm concerned, debt is the root of all evil. After paying off the debt, I had enough money left to get Ninja Bob a dog collar so he could wear his rabies tag.

I was going to let the whole thing go about the money, but then Mom noticed Ninja Bob's eye bandage and his very dashing collar and tag. Before she could get angry about having a bigger bill to pay than expected, I showed her the receipt for payment from the vet. Then came the twenty questions, and I ended up telling her about my secret savings stamp book, and how I had cashed it in. Mom didn't say anything. She just walked out of the kitchen and went to her bedroom, to get ready for work, I guess.

The next day was Saturday, and the guys showed up with birthday presents, and Aimee and Mom presented us with my birthday cake. My best present was from Beetle. It was *Night Crawlers* by a guy named Charles Addams. Now, this guy is a different guy than Beetle's great grand uncle who was in the Civil War. This guy spells his last name with two d's, and he's still alive. He draws these wicked funny cartoons of spooky things and creepy people. It has become one of my favorite books.

Mom looked tired, but she kept smiling the whole time we ate my birthday cake. Then she gave each one of us fifty cents, and she said that the Saturday matinee movie at the Falls Theater was on her. That was very, very cool, because *The Time Machine* was showing, and I love science fiction. We could all afford to get in, and we could all get popcorn, a small pop, and a candy bar, except for Poopy. Instead of a candy bar he got candy cigarettes. We stretch our money by using the candy machine in the lobby. The candy bar election is smaller than at the concession, but candy only costs a nickel out of the machine.

The underground cannibal guys in the movie were neat, and the girls who the cannibal guys fed upon wore fetchingly short skirts. But the whole thing about time being the fourth dimension lost me. I think space is the third dimension, but I'm not sure what the first and second dimensions are. We had a lot of fun, and there was a *Bugs Bunny* cartoon to start off with. We sat way up in the front row.

To tell the truth, other than my birthday and the last day of school I don't remember much about May, because there wasn't much to remember. We had assigned seating in the classroom and assigned seating in the lunchroom. I suppose that might have something to do with me passing the fifth grade. Aimee stopped having her fits at night, so May just came and went.

Oh yes, I had to get the garden out back started in May. Starting the garden is always a bunch of work. I start out by remaking the scarecrow out of Dad's old flannel work-shirt and bib overalls. I keep them in my closet, way in the back. Dad used to call the scarecrow a *butzemann*, which is German for scarecrow, I guess.

The first time I made the scarecrow using Dad's old clothes Mom get upset, and then I got upset. She said that all of Dad's clothes were supposed to go to the Salvation Army. I cried and asked her how I was supposed to make a scarecrow without a good big pair of clothes. But the secret is I just wanted to keep Dad's clothes. Mom finally let it go, but she said it was creepy. I didn't care.

Besides working in our garden, I started scouting out underneath the bleachers over at Hagan Field. That's where the baseball and football fields are, just down from Black Goose Falls Junior-Senior High School. I'd get over there before heading off to school, early enough before most prying eyes were awake. I'd always found change and pop bottles under those bleachers in the past. But now I was coming up with nothing, which was puzzling. Softball and baseball had started, and there should have been easy pickings under those bleachers. Morning after morning there wasn't a pop bottle to be found, and nickels and dimes were hard to come by. I realized I would have to expand my search to keep change in my pocket.

We finally got to the last week of school near the end of May, and things started to loosen up. We gave a flute-a-phone concert one afternoon, and then a few days later we all got to go over to the big auditorium at the high school to see an educational film about Minnesota Indian tribes and what it was like for them a long time ago. We all tried to clump together when we walked over to the high school, but Miss Lindquist outfoxed us. She held me back as we moved into the rows of seats, and I ended up sitting with another class, in a seat right next to Molly.

Some guy in a coat and tie talked for a while, and then they started the film. It showed how Indians dried fish, hunted deer and made clothes out of buckskin. Then came this part where a captive Indian from another tribe was burned at the stake, all while there was singing and chanting. Molly pressed her head into my shoulder during this part, and I wasn't sure what to do, so I held her hand. She squeezed my hand tight, but when it was over, she let go and sat up straight as an arrow. The film ended and the guy in the coat and tie said something about that was what it was like in Minnesota before the white man. We got to walk back to our school and have ice cream sandwiches. After school that afternoon Molly and me shared our very first Popsicle on the bench outside Swenson's Grocery.

I had just sat down on the bench and was getting ready to tear off the wrapper of an ice-cold double Popsicle when Molly came sauntering up with a big grin on her face. She didn't say a word. She just plunked herself down and continued to grin at me. I wasn't exactly sure what she was up to, but because I was practicing on being a gallant gentleman, I snapped the double Popsicle in two and handed her one, stick first, out of the wrapper so as not to touch it with my grubby fingers.

She slid the Popsicle out and proceeded to go at it with gusto, making these slurping sounds that were just as loud and good as anything me or Poopy were famous for. I got my Popsicle out and gave her a run for the money with my own slurping, and we both started laughing. I shall never forget that day. The Popsicle was a root-beer one, the finest flavor on earth.

The last day of school was real fun, and I didn't have to pay for anything. Manitou Mounds Park was the location of our end of year school picnic. The school bused us up there. When you get close to the park the tar road divides for incoming and outgoing traffic, and right where the road divides there's a stone teepee. It's painted to look like the real thing. It's funny to watch out-of-towners stop at it, only to find out it's made of concrete.

The five mounds that the park is named for are at the top of Liberty Hill, overlooking a ravine and Black Goose Falls: the falls themselves, not the town. The Park is cool place, but it's hard for us to get to, because of Liberty Hill. We've biked there a couple of times. Not only is it a long way to bike, but then you've got to peddle up Liberty Hill, which is no joke. We always end up walking our bikes. Of course, the way back down makes it almost worth it. Almost.

Nobody goes up on the mounds. There's this bronze sign along a rail fence that says to stay off the mounds because they're burial mounds. Next to the sign there's this plaque with funny symbols on it, kind of an L followed by a sideways q followed by a backwards C with a period mark over the C. The only people that go up on the mounds are out-of-towners, and then people yell at them to get down. Besides, there's an observation deck where people can look at the falls just off to the left of the mounds.

Of course, we know all this, so we ran over to the pavilion area where the swings and marry-go-round are. We had sack races, water balloon tosses, volleyball games, soft-ball games, and dodge-ball games. There was ice-cold pop, watermelon, hotdogs, and ice cream. When we took our bus back down the hill we were all as full as summer ticks on an old dog.

Oleanna

June started out hot. The gang was sitting out on Peachy's back porch having fresh lemonade, the kind that's made from real lemons, not the kind you make from powder. Beetle wanted to talk about a problem. His birthday was going to be in a few weeks, and he wasn't sure if all of us were going to be invited. His mom had a dim view of some of us. All of us had been invited the year before the bike accident and the scalding accident and the reports of misbehavior involving some of us.

Beetle's mom had bought invitations at the five and dime store, and they were sitting on the kitchen counter, but they hadn't been filled out yet. The Beetle said his mom was feeling cranky because tomorrow was her birthday, and he was worried that if she filled out the cards when she was feeling cranky, then it might mean some of us wouldn't get invited. Peachy got an idea. Beetle's mom's name is Oleanna. We all know bits and pieces of the song Oleanna, and Peachy suggested that we sing her that song as a serenade tomorrow morning for her birthday. Poopy felt bashful about singing, but Peachy was in fine form.

"You sang in front of the whole class all by yourself a few days ago. Come on! This is a good idea," Peachy insisted. The idea gained traction.

"We could all pick wildflowers and give her a bouquet, too," suggested Dingo.

We voted, and we were all in favor of the effort. Our next topic was about where the wildflowers were. We had ideas. We got on our bikes and went peddling off to check out where the wildflowers were, but in June there's not much except for dandelions. But as Peachy always says, desperate times call for desperate measures. While looking for likely places for wildflowers we also scouted out some fine neighborhood flower beds. We decided that, depending on our success gathering wild-flowers, that some of us might have to get an early morning start to visit a flower bed or two.

Peachy was quick to admonish us as to the notion of any early morning visits to neighborhood flower beds. This, he instructed us, would have to be an option of last resort, as we didn't want to muck up such a gallant and fine gesture. We were trying to get all of us invited to Beetle's birthday party, not trying to get some of us black-balled For Ever, and Ever, Amen.

The next day was a hoot. I said 'Bye' to Aimee after breakfast and headed out after getting my flowers from their hiding place in the base-ment. I had gathered them up at the crack of dawn from various neigh-borhood flowerbeds, but I had only taken one or two from each bed, so as not to be mean or obvious.

We had designated Poopy's house as our gathering place, because it was about mid-way for most of us, and because Mrs. Alighieri dose not tend to ask too many questions about whatever we are doing, at any given time. Even today, she pretty much takes things in stride, unless one of us is bleeding. As one of our moms, I like her a lot. Even so, once we gathered at Poopy's we remained somewhat furtive. We did our business on the backside of Poopy's garage.

We only stuck around long enough to make sure that everyone arrived, that we all knew the words to the song we were about to sing.

We all had reasonably acceptable bouquets. However, the bouquet business took some doing. Peachy sorted our various bouquets so that they were more balanced. While doing so he showed off by naming some of the wildflowers. As it turned out, we had Carolina Anemones, Field Pussy-toes, Red Columbines, Wild Indigos, Marsh Marigolds, Dutchman's Breeches, and Jeweled Shooting Stars. Just so you guys know, I only partly remembered the names of these flowers. I had to look them up here in Reverend Leverkuehn's study, out of a book about Minnesota wildflowers.

After getting sufficiently organized it was time to head off for our rendezvous with The Beetle. We biked out to Beetles, going slow so as not to wreck the flowers or ourselves because we were riding 'one handed' on a gravel and dirt country road. I hoped that The Beetle had had the sense to get his own flowers. I needn't have worried. The Beetle met us at the end of his farm's lane, where he had a bunch of flowers in the ditch by the mailbox. They were a mix of the same wildflowers we had, along with a few from his mom's flower bed. Beetle was excited. "Come on, she's in the kitchen!" he nearly squealed.

We peddled up the lane and parked our bikes. Beetle called for his mom through the screen door, and we gathered ourselves, along with our wits. Mrs. Gustavsson stepped out, blinking in the sunlight and shading her eyes. Her blond hair was tied back into a ponytail. She was barefoot, and she had on a blue cotton dress. With the sunshine on her face, she didn't look thirty years old at all. She looked more like one of the older high school girls, like the ones who do lifeguard duty at the lake. We stood there with our flowers. Peachy called out, "And a one, and a two, and a three," just like Lawrence Welk.

We launched into *Oleanna*, and by the time we got to the third verse about the roasted pigs running down the street, Mrs. Gustavsson was using her hand with her thumb and her index finger to wipe away the corners of her eyes. She looked like she was laughing and crying at the same time. When we finished, she scooped up our flowers and then went running into the house, letting the screen door bang shut behind her. We just stood there. Poopy asked Beetle if everything was alright, and Beetle just shrugged.

We heard a bunch of clinking and clanking coming from the kitchen, and then out came Beetle's mom with a big cold pitcher of lemonade. It was the kind that's made with powder, but we didn't complain. She went back into the kitchen and left us on the front porch enjoying our well-earned and ice-cold lemonade. After a few more minutes she came back out onto the porch with a bunch of little envelopes. We all got invitations to Beetle's birthday party. Aimee got one, too.

Speaking of Aimee, that night she went sleepwalking again. We had both stayed up a little late because it was summer vacation. And besides, we both wanted to be sure to let Ninja Bob in so he wouldn't be scratching at Aimee's window. Finally, he yowled to be let in.

We both went down to the basement just as brave as brass, made sure he was fed, and then we went back upstairs and hit the hay. I left my bedroom door open and sure enough, after a few minutes Ninja Bob bounded right up and onto my bed. With his big old long body across my feet, and him purring away to beat the band, I fell fast asleep. I remember smiling as I drifted off. I remember looking at Dad's picture in the shadows, and he was smiling, too.

In the middle of the night, but before Mom got home, I woke up because Ninja Bob had set his claws into my left foot. I kind of kicked him off my foot and turned over on my side. It was then I saw something move in the closet. I nearly jumped right out of my own skin.

It was Aimee, just standing there in her nightgown, standing there in my closet. Oh, my goodness, but my heart was pounding in my chest as hard as a drum. I swung out of bed just as Mom's car lights lit up my bedroom curtains. I took Aimee by the hand and guided her back into her own bed as I heard the kitchen door open downstairs. I pretended that I was going to the bathroom as Mom came upstairs.

Beetle's Birthday Party

The invitations to Beetle's Birthday Party were for Saturday from 1:00 pm until 3:00 pm. The Beetle explained although his real birthday was on Friday, his party was on Saturday so that everyone could be there. This made no sense until Beetle explained his whole clan was showing up. They were coming in from all over Arrowhead County. He went on to explain the kid's party was in the afternoon, and then we'd have to skedaddle to make way for the big party. The big party was going to have polka and beer drinking, and his parents wanted to make sure a bunch of us kids weren't underfoot. This now made sense. Besides, for the kid party there was going to be hot dogs, chips, cake and ice cream, games and party favors. This sounded good to me. To tell the truth, it sounded like an exhausting day for Beetle.

I can't imagine what it would be like to have so many relatives. I used to have Grandma Doris and Grandpa Fritz, but Grandma Doris died from a heart attack right after Dad died in the car accident. That left us with Grandpa Fritz and my Uncle Carl and Aunt Monica. Uncle Carl is OK, but Mom and Aunt Monica don't like each other at all, so we don't see them much. Besides, they live all the way up in St. Cloud. For a few years after Dad died Grandpa Fritz would come visit us. Sometimes we would even get to visit him in New Ulm, until he died from a heart attack, too. That's how it goes with some families. This is not the case with The Beetle's family, though. It sounded like a whole small town's worth of relatives was coming for the evening party.

It took all the money I had to get Beetle his present. What I got him were three hand-painted Union soldiers from the five and dime store. I had to do some looking to find the right ones, because Beetle's Mom doesn't allow him to have any toy guns or toy soldiers with guns. I found one guy holding a bugle above his head, another guy with a drum, and the last guy holding an American flag. I reckoned that Union soldiers would work well because of the picture of Major Adams in Beetle's house, and because none of the Union soldiers had any guns. I suppose that's why Beetle used to love our 'Massacre of New Ulm' game so much. We used to play it with plastic cowboys and Indians in Dingo's tack room on rainy days. Of course, this was when we were just little kids.

Dingo showed up at my house right on-time, and we biked over to Poopy's. Poopy was ready to go for once, and off we went. When we got to Beetle's place Peachy, and Molly were already there. Boy Scout Kurt, Hanna, and surprisingly, Regina Schlagle, were already there, too. All the girls were wearing summery dresses, and Peachy and Beetle were wearing short sleeved white shirts. But Boy Scout Kurt was wearing a t-shirt like me, Dingo and Poopy, so we blended in OK. The big picnic table had been pulled underneath the oak trees in the front yard, so we had some good shade.

Mrs. Gustavsson had the picnic table all set up with a birthday tablecloth, pitchers of ice-cold Kool-Aid, hotdog buns, chips, plastic cups, napkins and paper plates. Mrs. Gustavsson was lighting the grill when we got there. Beetle's cake was a nice big one with thick white frosting. Peachy told me afterword there was an even bigger cake for the big party set for the evening.

While Mrs. Gustavsson grilled hotdogs we played kickball in the drive between the main house and the barn. When she called us over to the table we came running, whooping, and hollering. There was a rush to get next to the cake. Molly got on one end of the table next to the cake, and Peachy got the other end next to the cake across from his sister. The Beetle, because he was the birthday boy, changed places with Peachy and got next to the cake, as was his right. Peachy shoved down one spot on the bench and the rest of us just sorted ourselves out. We made a pretty good ruckus. Over and above all the din Mrs. Gustavsson made some noise of her own, yelling out "Sven, get the chicken ready for tonight while I do this!"

On his hurried way past us Mr. Gustavsson greeted all of us by name and told us how pleased he was that we had come to the party. Then he trotted down across the drive, across the barnyard, and behind the barn.

Hanna took it upon herself to pour the drinks, and in so doing she added decorum to the proceedings, telling everyone not to reach, and not to grab. We loaded chips on our plates and then Mrs. Gustavsson told us to come over and pick out our hotdogs, because some like them burnt, and some like them not so burnt. We all got seated with our hotdogs and at about that time we heard very loud clucking and cawing coming from behind the barn. We looked out across the barnyard and were startled to see what looked like two crazy-acting chickens come running out from behind the barn, with Mr. Gustavsson right behind them. Then we realized that the chickens were missing their heads.

Regina screamed. Dingo jumped up from the table and took off like a shot down the drive to help Mr. Gustavsson corral the chickens. Boy Scout Kurt followed, hot on Dingo's heels. One chicken just ran around in circles in the barnyard, with Dingo and Mr. Gustavsson both after it. The other chicken made a beeline straight for our picnic table. Boy Scout Kurt made a dive for it and missed. Mrs. Gustavsson ran around the picnic table to cut off the chicken before it could get to us, but as she ran up to it the poor thing took flight, making a wide arc and then flying directly over our table.

Regina shrieked. Molly, on the far end of the table next to the cake, made a lunge and snagged the poor chicken. I will never forget seeing that for the rest of my life. Molly held it away from her dress and trotted down to where Dingo and Mr. Gustavsson had finally got the other bird. Boy Scout Kurt offered to take the chicken from her, but Molly just shook her head. The whole group of them all walked back behind the barn with the still fluttering chickens in tow.

Meantime, Regina had come unglued. She had left the table and was standing under one of the oak trees hugging herself and crying. Beetle, Hanna and Mrs. Gustavsson walked over to her to help her calm down. When Beetle walked up to her, she started screaming again, and it was because Beetle had a few little red spots on his white shirt. Mrs. Gustavsson looked up to the sky, as if she were maybe praying, and then told her son to go inside and put on another shirt.

While this was all going on, Peachy made eye contact with me and silently pointed out some little chicken-neck blood sprinkles on the birthday cake. Then he moved fast. Using his plastic spoon, he scooped out the little blood sprinkles from the cake, flinging dabs of frosting under the table. There weren't many blood sprinkles, and they weren't very large. They looked like what you might get out of a slightly clogged bottle of tabasco sauce.

While Peachy spooned away, I got in gear and started smoothing out the little divots in the frosting with my plastic knife. Poopy just sat there and grinned. Just as Peachy finished, and as I was making a last smoothing pass over the frosting with my knife, Hanna looked over at me. "Hey, no fair eating the frosting before we cut the cake!" she said in a loud voice.

I just smiled and licked off my knife. We all got settled back to the table, Beetle came back out wearing a light blue short sleeved shirt, and we waited for the others to get back from the barnyard, out of courtesy. By the time they all came walking back from behind the barn Regina had collected herself, with a lot of help from Hanna. Mrs. Gustavsson stood there with her hands on her hips and a smile on her face.

"Nice work, Sven honey," said Mrs. Gustavsson.

"You are most welcome, Oleanna, darling," replied Mr. Gustavsson.

They were both grinning at each other, but not laughing outright. Mr. Gustavsson turned on the garden hose and the chicken squad washed up before coming back to the table. Molly made a few dabs at her dress and came walking back to the table with a few wet spots here and there. I got my hotdog and decided not to put ketchup on it, preferring to just use mustard instead. Besides, you aren't supposed to put ketchup on hotdogs, anyway.

Captain Jinx

June stayed hot. The Gustavssons and the Petersons always used to send their kids to camp right after Beetle's birthday. This time around Beetle and Peachy got to go to a YMCA camp somewhere along the St. Croix River. They told me later that they got to play at being Indians at camp, building teepees, cooking meat over fires, and running around in the woods wearing nothing but war paint, moccasins they stitched together themselves, breechcloths, and feathers.

As for Dingo, he always has a lot of work to do on his farm in June. I had work to do in our garden, but nothing like the work that Dingo used to do on the farm. A lot of times in June, or at least for the first few weeks of June, it was usually just me and Poopy knocking around. I was careful not to let Poopy in on where I was finding a few pop bottles for cashing in, because times were tough.

One day in the middle of June Poopy decided to take the long way back from fishing off Grandma Lundgren's dock (no croppies that day, it was just too hot) by tagging along with me to Firefly Field. I showed him to what I considered to be an excellent place to lie in the shade right along the boundary of East Anderson's Woods right near to where the path runs to the crossroads at Hanging Tree.

Except for that trail, which is only along the wood-line, East Anderson's Woods doesn't have a cool riding path like West Anderson's Woods. All it seems to have are just these little game trails here and there, that sometimes just seem to stop short in the middle of nowhere. After East Anderson's Woods comes the state forest, but you can't really tell where Anderson's Woods stops, and the state forest begins.

We leaned are bikes against a big oak and I laid down in the cool, tall grass. Poopy wasn't interested in just lounging in the grass, so he went off exploring. He went in on one of those little trails that looked like it was going to disappear. I told him he was wasting his time, but then Poopy saw something off in the brush. It was a cigarette butt. But it was a funny looking one, all twisty looking. Poopy pulled it apart, and watched the tobacco fall out. Then he noticed what looked like a narrow little trail on the other side of the brush. It looked like another little game track really, like what whitetail deer make.

We followed the little trail, being really quiet, because we thought the owner of the cigarette butt might be near-by. The trail, if you can call it that, went a long way deeper into the woods. The little track went on so long I thought we might get lost in the state forest. Poopy in the lead stopped short. He turned to me. "Look!" he whispered.

There was a mound with grass growing over it, and next to the mound what looked like a stove pipe sticking out of the ground, almost next to the mound. The mound itself almost looked like a midget version of the mounds at Manitou Mounds Park, except for the thick grass all over it, especially on the top. Walking so very quietly, we snuck over to have a look.

A few feet in front of the stovepipe sticking there out of the ground was a doorway, or entryway, or whatever you would call a hole in the ground. I guess doorway works, because it was framed in with logs. There were a few log steps going down into the hole, and a piece of tan canvas held in place across the top of the door by nails through metal grommets. The canvas was pulled aside and tied off. Before I could say anything Poopy stuck his head in.

"Let's get out of here, Poopy!" I said in a kind of loud whisper. "Let's get out of here now!"

"OK, OK," said Poopy. "But look, there's a cot, a little stove, a can of cat food, a transistor radio, and a green duffle bag with a padlock on the top of it. It says Red Cloud J. on the bag, and there's a bunch of pop bottles underneath the cot next to the duffle bag," Poopy blurted out excitedly, just as bold as brass.

"Poopy," I said in exasperation, "That's somebody's stuff. Let's get out of here, now!" I spoke in a normal voice, maybe a little louder than normal, because I wanted out of there.

"Good afternoon, gentlemen," said a voice on the other side of the mound.

We froze. Around the side of the mound walked this skinny guy with long black hair tied back in a ponytail. He had on jeans, work boots, and a flannel shirt. He looked older than a high school guy, but not much. The guy didn't walk directly towards us, but rather to a big log nearby, where he sat down. I realized the log was probably his sitting log. But there wasn't a fire ring in front of it, which I found odd.

"Well," the guy said, "At least you aren't thieves. But son, listen to me. It's called a sea bag, not a duffle bag."

"We don't care about the bag, and we don't steal stuff," said Poopy. "But sometimes we use stuff that we find around abandoned farms and barns – we do that."

"Yep, me too," said the guy. While he talked, he rolled a cigarette. I had never seen anyone roll a cigarette before.

"I guess we need to parley," said the guy.

"Is your name Mr. Red?" asked Poopy.

The guy's eyebrows went up.

"Well, well. You guys really have scoped me out. Well, young sir, you're half right. My last name is Red Cloud. You can call me Mr. Red Cloud. Are you Poopy?"

"I'm Larry, replied Poopy. "Only my very best friends call me Poopy." The guy laughed.

"Some friends," the guy said, still laughing. "And what's your name, kid?"

"I'm Eric," I replied.

"OK, boys, let's parley," said Mr. Red Cloud.

"What's that mean?" asked Poopy.

"It means working out an understanding," replied Mr. Red Cloud. "You see boys, if you tell people about me camping out here, I'll have to move. I'd rather not for the time being, but I'm on state property where I reckon camping's perhaps not allowed, and I'd have to go.

"Are you poor?" asked Poopy.

"I've been better off," answered Mr. Red Cloud.

"Is that why you eat cat food now?" inquired Poopy. This was a very tactless question, but it made Mr. Red Cloud laugh suddenly, and hard.

"No, no son. The cat food is for an honored guest who comes by from time to time. I haven't seen him for a while, though."

"What's his name?" asked Poopy.

"I call him Jinx," replied Mr. Red Cloud. "He's this big old cat I first saw hanging around that old, dilapidated barn down the trail from here."

"Why do you call him Jinx?" I asked, finally saying something. "Is it because he looks like a lynx, or is it because he's bad luck?"

"Neither," said Mr. Red Cloud. "He does look like a lynx to be sure, except for the tail. And just as sure, he's not bad luck. The opposite, I think. He's got the Manitou in him, in a big way. Nope, I named him after Captain Jinx of the Horse Marines."

"Who's that?" asked Poopy. Mr. Red Cloud's eyebrows went up again.

"Are you Minnesota boys?" he asked.

"Yes, of course, we are," we both nearly shouted.

"Then you should know about Captain Jinx of the Horse Marines!" exclaimed Mr. Red Cloud. "He sports young ladies that are in their teens! I think he sported that girl in the prairie books. What was her name, Laura Winter, Weller?"

"Wilder," said Poopy crossly.

"Yeah, that's her," said Mr. Red Cloud, eyeing Poopy closely. "Miss Wilder talks about Captain Jinx enough in her books, is all I'm saying," said Mr. Red Cloud in a conciliatory sort of way.

I shifted the conversation a little because Poopy really likes the Wilder books, and he was still looking cross.

"You named the cat after a Marine?"

"Yep."

"Were you a Marine?"

"Yep."

"Did you fight in a war?" asked Poopy, breaking out of his funk.

"Yep," said Mr. Red Cloud. But when he answered Mr. Red Cloud wasn't smiling. Then *he* shifted gears. "Lads, like I said, I'm camping here on state property, and I'd like to stay a little longer. What do you guys think?"

"Did you ask permission?" asked Poopy.

"Nope, wasn't sure who to ask."

"Well, this place is called Anderson's Woods, but I'm not sure if it really belongs to Anderson, but I'm not sure if we're on state land," I told him.

"If we find out, we can leave you a note," said Poopy.

"Look boys, I'm sure you'd like to be getting along. To tell the truth, I'd like it if you were getting along, too."

Then Poopy blurted out, "I think you should stay."

"And you, sir?"

"Stay," I said.

"OK boys. I'll sit tight for now. I think I'll be moving on in the fall."

"Where were you before here?" asked Poopy.

"White Earth," said Mr. Red Cloud. "But I didn't fit in there very well after the Marines. Seems I don't fit in anywhere very well anymore. Well, get the devil out of here boys, and thanks for not stealing anything, and thanks for hearing me out. Maybe if I see you in the woods, I'll show you where some good berries are."

We talked a little longer, and Mr. Red Cloud explained that he felt a strong kind of force around these parts, and that's why he picked a place near the Manitou Mounds to get his mind straight. We asked him about the Manitou, and he tried to explain, but neither of us really got it. I mean, how can rocks and trees have any kind of spirit inside them? He did make me think about how the crack in the ice that sunk me on the Swamp seemed like something alive. Yeah, that got me thinking about nature spirits, but like I told people then, and like I tell people now, I'm not religious.

After a little more dawdling we did as he asked, and we got out of there. As we walked back down the narrow little trail we came across an old black Schwinn bike, with a basket on the front. The guy must have quietly set it down and snuck up on us. Poopy pointed out that of course he knew we were poking around his camp, because we had left our bikes parked at his trail entrance. "*I'm a dumb bunny,*" I thought to myself.

Time had flown by, and it was time for supper. Poopy headed off, but not before reminding me that he'd be gone for a few days visiting family up in the Twin Cities. I turned for home. I felt a little jittery, but I reckoned things would be OK. Poopy would keep his word, and so would I.

The thing was, when I realized the guy had been taking care of Ninja Bob in a hit and miss sort of way, it reduced my suspicion about him a little bit. Plus, he said he had been a Marine. Well, maybe he had, or maybe he hadn't. I mean, he was living in the woods like a bum, which didn't strike me as very Marine-like. I decided to let it all ride for the time being. I also decided to give him a wide berth. And darn it, now I knew why all the pop bottles were disappearing from around town.

Supper was pretty good, as Mom was getting some good tips out at the OKK. It was fried chicken and mashed potatoes, always a favorite. Soon the garden would start producing lettuce, radishes, onions and carrots. I knew we would be living high on the hog once I started back to mowing lawns in earnest; the lack of pop bottles was just a temporary dry spell as far as pocket change went. After we finished supper, I want out to check on the garden, and saw Ninja Bob strolling up from the Swamp. I called out to him, and he meowed back. He came over to me and I scratched him behind the ears.

Come night I thought about what the Red Cloud guy had said about the Manitou. Maybe I'd look it up in the next day or so. But I felt way too lazy to look it up that evening. As it turned out I was to learn a little more about Indian spiritual beliefs within the next few nights. And not from the encyclopedia, either.

The Wendigo

A few days after first meeting Mr. Red Cloud Aimee got invited to a sleepover at her silly friend Mary's house, which left me alone with no responsibilities other than taking care of myself. That evening there had been a double header with our softball leagues over at Hagan Field, and I was eager to check under the bleachers for pop bottles before Mr. Red Cloud got over there. Timing is everything. I didn't want to go over there while there were still people around, because then everybody would know my business. I also needed to be able to get back in plenty of time before Mom got back home around 1:00 a.m. in the morning. I figured around 11 at night would work just fine. All the teenagers would be gone by then because of curfew.

I set out just before eleven. I looked for Ninja Bob down in the back yard first, but he wasn't around. The night was warm, but dark. With no moonlight the night stars were very bright. Looking up at the sky, it seemed like you could see all the way through the universe. I made my way to Hagan Field staying in the shadows and avoiding street and house lights. Once at Hagan Field I took my time and looked around, or rather crawled around. There were only a few lights on at Hagan Field itself, one by the restrooms, and one by the gate.

I'll tell you something. Finding pop bottles in the dark under the bleachers is no easy task. I only found a couple bottles, but two are better than nothing. Then I heard the yowl of a cat, way off and up the road from Hagan Field, in the direction of Firefly Field and the Hoot Owl Barn. I thought it might be Ninja Bob, but it sounded strange too, almost otherworldly. I scuttled out from under the bleachers and found a place by a concrete support to leave the bottles. Then I snuck up towards Firefly Field.

It was easy to stay in the dark. The old highway doesn't have any streetlights after Hagan Field. It's all dark and spooky once past Hagan Field, with woods and groves on both sides of the road. I wasn't going to go far. I for sure wasn't going to go as far as the crossroads at Hanging Tree. I'm not nuts. Just as I was about to turn around along the road at where the old farm lane runs up to the Hoot Owl Barn, I heard the yowl again. It sounded like it was coming from up the lane, or maybe among the windbreak trees along the side of the lane. Well, I'd been to Firefly Field at night before, but never alone. I called out "Hey, Ninja Bob!"

I didn't hear a return yowl, so I walked up the old lane, staying right smack-dab in the middle of the lane, you bet! When I got to the end of the lane I heard the yowl again, much closer. It sounded like it was coming from around Firefly Field, which concerned me just a little bit, because it was so dark. I felt like staying way out in the open. I decided to find a place in the field and just wait. I sat down and stretched out on the grass, and then looked up. There were shooting stars. First one shooting star, then another, and then another. It was wonderful.

Suddenly there was a flare of light a way off to my right. "Good evening," said Mr. Red Cloud.

That made me jump. But then I smelled tobacco and for some reason it made me settle down. Mr. Red Cloud asked me what the in the heck I was doing out so late at night. I made up as I went, telling him that I was out looking for my cat, the one he called Jinx. Mr. Red Cloud told me that Jinx was around somewhere close, but that he hadn't seen him yet. Right about then something bumped up against my right hand and I let out a squawk.

Mr. Red Cloud moved fast and was over next to me right about when I realized that Ninja Bob had found me. With Mr. Red Cloud standing over me, Ninja Bob started purring like a little outboard motor. Mr. Red Cloud sat down near me just laughing away, and Ninja Bob took up a position between us. I was feeling cheeky, so I asked Mr. Red Cloud what *he* was doing out in the middle of the night. "Meteors, sonny! On a clear, moonless night like this, you can see em, now and then. Not like last month, though, but you can still see a few."

Then he paused, looked at me, and went on to admonish me, telling me how unsafe it was for me to be out so late. Shifting gears, I told Mr. Red Cloud that I liked coming out here at dusk to watch the bats chase the fireflies.

"Bats and whippoorwills," said Mr. Red Cloud. "Bats and whippoorwills chase the fireflies, son."

"How can you tell one from the other in the dark?" I asked Mr. Red Cloud.

"One swoops, and the other one darts," Mr. Red Cloud replied. Then he said, "Well, there's no fireflies now, and it's not safe to be out here this late."

Still feeling cheeky, I made a remark about lions, tigers, and bears. He got quiet for a while. I guess he was watching for falling stars, because while we were talking, we saw one. Finally, he started talking again. He said for me not get stupid about tigers and such. He said he was talking about people.

I countered that people were nice around these parts. Then when he told me about The Wendigo. What he told me scared me enough to make me weep, but not right away. That would come later. He told me about it while he smoked his smoke and while Ninja Bob purred away. The smell of tobacco along with Ninja Bob purring and the all the shooting stars made it seem like a wonderful spooky story in the middle of a warm Minnesota summer's night, and that's all.

He told me that The Wendigo is an evil and ancient being who fell from the stars during a comet storm eons ago. The thing is a shapeshifter, and if it's near enough to a sleeping person, it can see that person's dreams. Mr. Red Cloud went on to say that if the thing spends enough time watching another's dreams it can enter that person's dream-world. When a person's dream-world is violated by The Wendigo, that person starts to have nightmares about being tossed into the air and being set on fire. When The Wendigo eventually leaves a person's dream-world, that person's spirit is forever corrupted. First, they become reclusive. But then after a while they go insane and become a cannibal.

I told Mr. Red Cloud that that was quite a story. I told him that if he had spent any time around these parts that he would know that there were no such things as cannibals in farm country. He got quiet for a while, and I could hear him rolling another cigarette. When he got done, he lit it up, and then asked me if I had ever heard of a guy named Ed Gein. I told him that I hadn't. He said he wasn't surprised, because everyone tried to pretend that there was no such thing as The Wendigo. Then he asked me if I knew anything about the tree at the crossroads farther down the old highway, and I told him that everyone knows about the Hanging Tree. He got quiet, so I asked him what he meant about Ed Gein.

He told me that Ed Gein used to live on a farm in southwest Wisconsin. He told me that several years ago Ed Gein was possibly possessed by The Wendigo. Mr. Red Cloud went on to say that Ed Gein started to range around at night, and that he covered a lot of ground, maybe over a hundred miles. He said that he hunted for people and robbed graves as far over as La Crosse, and parts of Houston County. He told me that when the police finally caught up with Gein just a few years ago, that he had killed and eaten some people, and that he had robbed a bunch of graves. He told me that when they searched Gein's farmhouse they found pickled human remains put up in canning jars down in the root cellar. When Mr. Red Cloud finished telling me this outlandish story, I told him that I thought that the whole thing was just a bunch of baloney.

He got quiet again for a moment, and then he told me to take off. He told me that I needed to get the hell back home, because he didn't need the trouble of having anything to do with a young punk who was breaking curfew. He also told me to take my damn cat with me. I excused myself. I didn't want to try picking up Ninja Bob, so I tried something else. "Come on, Ninja Bob," I quietly said.

I know this next part is kind of hard to believe, but I swear to God, Ninja Bob followed me back into town just like a dog. I got back in plenty of time to beat Mom home with my two lousy pop bottles and my big old cat. I went to bed feeling a little amused that Mr. Red Cloud had tried to scare me into not running around by myself late at night. How funny.

Troubling News

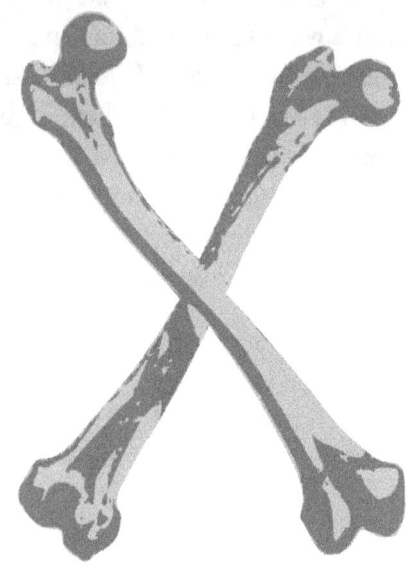

I woke up the next morning to the sound of bells ringing. This sometimes happens, but not often. What I mean is that the Church of Christ across the road does have a steeple, and they do ring their one church bell on Sunday mornings. I've watched them ring it. The bell rope comes loose just inside the church entryway, and different people take turns pulling on the bell rope. It looks like fun. The thing is, it's just one bell, and sometimes I hear bells ringing, and sometimes not on Sunday. As I said, it doesn't happen often. The truth is, when I was a little kid, I thought the church next door had a lot of bells in the belfry. As it turns out, I'm the one with a lot of bells in the belfry, but I've learned to shut up about it. I just stayed in bed and listened to the bells until they stopped ringing, and then I got up.

Aimee wasn't back yet from her sleepover, Mom was still sleeping, and Ninja Bob wanted out. I was left to my own devices. I called Poopy and no one picked up. I made toast and peanut butter and then headed out, this time on my bike. I decided to just peddle along looking for bottles, and maybe stop off at the library. I like going to the library during the summer. I don't like school, but I go to the library during summer vacation. That's just the way it is. When I'm there I always read my horoscope.

Outside the library, there's this sign that says it's a Carnegie Library. I have no idea what that means. But it's for certain a very impressive library for a town our size. The place is one block down from Main Street, and it sits on the corner of Silk Stocking Street. Silk Stocking Street is where all the big houses are, where the big oak trees are, and where most of the old rich people live. When you look down Silk Stocking Street you could easily think you were in a much bigger town, except that way down at the other end of the street you can see a cornfield. It's like looking at a cornfield through a long leafy tunnel. Grandma Lundgren's house is right in the middle of Silk Stocking Street.

I parked my bike and skipped up the library steps and went in through the big doors. The librarian's desk is front and center as you walk in. I'm a regular there on Mondays during the summer because I can read the Sunday comics in a big leather chair by the window. The place had just opened for the day and there was hardly anyone there. I walked over to the desk to ask my question.

"Yes, Eric?" the librarian said.

She always remembers my name, but I don't remember hers. I asked her where I could find out information about The Wendigo, and Ed Gein. Her smile vanished.

"I believe you are referring to American Indian myths and legends, and I can show you where to find that material," she said.

"What about Ed Gein?" I asked.

She told me that that was not a subject for young people and that there was nothing about that *situation* in the library. She also advised me to engage myself in wholesome research pursuits, and to steer clear of the morbid and the unwholesome. She then led me over to the area where all the books on Indians are kept, and then she left me on my own. After she moved off, I pretended to look at a few books, and then I left. She had told me something by *not* telling me something.

When I stepped out of the library, I heard music coming down from Silk Stocking Street. It was the most beautiful music I had ever heard. It sounded like church music but was played by a whole orchestra like when there's a Christmas Special on TV. I walked quickly down the steps, trying to catch all the music as I went. When I got to the bottom I quietly got on my bike and peddled towards the music. As I got farther down Silk Stocking Street, I realized that the music was coming from Grandma Lundgren's house.

I stopped on the curb behind an oak and just listened. The old lady saw me anyway. She must have been sitting by one of her open living room windows, catching the breeze. She stepped out onto her front porch with Lilith, her old black cat, slinking along right behind her.

"That you, Eric?"

"Yes ma'am," I answered.

"What are you doing?"

"I'm listening to your music, ma'am. I've never heard anything like it. It reminds me about how I feel when I'm in the woods by myself."

"Come on up on the porch son. I've got cold lemonade. I was thinking about having some out on the front porch. Come on up here and join me, please."

"Yes ma'am," I said.

I've found it's always best to stay on the good side of The Beetle's grandma. She has that nice dock to fish off right in the back of her house. I pulled my bike up off the curb and leaned it against the oak and then went right up to the porch. Grandma Lundgren pointed to one of the wicker chairs and I took a seat. She went back inside, and I stood back up and watched her go into the kitchen. Right inside her front door Grandma Lundgren has this wooden stand with glass doors and glass shelves. On the glass shelves are a bunch of these different kinds of owls. Some are made of wood, some are made of stone, and some are made of ceramic, I guess. I didn't want her to think I was nosey, so I got back in my seat before she turned around. Lilith meowed at me, and then rubbed against my leg.

I finished listening to the music. It was done by the time Grandma Lundgren came back out. She had two big ice-filled glasses of lemonade and a note. She gave me a glass and the note. The note said: *Ralph Vaughan Williams: Tallis Fantasia.*

"That's the music that stopped you cold on this hot summer's day," said Grandma Lundgren.

I put the note in my pocket to be polite. We don't have a record player. I've still got the note in case we ever do get a record player. We sat there and sipped lemonade, and then she asked me if I was staying safe and not getting into mischief. I told her that of course, I was staying safe. We sipped more lemonade, and then she asked me if I was running around town late at night. I looked down. "Eric, don't fib to me, boy. I do everything I can to help the friendship along between you and Godfrey, but don't lie to me, son," said a frowning Grandma Lundgren.

I gulped my lemonade and then I told her I didn't usually go out by myself late at night, because I'm always babysitting my sister. I explained Aimee had a sleepover, and there had been a double header at Hagan field and so I went out looking for pop bottles under the bleachers. I waited until after all the teenagers had left because I was indeed being sneaky. She seemed to buy it.

"I'm glad that you're honest with me Eric. I saw you last night while I was sitting up with poor Mrs. Noble. I'm going to have to mention this to your mother. We just want you to be safe. Mrs. Noble by the way thinks the world of you, for shoveling her walk during the winter."

I smiled, nodded, and sipped my lemonade. Old ladies seem to like me a lot. Grandma Lundgren smiled back at me and kept on talking. "When I saw you walking to your house, you had your head down. You seemed to be deep in thought. You looked the same way when you were outside here. Is everything OK, Eric? Please tell me the truth, son."

I answered her. I told her I had gone to the library to find out about a guy named Ed Gein, but the librarian refused to talk about him or to show me where I could find out anything about him. Grandma Lundgren set her lemonade down and looked off into the trees with a frown on her face. Then she got up and went inside. I didn't know what to think. She was gone for a while. When she came back out, she had a newspaper. It was kind of yellow looking, so it wasn't fresh. The paper made a rustling sound. She looked at me hard, and then she handed me the paper. It was the *Minneapolis Morning Tribune*, dated November 18th, 1957. The paper was only a few years old, but it looked older.

It was a story about Edward Gein. It said that he had been arrested, and that police had found the body of a woman in his farm shed that had been strung up and butchered like livestock. It said that they had found a human heart in a pot on the stove. It said that Edward Gein was probably responsible for other murders and disappearances, including that of a fifteen-year-old girl from La Crosse.

My hands were shaking, making the paper rustle. I folded the paper and handed it back to Grandma Lundgren. My eyes got all wet, and Grandma Lundgren put her hand over her mouth, and suddenly her eyes got all wet, too.

"Oh, sweetheart," she said. "I'm so very sorry. You're much more sensitive than you look."

"It's not that," I said. "I have to be able to go into the woods. I can't *not* go into the woods. I can't be afraid to go into the woods. The woods are the closest thing I've got to a church. I just can't be afraid to go into the woods," I told her over, and over again.

I was just sitting there with tears dropping into my lap. I was so very embarrassed, but I couldn't make the tears stop, and I didn't want to acknowledge them by trying to brush them away, either. Grandma Lundgren took the newspaper and went back inside. Lilith jumped into my lap and started purring. When Grandma Lundgren came back out, she had a box of Kleenex, and she was using some herself. She handed me the box. I put myself back together and told her I had to be going. She stood up and hugged me.

While hugging me she told me to go right ahead and go into our woods, but to just please not go wandering around by myself late at night. She told me that if I would just do that for her that I had nothing to fear. I told her that I would never go wandering around at night by myself, ever again. Then I got on my bike and took off. When Grandma Lundgren hugged me, she smelled like a summer meadow full of wildflowers.

The Singing Shirts

Finding out that real monsters exist in and around our safe, quiet farm country really kicked the stuffing out of me for a couple of days, and a couple of nights, too. The scolding I got from Mom about breaking trust and catting around town when I was supposed to be safe at home didn't help, either. I got to go on a good guilt trip with that one, I can tell you. I wasn't grounded, but I went to ground just the same, so that I could mull things over. I let my logic kick in for all it was worth, just like I had done in figuring out the whole business of the scratching sounds at Aimee's window. I remembered the movie we had seen on my birthday with the underground cannibals in it, and I worked things out from there. I curled in bed and thought and thought about it, with Ninja Bob at my feet and my bedroom door wide open.

The first night thinking about it I decided that there was no such thing as the Wendigo. Like any myth, it was an explanation for something that was hard to understand. I decided that the Wendigo was just an Indian explanation for what happens to a person if they go insane. The following day I felt better, but still not quite one hundred percent. Dingo called and wanted to know if I wanted to help walk the bean fields for a nickel a row. I told him I'd think about it. I didn't call back. I stayed close to home and tended our family garden. The truth is, I really hate walking bean rows for a nickel a row.

The next night I really let the logic come home to roost. First off, the Gein guy was in jail, and he wasn't ever getting out. And second off, I wasn't going out by myself late at night anymore, ever again. There. I had it. I had my woods back. I woke up the next morning to singing voices in my room. The sun was coming in through my bedroom window, and there were sparkling little dust motes in the rays of sunlight. The singing seemed to be coming from my closet. Ninja Bob was lying on the foot of my bed and staring straight at the closet.

The voices were singing in a language I couldn't understand, but it sounded like Indian words. The tune was the same as the music I had heard at Grandma Lundgren's, only it was just voices, no instruments. I sat up in bed a little and looked at the closet. Two of my long sleeve shirts were hanging in there. The shirt collars were opening and closing like mouths, and the arms were moving up and down. I had heard bells before, sure. But I had never, ever seen or heard anything like this. Then suddenly the singing stopped. Ninja Bob looked over at me and meowed. "Yeah," I told him, "That was weird."

And it was weird; but weird, not scary. I tried really hard to hold onto some of the words. But *Knee go on no keg* and *Neesh way swish* were all that I could hang onto. I found a pencil and an envelope and wrote the words down while I could still remember them. I have no idea about the spelling. For the next few mornings, I tried to bring the singing back, but that never works. I can't just make my hallucinations happen, try as I might. When it happens, it just happens.

The whole business in my bedroom that morning told me two things; I had my woods back (during the day at least) and I also had to make amends. I didn't believe in The Wendigo. And I really, really hadn't believed that some crazy farmer had been roaming around in farm country killing and eating people. As far as I was concerned, I was half-right and half-wrong. But as things stood, I had to make amends. Giving up an apology is kind of like a debt; if you don't take care of it, then it becomes debt-like, and that leads to nothing good. I also felt a twinge of guilt about the two pop bottles I had harvested from under the bleachers. I determined to pay Mr. Red Cloud a visit.

I humped on out to East Anderson's Woods on my bike and then cut over to the trail that connects with the trail me and Poopy had discovered leading to Mr. Red Cloud's camp. The morning had started out hot, quiet and sunny, but a breeze was picking up. It felt good. Clouds were coming in, too. I peddled on up to the top of the trail and then walked my bike along the little game trail to Mr. Red Cloud's hooch. Even before I got there, I could hear his transistor radio. He was listening to what sounded like a baseball game, but it seemed too early in the morning for that, unless it was from another part of the country. I could smell tobacco. His old black bike was leaned up against one of the big sugar maples that were all around his dugout.

I guess he heard me come up, because he stepped right out. I gave him my prepared speech, and it didn't go like I expected. When I set down the pop bottles next to his sitting log, he started to look angry. When I got to the part about how I really didn't need to go under bleachers to get pop bottles or pennies and dimes, he looked even angrier. Speaking as fast as I could, I told him I'd probably start mowing lawns or even go over to the Wilcox farm and do bean rows for a nickel a row, although walking bean rows really sucked. Then things really went sideways. Mr. Red Cloud swore at me. "You feel sorry for me, boy? Is that it? You feel sorry for me, you little ****ing punk?"

I would never, ever use language like this, and I've only heard Mr. Red Cloud use this kind of language only one time. I've heard rough language before (You know what I mean, don't you Constable Benny?) But this outburst frightened me.

I backed away from him, and as I did a long gust of wind came along, making the sugar maples groan and bump into each other. The trees bumped into each other so hard that we both looked up. Something from way high up in the tree-top branches tumbled straight down at me. I ducked my head, and it was like getting hit with a dry clod of dirt and twigs. It was half of an old dried-up bird's nest. Stuff from it was in my hair and down my back. Mr. Red Cloud started laughing, which was a damn sight better than him being all angry and swearing at me. I started brushing the crud out my hair, and Mr. Red Cloud stepped forward and reached out towards my head.

I kind of jerked my head away, but he managed to grab something out of my hair. It was a black feather. He stopped laughing, and just stood there, twirling the black feather back and forth between his thumb and forefinger. Then a strange look came over Mr. Red Cloud's face. It wasn't a smile, and it wasn't a frown. His mouth just took on a hard look. Like maybe how I looked the first time I had lutefisk on a Ritz. "I apologize, young master Eric," said Mr. Red Cloud. "I'm ashamed of myself. The way that I talked to you was uncalled for."

Then he turned around with the black feather and went into his hooch, or hogan, or dugout, or whatever you might call a sod covered hole. The radio got shut off, and then he came back out. He sat down on his sitting log with his tobacco pouch. He offered me a seat, and a hand rolled cigarette to go with it. I accepted the seat but declined the cigarette.

He rolled his smoke and then sat quiet for a while and smoked. I've kind of gotten used to how he goes quiet, but I didn't know what to expect back then. After a minute or two he looked over at me and asked about the bean fields and a nickel a row. I drew him a map in the dirt to show him where the Wilcox farm is. When I explained to him the bean field up the road from Firefly Field and the Hoot Owl barn is part of the Wilcox farm, he got it.

He tore up the little bit of stub that was left of his cigarette and put it into his pouch. Then he said time was wasting and he was going to strike while the 'iron was hot'. He shook my hand, then got on his old black bike and peddled off. "Don't steal anything, punk!" he called over his shoulder, but he hollered it with a smile on his face.

I was having quite a morning. I walked over to where the chunk of half-nest was and picked it up. It was pretty busted up, and it felt real brittle, like it could crumble apart with the least bit of pressure. I wondered where the other half was. Then I noticed something. Along on the inside was something that looked like an oblong white stone. I very, very carefully pulled it out. It wasn't a stone at all, but some sort of bone. I sat on the sitting log and pondered. Maybe it was the boney part of a raccoon paw. But it was too big for a raccoon paw. Maybe it was the boney leftover part of a bear paw. I wondered how the devil it could have become part of a crow's nest. I put the bone in my jeans pocket for further consideration.

Because Mr. Red Cloud was so interested in the feather, I set what was left of the nest on his sitting log. I resisted the urge to look inside his place, and I felt good about being good. I shook my shirt off, but I still felt I needed a swim or a shower. A swim sounded a lot more fun than a shower, so I decided to ride my bike over to Poopy's and see if he wanted to go over to Salt Lick Lake for a swim. Salt Lick Lake is on The Beetle's side of town, but that's how bad I needed a swim. Plus, it didn't hurt I had thirty-five cents in my pocket – enough to get into the lake concession stand and buy a bottle of pop if I wanted one.

When I got to Poopy's it was clear that rain was heading our way. There were a lot of big purple clouds coming up from the south. There was a wind coming up too, but the sun was still shining and when it hit you it was hot. Both of Poopy's sisters were out on the front lawn playing in the sprinkler, which I took as a good sign that Poopy would want to go for a swim. He came to the backdoor and talked with me through the screen. He didn't want to go swimming. He was working on a model. He asked me if I wanted to come in and I told him no, I was going swimming before the storm came. About then Poopy's Mom came bustling to the door, and she asked me if I wanted to come in. I'm treated like almost family at Poopy's. I told her no, and then she yelled for the girls to come in.

The girls came scampering in all wet and full of grass, and Mrs. Alighieri told them to strip right down in the kitchen before they made a mess. This was met with squeals and giggles because I was standing right there at the screen door. You would think that this would have slowed the process down a bit, but the girls stripped down 'toot sweet'.

I picked that moment to get out of there, pronto. I was on my own for the afternoon.

I got to Salt Lick Lake in record time. Once you're over the tracks and past the tractor dealership there's that row of metal silos, then the corn fields on both sides of the road, and then the little turn-off sign for Salt Lick Lake. It's easy, flat going to get there on a bike. The lake is an almost perfect circle. There's a little changing building and one lifeguard chair. Normally there's some high school girl on lifeguard duty, which is a bonus. There's a little sandy beach and a floating dock. The water is clear, and the bottom is sandy.

I kicked off my shoes, tossed off my shirt, and pulled off my socks. I rolled up my jeans and jumped in. I went a couple of strokes under-water, and then did the crawl the rest of the way to the float. While swimming I got rid of most of the bird nest crud that had gone down my pants. I pulled myself up on the dock and then just laid myself down on the warm wood. It was just me. There were a few families on the little beach, but not many kids, and none of them my age. I didn't get to be on the dock for long. The lifeguard blew her whistle and called out that the beach was closing because a storm was on the way. I jumped back into the water, swam to shore, said hello and goodbye to the lifeguard, and almost made it home before getting drenched. But I was wet anyway from swimming.

I said hello to Mom and Aimee, and then changed into my clean but worn-out spare jeans and t-shirt. I remembered the bear toe-bone in my pocket. I fished it out and set it on my nightstand. I decided I'd run it over to Peachy's in a day or so and have his dad look at it, since he's a science teacher.

I felt good. I felt clean. I felt like my old self again. I parked myself in the living room and watched the thunderstorm. A thunderstorm is just as entertaining as TV, and besides you can't watch TV during a thunderstorm anyway, because the picture keeps going out. We had chili for supper, which really hit the spot after swimming and a thun-derstorm. Mom went to work and Dingo called with interesting news. He said that some Indian guy had come right up to the house while his dad was out in the yard and asked for work walking the bean fields.

Dingo said at first his dad had an angry look on his face, but then they got to talking about each other's tattoos. Dingo said that the Indian guy had been in the Navy or something.

I didn't let on to what I knew. I figured things would just sort themselves out. Dingo said that when the thunderstorm hit, his dad and the Indian guy sat out on the front porch and drank beer and smoked cigars. When the worst part of the storm let up the Indian guy got on his bike and took off, but not before Dingo's Mom fixed him up with a brown paper bag full of cold chicken and biscuits. Dingo said it looked like he had help in the bean rows, and I had waited too long.

I told Dingo it was OK. And it was OK. I truly hate walking bean rows. That night I fell asleep and dreamed about walking bean rows. I remember the dream because I woke up in the middle of the dream because I heard what sounded like a crying baby. I sat up and looked around in the dark and listened real hard. I didn't hear anything more, so after a while I went back to sleep.

The Witch Trees

A few days after Mr. Red Cloud got hired on at Dingo's farm Peachy and The Beetle got back into town with their exciting stories about how they had got to live like Indians while at camp. And, speaking of Indians, just as Dingo had hoped, the bean fields got along without him now that there was this fast-moving Indian guy walking the rows. He could now enjoy a big chunk of the summer with all the rest of us. Being mindful, Dingo suggested a campout on the border of the woods on what he calls the 'back forty'. The back forty is a part of his farm that's mostly cornfield and a bit of woods that borders up against the Durr place. We had scouted it out as a good potential spot, close to the homestead but with a remote feeling because of the cornfield.

Last year we had even prepped the area with a fire ring. Back then we thought that we could use our bikes as cargo vehicles and just wheel them through the corn rows until we got to the woods. Our designated camp spot wasn't too far into the trees, because the brush, roots and creepers were all thick and tangled farther back. And we weren't supposed to go back there anyway, because it was Durr property. But the spot that we had picked out was under enough trees to still feel like we were in the woods, but we had to use imagination. Our spot was indeed under a few trees, but we could see the cornfield, and beyond the cornfield we could see the farm's silo. We all called each other over the phone and talked about our exciting plans for our first camp-out of the summer.

The Beetle had to bow out. His momma wouldn't let him camp with us since the scalding incident during our camp-out last fall. I got permission from Mom (everything about my last transgression was forgiven) and set to work getting my camping stuff together. It was easy. My dad's old Army sleeping bag was still in his duffle bag. After using it I always gave it a good cleaning and drying, and back into his duffle bag it would go. But obviously, the duffle bag and sleeping bag are mine now. Also in *my* duffle bag: a mess kit, a pistol belt, a canteen, and a shelter half, all of it Army issue. Chow wouldn't be a problem. I had enough change to get a loaf of bread and a couple of cans of chili or beef stew.

We all assembled at Dingo's house, where his mom gave us the once over, and the 'safety talk'. The thing about Dingo's Mom is this; she seems to really like me a lot. She always gives me a hug, and she puts her arm around me a lot. I've noticed that none of the other guys get the same treatment, except for Dingo himself. What's also odd is that my mom and Dingo's mom really don't like each other one little bit, even though they used to be very good friends in high school. Dingo's dad just barely puts up with me. He mostly just ignores me.

Molly begged to come along, just like last year, and just like last year she was told that she could hang out with us until supper time, and then she had to go home. We got our gear tied down on the handlebars of our bikes and then headed out. It was a fine, clear, and warm summer afternoon.

It didn't take us long to get camp set up, as our fire ring and sitting logs were already in place. As it turned out, Poopy probably found the new trail because he had time to poke around in the brush on the other side of the thick stand of white cedars that is sort of the boundary between Dingo's farm and the Durr place. The real boundary is the dilapidated bob-wire fence that runs along the woods just on the other side of the cedar trees. It was the cedars that drew us there in the first place.

We had been exploring the old rutted and overgrown track that runs along the fence line around that side of the farm when we came upon them. At the time, Dingo didn't think they were anything special. They were just a bunch of trees. The cedars are all twisted up and clumped together on a little hill just inside where there are a few other trees on the other side of the old lane. When we first came upon them last year Poopy commented that they looked like they had been trying to dance the hula when they suddenly got frozen.

Just beyond the cedars is that old fence line that's the boundary between the Wilcox and Durr farms, but it's all but gone. There are only a few places where the barbed wire still runs from post to post. Some trees must have fallen on parts of the fence during past windstorms a long time ago, and in other places, the fence posts just sort of rotted away. You would almost never know that there was a bob-wire fence through there, because so much of it is all overgrown. Of course, a couple of us have tangled up with that fence in very unwelcome ways. It was along part of the fence that Poopy noticed the little game trail.

I do not know what it is about Poopy and little, almost unnoticed game trails. Once, when we were little boys, Poopy wanted to explore a little break in the brush because there were little pellets laying there in the snow right in the middle of the break. Peachy told Poopy they were raisons, so Poopy tried one. Poopy made a face and spat it out, because it was a rabbit dropping.

Anyway, Peachy pointed out a couple of turkey buzzards floating high over the woods ahead of us, in the direction the trail seemed to go. Peachy opinioned that there might be something dead in the woods up ahead, and we could follow the little trail and find out. Dingo was apprehensive about following the slope down along the trail, because he knew it was Durr property. Peachy told Dingo to take it easy, because the trail was obviously not a people trail; it was simply no more than a game trail. It was thin and barely visible, just like the other trail Poopy had discovered that had led us to Mr. Red Cloud. We decided as a group that we had to follow this new-found trail, Molly bringing up the rear just in case we ran into a bear or coyotes.

The woods there are thick, and the trees were some of the tallest I've ever seen. There were a lot of red oaks and sugar maples, and a lot of fallen logs and brush. It was kind of hard going. Then we smelled something nasty and ripe, and at the same time a cloud of horseflies swarmed over us. I'll tell you what, it's no picnic being eaten alive by a swarm of horseflies that have been gorging on carrion. We did an about face and got the heck out of there. We chugged our way back up the trail and pushed back through the white cedars.

"Man, what do you think that was?" asked Poopy.

"Don't know," replied Dingo. "Probably a dead bear or deer, something like that. Whatever it is, it'll stop smelling so bad in a week or so, and then we can check it out."

Molly made a face but didn't say anything. Right about then Bernard Who Is Not A Saint Bernard showed up, which was Molly's cue to head on home. You see, one of Bernard Who Is Not A Saint Bernard's jobs, is to escort Molly home. Her Dad will tell Bernard to go find Molly and get her home, and he will do so. Molly peddled off with her good dog following behind her. We knew Bernard Who Is Not A Saint Bernard would be back in a while, which is always a comfort when we're camping at night in the woods.

We set about gathering wood. You can never, ever have enough wood for the fire when you're out camping. This time around Peachy had brought along a hatchet, which made things easier. After we had a good pile of wood, we did an inventory of our provisions. I had my loaf of bread and two cans of chili. Dingo had a package of hot dogs along with a bag of hot dog buns. Peachy had a dozen eggs, still in the carton and all miraculously unbroken. He also had this odd little lightweight folding grill (odd, but cool).

Peachy also brought the bacon. Poopy brought the wholesome food groups; potato chips, marsh-mellows, gram-crackers, and a bag full of stale little Halloween chocolate bars from last year he recovered from behind the bookcase in his room. He uses the bookcase as a kind of plastic model display case, and as a sort of safe, except he sometimes forgets what he hides behind the bookcase. Anyway, as far as chow, we were set.

Of course, all of us had canteens. You got to have clean water when you're camping. Me, Dingo and Peachy all have the Army kind of canteens, and we also have the pistol belts to hook them onto. Poopy's Dad had been 4-F, so Poopy doesn't have an inventory of military gear like the rest of us. He does have an old green poncho, the snaps of which fit my shelter-half so we could make a sort of pup tent. Poopy also has this cowboy looking oval kind of a canteen that has a strap that you must hang over your shoulder in an awkward way. It bumps along when he rides his bike. However, his canteen *is* light weight.

Besides our canteens, me, Dingo, and Peachy also have the GI kind of mess kits. I must admit, these mess kits have a strap that you hang over your shoulder, also in an awkward way, and they do bump along as we ride our bikes. But they are gosh-darn cool. As to Poopy's mess kit, well, Poopy makes do with a Hopalong Cassidy pocketknife, tin foil, a little silver-plated teaspoon he found one day when we had been exploring the town dump, and a big tin cup.

It was starting to get dark. I don't mean that it was pitch-black dark, just kind of twilight dark. It was then that we heard the clanking and clacking sound of a bike coming up the old farm-truck lane that in fact runs from the culvert on the farm road and then goes along the border of the cornfield. After pushing our bikes through the cornrows, we all knew that lane would have been the easier way to transport our loads; longer, but easier. Anyway, we just waited. We surmised it might be Molly, coming back to tell us something important, or less likely, it might be The Beetle, because the bike had a light. Peachy had got the fire going, and we were busy whittling away on our marshmallow sticks. The bike rider got closer, and we looked up.

Out trotted Bernard Who Is Not A Saint Bernard. He was grinning, like dogs do when they're happy. Bernard grins like this pretty much whenever he gets to be with a bunch of us; the more of us, the better. Then along came Mr. Red Cloud. Well, this was a surprise. And it got even better, because he had something with him that greatly enhanced our evening campfire, Jiffy Pop!

"Your momma asked me to come out and check on you," said Mr. Red Cloud looking at Dingo. "And she sent this along," he said, twirling the Jiffy Pop pan by its handle.

"Hiya, Mr. Red Cloud," called out Dingo.

I felt a twinge of annoyance that suddenly Dingo was on such familiar terms with Mr. Red Cloud. But Mr. Red Cloud made my bad feeling go away by greeting me and Poopy. Then he walked over and introduced himself to Peachy, who was looking back and forth at us in a puzzled sort of way. Peachy stood up and they shook hands. After these niceties, we got going on the Jiffy Pop. Mr. Red Cloud stated that he was darn-sure going to stay for the Jiffy Pop, since he was the one who 'brang' it.

I'd never tried Jiffy Pop on a campfire before, but it worked, sort of. The bottom kernels got burnt. Not badly burnt but burnt just the same. We all made sure that we all got the good and the bad, and to tell you the truth, it was mostly pretty good. While we were munching away Mr. Red Cloud kept looking over towards the little hill with the clump of white cedars. It was kind of weird, like he almost knew what we had been up to earlier that day.

After a while he said in an absent and off-hand kind of way that those cedars were maybe hundreds of years old, and it certainly was an odd little hill they were sitting on. He called them 'witch trees', and he said that they normally don't grow this far south. We all looked back at the trees while he talked about them. As we looked back a little bit of a breeze made them move gently, making them creak and groan.

"I wished I understood what they were saying," mused Mr. Red Cloud. "And look at all those big stones sleeping there under the trees on this little hill. Odd, isn't it?"

"They probably just got set there by however first cleared this cornfield," guessed Peachy.

Mr. Red Cloud got quiet again and rolled a smoke. Like he always does, he asked if anyone would like one. We all said no, but Poopy almost took one. Now, we normally just chatter away around a campfire, but for once we just sat there quiet while Mr. Red Cloud smoked his smoke. I recommend being quiet like that. We heard owls hooting, leaves rustling, and the fire sizzling and popping. Mr. Red Cloud finished his smoke. He got to his feet and wished us a pleasant evening. "Watch out for the Boogey Man!" Mr. Red Cloud called over his shoulder.

Then Mr. Red Cloud was gone. Bernard Who Is Not A Saint Bernard stuck around however, like we knew he would. We cooked our hot dogs over the fire using our sticks, and I heated up a can of chili. We feasted on chili dogs and potato chips, followed by some-mores for dessert. After we were done, we told each other the same old lame ghost stories, and then some even lamer new ones that we made up. Poopy's story was by far the grossest. It wasn't really a ghost story. It was rather a horror story, and we laughed hard when he told it.

His story was about his uncle Romeo (funny already, right?). Uncle Romeo was sitting on the biffy one fine day, and at the time he had a bad cold. He blew his nose with a tissue, and then wiped his butt with the same bit of tissue. As a result, he gave his butthole a very bad cold. For the next week, every time he would fart, he would blow a bunch of snot into his skivvies. I know, I know, this is gross, but there are two things I would like to mention. The first is that we all laughed ourselves silly when Poopy told his story, and the second thing is that I shall never blow my nose and then wipe my butt with the same tissue.

For my part I said nothing about the Booger Lady, The Wendigo or Ed Gein. I did not wish to. I did not wish to scare the pee-wad out of my own darn self. As it was, I still got spooked later anyway, and so did Bernard Who Is Not A Saint Bernard.

We had all got done pissing on various nearby trees and then we bedded down. Me and Poopy shared one puptent, Dingo and Peachy the other puptent (a real puptent, as it was made with two G.I issue shelter halves). Sometimes Bernard Who Is Not A Saint Bernard bunks with us, but not on this night – at least not to start out with. He decided instead to sleep outside next to the fire.

It had gotten very, very dark, as there was no moon. At the back end of our shelter, it was pitch black, which suited me just fine. I had a good sleeping bag, and I was tired. Poopy was already snoring. I drifted off. What woke me up in the middle of the night was the sound of a growling dog. It was our dog. I was the first one to get moving. I almost kicked my way out of my sleeping bag, giving Poopy a good thumping in the process. It seems to me once Bernard Who Is Not A Saint Bernard was sure we were awake he decided to really put on a show. His growling took on a higher, almost frantic kind of pitch. But he didn't bark. I found his behavior odd. By just about then I had got myself turned around so I could look out.

The fire was almost out, but the embers were still glowing red. The dog was looking out towards where the white cedars were. He was hunched down; not exactly laying down, not exactly sitting up. Moreover, he was very still, and his ears were back. Peachy yelled "Bernard!" The dog looked away and stopped his high-pitched growling. Peachy, his head poking out of the tent, swung his flashlight around the camp. Seeing nothing, he then swung the beam of light towards the cedars. There was nothing there, either. "Just some critter, probably a skunk," muttered Peachy.

Peacy's flashlight went off. I could dimly see the shape of Bernard Who Is Not A Saint Bernard move off towards Peachy and Dingo's hooch. I heard them laugh and complain as Bernard made himself comfortable inside. I felt that a bit more could be done about the situation. I pulled myself out of my bag, located a couple of good-sized chunks of wood, and set them on top of the glowing coals. Then I snugged myself back in, but not like I had gone to bed to start with. I rearranged myself so that my head was almost outside of the tent, so I could watch the fire. Oh yeah, I also had the hatchet we had used to chop wood next to me.

Once the fire got going well, I felt better. I couldn't quite see the cedars, but I could tell where they were because of the night sky. The stars stopped where the cedars were. I just lay there listening. The crickets were chirping, and there was a hoot-owl way, way back in the woods. Once I heard Bernard Who Is Not A Saint Bernard start snoring, I felt good enough to let myself fall back asleep.

The next thing I knew, something very cold and very wet splashed into my face. I woke up gasping, trying to get myself orientated. It was light out, but at first glance, I couldn't figure out what I was seeing. Then I realized I was looking up a girl's dress. I shifted my gaze to see *what* girl, just in time to see Molly's grinning face and to also catch another big dollop of cold water right between the eyes. She was using Poopy's canteen with a great sense of aim. I fairly shot out of my sleeping bag. I mean, I don't even know how I got out so fast. It was like I was propelled out. I was going to grab that girl and pour water right over her head.

Molly skipped back, and then let out a hooting sound. She grabbed herself around the waist with one arm, and her other hand shot up and covered her mouth. Her eyes were wide as pie pans and her pig tails were sticking straight out. It was then I realized I was standing there in my skivvies. I wear boxer shorts. You know, the kind with a great big open barn door in the front, if you know what I mean. I dove back into our shelter and frantically worked on finding my jeans and pulling them on, toot sweet! I guess I kind of bumped and elbowed Poopy in the process, because he swore and slugged me in the ribs good and hard, so I slugged him back. His arms were out but he was still in his bag.

Poopy reared up like a kind of giant worm and he rolled on me bag and all. He knocked out the front support pole in the process, so we were grappling each other underneath fallen canvas. I heard Molly, Dingo and Peachy all laughing, so I concentrated on pulling on my jeans, while Poopy continued to punch me. After a few more seconds he realized that I wasn't punching back, and he stopped. I got my pants on, and we threw back the collapsed tent. Peachy and Dingo were standing there both laughing, and Molly was sitting on a log doing something at the fire. Oh yes, and she was laughing hard, too.

As me and Poopy struggled out and stood up, Molly announced that she was making blueberry pancakes. Dingo and Peachy jumped for their mess kits. Dingo got in line first, with Peachy right behind him. I just stood there, trying to process what had happened, and what was now happening. Then Poopy lurched up from behind me and jumped in line behind Peachy, tin cup and little spoon at the ready. I ended up last in line and fuming to beat the band.

I'll have to admit that I cooled off as I watched Molly cook up those flapjacks. She had packed this gigantic purse (the kind old ladies have) with a pan, a spatula, a plastic container full of batter, a bottle of syrup, and a half stick of butter. The batter was all lumpy full of blueberries. Molly somehow knew exactly when to flip those pancakes. I noticed Bernard Who Is Not A Saint Bernard was just as happy as a clam, grinning and wagging his tail. I wondered why he hadn't barked when she had biked up. Traitor! But then Molly served up my first pancake along with her dimply smile, and all was forgiven. She kept making pancakes until she was out of batter, saving the last one for herself. She ate it right out of the pan. When she was done, Peachy grabbed the pan. It was time for scrambled eggs and bacon.

While Peachy worked on the eggs and bacon, I got out his little grill and got going on the toast. Dingo and Poopy tore down the shelters. I'm going to tell you this right now. That morning I had one of the best breakfasts I've ever had in my entire life. After we were done, we spread out the chunks of wood in the fire ring, and then cleaned our mess gear over the ashes to help put the fire out. We dumped dirt from the cornfield on the fire pit as a final measure. We all smelled like wood smoke. Peachy suggested that we could all blow off the smoke by taking a swim out at Salt Lick Lake. We all loudly agreed, including Bernard Who Is Not A Saint Bernard. Dingo said that he would catch up with us, as he still had to do his morning chores. We told him we would take our time. We all of us had to check in anyway.

When I got to the house Mom was sitting at the kitchen table in her bathrobe waiting for me. She always does this when I go camping overnight, because of the various burns, puncture wounds, and gashes that sometimes seem to go along with a night of camping. She looked me over, saw that I was sound, and turned to go get more shut eye before her shift. I told her I'd be off swimming with the guys over at Salt Lick Lake. Mom said OK just as Aimee squealed that she was going too. Aimee had been in the living room and had heard everything. All Mom did was look at me in a way that said, 'your sister is going, too'. Darn, and double darn.

Aimee went bounding off to change, and I plodded upstairs to do the same thing. Ninja Bob was lying on my bed, just as comfortable as you please. He gave me one 'meow', then curled back up and dozed off. I got into my trunks and took my smoky smelling clothes down to the dirty clothes basket in the basement. By the time I got back upstairs Aimee was changed and ready to go, towel and everything. Will wonders never cease?

We ran outside and jumped on our bikes. I had to peddle kind of slow, because Aimee's bike is a little girl's bike, with dorky pink tassels fluttering off both handlebars. She goes kind of slow. I just had to poke along. About halfway to Salt Lick Lake the others caught up with us (except for Dingo). They all passed us by, laughing and jeering. Molly and Bernard Who Is Not A Saint Bernard were the last to pass, and Bernard decided to drop back with me and Aimee. I looked down at him. He had dropped into a trot. He met my gaze and gave me a big doggy grin along with a small 'woof'. He trotted along with us until we got to the turn for the lake, then he took off.

Once we hit the parking lot, I wasted no time. I dumped my bike on top of the others, paid my twenty-five cents at the concession stand, and sprinted towards the water. The sand was hot on the bottoms of my feet. I almost barreled over a little kid digging a hole in the sand, but I jumped over him. I hit the water running. The lake was fantastic. I slogged forward a few steps, and then went into this slow-motion thing water does to you when you try and run in it. I dove forward and started to swim.

Everyone else had made it up the ladder of the floating dock. Well, everyone except for Bernard Who Is Not A Saint Bernard. He was just starting up. He knows how to climb the ladder, except that he usually needs help the last step or two. Someone usually pulls him up by his collar, or if you are not so lucky, you get to push him up from behind. I got to the ladder just in time to get a good look up wet dog-butt.

I worked so hard to get up there because I wanted to get in on the first group jump-off. We all lined up (including Bernard), gave a yell, and all ran forward off the dock. Poopy did a magnificent belly flop. Me and Molly did cannon balls. Peachy dove in headfirst. Bernard Who Is Not A Saint Bernard always does this odd thing where he looks like he's still running when he hits the water. It's always fun to watch him do it, if you have time. Timing is everything.

We all clambered back up, helped Bernard up, and then helped Aimee up, as she finally made it out there. Aimee wanted to be part of a group jump and we were only too happy to oblige. We lined up hooting and hollering, and off we went. I dove this time around and went down to the bottom. Because Salt Lick Lake is clear, and the bottom is nice and sandy, I like to coast around down there, and I like to hold my breath for as long as I can. The water is cooler down there, and my ears kind of pop. I came back up blowing bubbles out of my nose. I surfaced just in time to miss a cannon ball from Dingo, who had finally shown up.

For the next hour or so we jumped or dove off on our own. After a while Aimee and Bernard headed back to land. I was feeling kind of tuckered out, so I lied down on my belly and dozed off. The warm dock on my belly and the warm sun on my back felt so very good, I must have fallen asleep. I woke up because something cool touched my back. It was Molly's hand. "You're burning," she said. "You're going to have to go in."

I looked over. She was sitting next to me with her knees drawn up, as if she was cold. She wasn't cold though, because she didn't have any goose bumps on her arms or legs. She was looking off over the lake, like she was daydreaming.

"I wish we had our own private swimming spot, like in the Tarzan movies," she said.

"Well, yeah, that would be cool, except there's always lions and tigers and cannibals close by," I pointed out.

"There are no tigers in Africa, and I've never seen anybody thrown into a cooking pot in any of those movies," said Molly a bit crossly.

"Molly, the reason they use palm trees to split those guys in half is so they can get to the meat easier," said Poopy in a laconic and off-hand way.

That did it. Molly shut up. I could feel that my back was starting to burn, and the sun was getting low. It was time to go. I stood up, said my good-byes, and dove into the water. The water felt good on my back. Aimee had finished an almost impressive sandcastle. Bernard Who Is Not A Saint Bernard had found himself a very nice piece of shade and was on his side sleeping with one eye open. Aimee knew it was time to go without being told. She wrapped her towel around herself and peddled off. I tied my towel around my neck like a cape to sort of protect my back.

We got home in time to get last minute instructions from Mom before she headed off to work. There were ham sandwiches in the fridge for supper, and I was instructed to go out to the garden and bring in radishes, onions, lettuce and carrots to go with the sandwiches. Aimee could make Kool-Aid while I got the veggies.

I sprayed bug dope on my back (that's one thing we *always* have in our house). I got to my bedroom and threw on a t-shirt. Ninja Bob was still laying on my bed. He looked up, stretched, and went back to the important work of sleeping all afternoon. For my part, I got to work out in the garden. I wedged the basement door by the deep sink part way open so I could just drop the veggies in the deep sink as I pulled them out of the garden. I rinsed the little carrots, radishes and onions in the deep sink and ran them upstairs.

Aimee was done mixing the Kool-Aid, so I ran out back to the garden by way of the kitchen door. Now I could use the kitchen sink, and I didn't feel like going all the way back down into the basement. I picked the lettuce leaves, ran back, gave them the quickest of rinses in the kitchen sink, and then stuffed most of them into our sandwiches. We ate early because we were both very hungry.

I Hatch a Plan

After we finished supper, I was feeling a bit restless, I suppose because I napped on the dock, and because the lower part of my back was burning hot. You know, the place where my towel didn't quite reach down across my back during the peddle home from the lake. I told Aimee she could watch whatever she wanted on TV, because I was going for a bike ride. She asked me if I'd be back by dark and I told her of course I would, and then I teased her about the Booger Lady. Aimee replied that I was being stupid because the Booger Lady only came during snowstorms in the winter. Her answer spoke volumes. It told me that Aimee wasn't yet done with the Booger Lady business, and I still had a bunch more work to do on the problem.

I headed out with this problem rattling through my head. As I've mentioned, Firefly Field is one of my haunts, and I just sort of absently headed off in that direction. When I found myself there, I wondered how I had got there without realizing *how* I got there. It was very late afternoon and absolutely nothing was going on, except for what goes on in a very quiet Minnesota field on a summer afternoon pushing towards sunset. I decided to cruise on into the woods towards John Red Cloud's hooch. I wanted to talk to him about why he had called the old cedars near our camping spot 'Witch Trees'. Well, to tell the truth, I just wanted to talk to him.

I had to push my bike most of the way because the little trail had become so overgrown with ferns and grass and weeds. It seemed strangely quiet as I approached his place. The sun was setting, and reddish-orange rays of sunlight were slanting in through the trees from the west. I got to his place and then just stood looking around, suddenly feeling lost. His hooch was missing. I was sure I was in the right place. I moved in closer and saw that there was a sort of wide circle of dirt where his hooch used to be. I almost couldn't make it out because it was covered with branches and leaves. Even the sitting logs and the stones of the fire ring were gone. I was confused and flummoxed.

I stood in the middle of the spot where Mr. Red Cloud's hooch used to be. I calmed myself, figuring he had probably found better accommodations over at Dingo's farm. I thought of him as now probably living in the barn or workshop or something. Then I noticed something. All the sugar maples were in a circle around where the hooch had been, and they were all about the same height, give or take. How weird. I hadn't noticed this because of all the other trees and brush and stuff. I looked around to identify the sugar maple that had dropped the nest on me, and when I found it, I walked over and around the tree. It was a big one alright, with a crotch way high up there towards the top.

I decided that I'd climb the sugar maple and look in the crotch way up there for the rest of the nest. Maybe there would be another piece of bone up there. Who knows? But my mission would have to wait, because the lowest branches were too high for me, and I'd have to get a rope to get up there. By now the sun was down and I had to get going. I knew Aimee would probably have a fit if I didn't get back pronto.

I pushed through the woods and made my way to Firefly Field and saw a firefly low down and in the brush. This made me want to hang around of course, but it also made me quicken my pace. I got back home just as the light in the west was all but gone. Aimee was standing on the back step looking down the street, and I waved at her. She saw me but turned her back and slammed the screen door behind her. Well, well.

Aimee was pissed, and I hung onto the flimsy technicality that it wasn't truly dark yet. She remained grumpy so I made nice by producing a treat in the form of cinnamon toast after supper. I used up the last of the loaf of bread I had got for the camp-out, which I had tucked away in my closet underneath the singing shirts. That's how it goes.

I snagged a couple of sugar packets from the little cup in the cupboard (Mom brings home the sugar packets from work) and a little cinnamon from the spice rack. I also made tea, because tea goes well with toast. Aimee wolfed down her two pieces of cinnamon toast, gulped down her tea, and all was forgiven. I was bone-tired, so I wished her good-night and went to my room.

I had to push Ninja Bob over so I could get into bed, and then he stretched out all along my right leg and started purring like a well-tuned outboard motor. Having Ninja Bob nudged up against me purring away felt good, and right. One minute I was thinking about the camp-out and Salt Lick Lake, and the next minute I was fast asleep. I know I slept hard, because I didn't hear Mom come home and I didn't wake up until it was broad daylight, and the birds were singing.

I scratched my ear and felt something cold and wet against the side of my hand. I turned my head on the pillow and found myself looking at a small dead bird about an inch from my nose. I yelped and sort of speed levitated out of my bed. One second, I was looking at the open mouth of a dead bird. Then, in what seemed like that very same second, I was standing next to my bed in my skivvies. I was confused and shocked.

The little dead bird was lying there on my pillow and there was this spot of wetness all around it. It was a young whippoorwill. It was blotchy looking. It was also chewed up looking. The dead thing lay there on my pillow, and the birds sang and sang and sang outside my window. Then I noticed Ninja Bob. He was lying on the foot of my bed, looking up at me and purring. His tail was twitching, too. I stared at the thing on my pillow as I pulled on my clothes. Then I took my pillow, dead whippoorwill and all, and went down to the basement. Wow. The basement door was still propped part way open. I had left it like that all night.

I walked outside past the garden to our burn barrel. I burn garbage about twice a week. I would be burning some today, I thought to myself. I dumped the poor little bird in, then stripped down my pillow and threw pillow and pillowcase all in the washer, with bleach and detergent. Yuck, yuck, yuck. I didn't feel like breakfast.

What I had my mind very set on was getting up an intriguing sugar maple tree. I needed rope, and I thought of the Aldrich place. Peachy had found rope there. I had found pop bottles there. I hadn't gone into the barn because of the funny smell in there, but that smell was probably gone by now, I reckoned. The morning was getting away from me because I had slept so long. I thought about calling one or two of the guys but decided to forget about it. Any one of them can get me sidetracked, and I wanted up that tree. I headed to the Aldrich place.

The sold sign was down, and the buildings looked abandoned. I knew the fields were being worked, but no one was living in the house. I could look around, but I had to be sneaky about it. I dropped my bike into a culvert, and then ran up the ditch alongside the lane to the house, hunched over like a hunchback. The barn door was wide open, so I darted in. The bad smell was gone, but there were no ropes. I cut through the barn over to the tractor shed and eureka! Rope!

It wasn't thick, and it was old. But it was still strong and plenty long enough. I coiled it up and hotfooted out of there. Once on my bike I felt like some sort of cowboy, with the coiled rope hanging off my side. It must have been early afternoon by the time I got to the little clearing with the circle of sugar maples.

I steadied my bike up against the tree and put down the kickstand. I could do this. I found a big rock and tied it to one end of the rope. After a few tries I got the rope over the lowest limb of the tree. I made a simple slip knot and pulled the rope tight. I clambered up first using my bike and then the tree itself for leverage. Once I got to the first branch, I knew I was going to make it all the way up.

As I started climbing the music I had heard at Grandma Lundgren's started playing in my head. I started to think then maybe Grandmas Lundgren's music had put some kind of spell on me. Then, Indian drums started playing in my head. Then Grandma Lundgren's music, then Indian drums, and so on back and forth. There was this one place where I really had to stretch up to get to the next limb up, but I did it. Suddenly the music and drums stopped.

I was high up. And I really hadn't thought about the getting back down part. As I was getting up there, I started to notice whiffs of cooler air. Big black clouds were moving in from the north. They were a good distance off though. Big white puffy clouds were right overhead, and sometimes they blocked out the sun. But then they'd move, and the sun was back out.

I climbed up and up towards the crotch. I pulled up to the crotch of the tree and peeked into what was left of a big, old nest, with a tree branch lodged across it. I looked around for any other pieces of stuff (or bones) but didn't see anything except a bunch of old feathers, twigs, leaves, bits of bark, and what might have been bits and pieces of old nests. There was a lot of that stuff. It didn't smell bad, but it looked gross. I didn't want to touch the crud; it looked like it went down deep into the crotch of the tree. It looked like it had been collecting there for a long, long time.

I grabbed off a twig and poked it deep into the stuff. The twig went in deep. I pushed down against something hard and unyielding. I heard a rumble of thunder way off and looked over to the north. There were a couple of turkey buzzards circling way up almost over my head. There were a few more circling over by what I reckoned was the Durr place.

When I looked off to the north towards the storm clouds, I noticed something odd. There were a bunch of pine trees, here and there, some close and some further off, and they looked like their tops had been stepped on. That's the best way I can describe it; like their tops were squished down. There was one which had a black and charred looking top, like it had been struck by lightning. Right behind it I saw lightning in the storm clouds moving towards me and decided it was time to get down.

Climbing back down I got to that part of the tree where I had had to stretch up, and I was forced to hang down and then balance on the limb below me. It was dicey, but I did it. It scared me bad however, and I decided I wouldn't be going back up. I got down to the rope and undid it. The thunder was getting closer, and the dark clouds were moving in. I got going.

I was pulling past Firefly Field when the siren went off. I looked around and didn't see any tornado, but I knew I really, really had to get going. I peddled for all I was worth. The sky was dark, and a gust of wind nearly knocked me off my bike. I pushed past Lucky Lurky's while this guy in the doorway yelled for me to get off the street and find cover. I really got going.

Mom was standing in the kitchen doorway yelling at me to get my butt in the house and down into the basement, *right now*! I got down there with Mom and Aimee and Ninja Bob, and we turned on the radio. Every time it thundered outside the radio would go all static. There was a huge thunderclap, and the lights went out, but the radio stayed on because it was on batteries.

The guy on the radio said that tornadoes had been sighted near Black Goose Falls. We rode the storm out and didn't see or hear any tornadoes. Mom looked frightened, and when we started to catch hail, she jumped. Eventually the lights came back on, but it was late enough and blustery enough that I knew I was inside for the rest of the evening. Mom headed off to work and left me in charge as usual. We had chicken pot pies for dinner.

A Little White Bone

The next morning the phone rang while Aimee and I were having breakfast. I picked it up right away so Mom could keep sleeping. It was Poopy. "Hiya Eric, what ya think me and The Beetle found yesterday morning by our new camping spot?" Poopy inquired. Poopy then proceeded to tell me all about it.

The Beetle, having missed the camp-out, was curious about the little trail and wanted to explore it some more. Him and Poopy rode their bikes out there at about the same time as I started up the sugar maple tree. I felt a little twinge that they hadn't invited me along. I said as much. "I called," said Poopy. "But Aimee said you were already gone."

Feeling better, I listened to Poopy's story. He said when him and Beetle got to the camping spot, they poked around the fire ring and then Poopy and Beetle investigated the little game trail that Poopy had discovered behind the stand of witch trees on the little hill. Poopy said that it was hard going because some trees on the other side of the old fence line had been knocked over, and part of the woods looked like a big bomb had been dropped and blew up.

They climbed over broken branches and tree limbs and managed to follow the trial until they got to where Poopy thought the bad smell had been, but the smell had gone away. Then they went further down the trail. Poopy said they came across what they first took to be a mangy thin dog with a dead pidgin in its teeth. Looking at it more closely they realized it was a coyote. Poopy said it growled at them and jumped off into the underbrush. Poopy said it had a snarl on its mouth, its lips all pulled back from its teeth around the pidgin, and that it had yellow eyes.

I was at a loss for words, because this was so very much cooler than my climb up a sugar maple tree. So, I tried to add dignity to my adventures by telling Poopy that I had found what I thought was the bone of a bear's toe. My comment made Poopy laugh. "Well, bring it over and we'll look at your bear's toe bone," he said. "Peachy wants us to meet over at his house," Poopy continued. "While we're there, you can let Peachy's Dad look at it. He'll know what kind of bone it is."

Poopy hung up. I smiled. It looked like it was going to be a fun day. It was in an interesting sort of way. I put the bone in my pocket and headed out. It was hot and muggy outside, what with all the rain we had the night before. There was no wind, not even a breeze, which made it feel even hotter and muggier. By the time I got over to Peachy's I was sweating like a pig. It was a relief to get into their big, cool house. Inside the fans were on and the windows were open.

Back then I could come and go to Peachy's house. I wasn't like almost family like over at Poopy's, but I could come and go, unless somebody was grounded. Like I think I've already said, I always had to be accompanied by Dingo to go to over to his place, and it was very rare indeed for me to get over to The Beetle's.

Walking into Peachy's big cool house was like bliss. Bernard Who Is Not A Saint Bernard came up and bumped against my leg. I walked on into Mr. Peterson's study. You can tell right off the bat that Mr. Peterson is a high school Science teacher. His study is full of books and framed butterflies, turtle shells, arrow heads and fossils. On the big reading table in the study there was a big map of the township. The study also has all kinds of maps. There is even this map drawer thing. And in one corner of the study is this big roll top desk with all kinds of drawers and compartments.

Everyone was in the study, including Molly. Everyone had a big cold glass of lemonade with ice except for me. Mr. Peterson walked in, saw me, and turned right around and left the room.

"Does he know?" I asked.

"No!" they all said together in hushed tones.

See, there are just things we do not talk about to the adults, like finding a coyote on somebody else's property. Peachy and The Beetle had been studying the map of the township, and they had noticed this little L shaped lake on the map, right above where Dingo's farm is, and next to a big marsh that's a state waterfowl sanctuary. They showed me the lake on the map. That's the first time I really had anything to do with Klammer Lake.

Mr. Peterson came back in with my glass of lemonade. That's what he had gone out of the study to get. He had been showing everyone the boundaries of the township, and where Peachy's place was, where The Beetle's place was, and where Dingo's place was. He went over it again quickly for my benefit. That's when I realized that the little pond in the back of my house is part of the bird sanctuary, too. I became more interested in that map, while Dingo talked about how his family rode out the tornado in their root cellar, and how it tore up one of their cornfields. I almost didn't hear Mr. Peterson when he asked us what we were up to this fine day, and we told him we were just going to go riding around town on our bikes, and then maybe go swimming.

Mr. Peterson agreed that it would be a fine day to go swimming, indeed. Then I looked at Mr. Peterson and told him I had something interesting to show him, and I wasn't sure what it was. "This is what it is," I said. "I found it in East Anderson's Woods."

I put the little white bone right down on the map, almost on Klammer Lake, like the bone was pointing to the lake. Mr. Peterson was very interested in the bone. He picked it up and asked me if he could keep it for further investigation. I told him it was fine with me. Staring at it he asked me again where I had found it, and I told him again that I found it out in the middle of East Anderson's Woods.

Mr. Peterson got one of his sample tubes and plunked the bone right into it and closed the lid. He then put the tube in his pocket. He wished us all a fine afternoon and then left the room. I heard him in the other room talking on the telephone, and I heard him say something about the fire station. There was a lot of coming and going at the fire station, all because of the twister the day before. We all got on our bikes and headed to Dingo's farm, while Mr. Peterson got into his car and headed the other way into town.

Night Crawler Lake

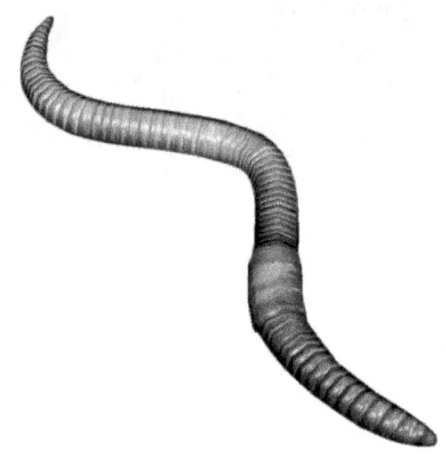

We got to our camp spot and dropped our bikes at random. Bernard was panting very hard after keeping up with us. The whole darn area had taken a beating. There was a big swath through the cornfield where a twister had run clean through it. There were corn stalks everywhere. There were places where batches of corn stalks were flat on the ground. There was this one tree that had part of a barbed wire fence wrapped around it, posts and all. Further back in the woods we could see fallen trees, but the witch trees were all still standing on their little hill. Dingo took a good look around to make sure nobody was watching, as he was still skittish about going onto Durr property.

Molly on the other hand, was very excited about discovering what Klammer Lake looked like. She was thinking that perhaps it could be our secret swimming spot like in the Tarzan movies. We hadn't exactly told her about how thrilling it was that a coyote was prowling around, but when we did, she didn't blab. Molly being Molly, we knew that once she was in on a secret, she would stay in on the secret. Besides, she was going to see what she was going to see. So off we went on safari while keeping a lookout for cannibals, much to Molly's annoyance.

I've got to say, it felt like cannibal country. It was around high noon. The sun was out in full force and the woods were hot, muggy, and still wet from the rains. Also, there were all the fallen trees that we had to climb over and round to follow the trail. I knew we were getting close to the spot because I recognized some of the trees around where we had first smelled that awful smell. But I didn't smell anything yet, except for wet woods. Then Poopy and The Beetle stopped.

They were puzzled. The smell was gone as they had reported, and for that matter, so was the log that they said the coyote was partly hiding behind when they spotted it. There were split trees and limbs everywhere. They scratched their heads and looked around and scratched their heads and looked around some more. They both seemed confused. "I guess the twister just picked up stuff and blew it every which way into the woods," said Peachy. "Wanna go off trail and look around?"

Nobody wished to go off-trail into those muggy and damp woods looking for coyote tracks, much less a coyote with yellow eyes and a snarling mouth full of teeth, and we all said so. Molly was kind of ticked off that we hadn't told her about the coyote, and she let us know she was ticked off. Peachy talked her out of her growing umbrage by suggesting that we push on and see if we could find Klammer Lake, and perhaps a secret swimming spot. Molly got all excited again, and so we continued our safari.

We had to crawl over more downed trees, and there were places where we lost the trail. It was tough going. At last, we caught sight of the lake up ahead, sparkling and glittering through the trees. From that distance, and through the trees, it looked wonderful. But when we got to the shoreline, we were all sorely disappointed.

The shore, if you can call it that, was all marshy and gross. Grossest of all were all the big worms piled almost on top of each other where the little waves lapped up against the muddy shore. Right then and there, we dubbed the place 'Night Crawler Lake'. We looked around and at first just saw woods all around the lake, but we all knew we were on Durr property, so we tried to be sneaky.

We explored along the shore a bit further, but it was mushy going. Then we came to a stop because a little dock and shed came into view across the lake, and we didn't want to be seen by anyone, especially old man Durr. We backtracked in the opposite direction until we got back to where we had come in and voted to get back onto Dingo's farm. Poopy didn't pay attention to the vote. He kept on slogging through the muck, but we didn't want to call him over, because we didn't want to make a lot of noise. Then, he turned and started waving to us to come over to where he was standing. We trooped through the shoreline mud, expecting to find something gross, like a dead coyote half sunk in swampy water surrounded by a bunch of dead worms. Molly hung back.

Poopy had found a boat. It was an old rowboat, with peeling light blue paint. Its bow was up in a bunch of cattails, and its stern was in the muck. There was water in the stern.

"It has a leak. It's not seaworthy," opinioned Peachy.

"It might be rainwater," countered Poopy.

"It's kaput," stated The Beetle.

"Let's pull her up and see," suggested Dingo.

Then, from Molly standing way back, "Is it something gross?"

Me and Poopy were already pulling the boat up by the bow, up by a few inches, anyway. She was stuck in the mud good and tight. And it was hot. And the horseflies found us. Molly finally came over and we all got to work. We all pushed and lifted and pulled and shoved. We got the stern out of the water, but by that point the flies were eating us alive.

We voted to retreat, although Poopy wanted to stay and see if the water in the stern stayed, or drained. Then he discovered a leach on his leg and decided that our vote to leave was a good idea after all. But he said he wanted to come back and check on the boat, and that he was darn sure going to have bug spray with him when he did. We climbed back over fallen trees and branches and made our way back to the witch trees and our camping spot. We were all a hot, muggy, sweaty mess. We decided to get our swimsuits and meet at Salt Lick Lake and plan our next move.

My tennis shoes were still a muddy mess when I got back to the house, and they smelled funky. I hosed them off outside by the basement and Ninja Bob wanted out. When I let him out, he came over and sniffed my shoes. I let him sniff, then went back in and tip-toed upstairs in my bare feet because I wanted to get out of there without letting Aimee know that I was heading to Salt Lick Lake. I tip-toed back to the basement and let myself out, ready to go with my swimsuit and thirty-five cents for entry and a cold bottle of pop after our swim. It was roasting hot by that time, and heatwaves and water mirages shimmered off the asphalt as I peddled through town. When I got to the lake everyone was there except The Beetle, who showed up after everyone else was on the floating dock. Once he got on the dock, we plotted and planned.

Peachy said that back in the old days tar was used to patch up leaks on wooden ships, and that maybe that would work on the boat, but first we should determine if it was leaky. We had pulled the boat all the way up on shore. If we went back and the water in the stern is gone, it's got a leak, he reasoned. If not, and there is still water in the stern, then there's no leak. The Beetle pointed out that none of us had any tar, and that tar would cost too much, anyway. Poopy, who had just been staring into the water, looked up and said that he knew where there was some tar, but getting at it might take some doing.

Poopy went on to tell us about the street behind the theater and one block down from his house where a street crew had put little iron bomb-like looking things that would get lit up at night, because they were patching the street. Poopy said they were using hot tar. He went on to tell us that he knew it was hot tar because he wasn't paying attention and he had run across the street with bare feet. Poopy showed us the bottoms of his feet, and they looked as if someone had painted them black. A plan started to take place.

First, me and Poopy would steal a bucket full of hot tar from the street work site during lunch, when all the crew would be over at Jenny's Diner gulping down their big ice teas and hot roast beef sandwiches with mashed potatoes and gravy. That had to be the first thing, because we didn't know how many more days they'd be out there patching the street. Also in the morning, Peachy and Beetle would check on the boat, while Dingo did chores, so his dad and Mr. Red Cloud wouldn't get suspicious about a bunch of us all hanging around our camp site in the middle of the day, without setting up a camp. We were all feeling a bit paranoid about our upcoming adventure. Molly, for her part, didn't want anything more to do with the boat, or Night Crawler Lake. But we swore her to secrecy.

We swam some more, and all took turns jumping off the dock, including Bernard. I almost hit Peachy because he likes to swim under the dock, which we're not supposed to do. Because of this the lifeguard blew her whistle and told us all to get out. On our way in we voted on getting some cold pop. We ran past the lifeguard who was still shaking her finger at us and hit the little concession stand. We were told, much to our dismay, that the pop machine was busted. We all had of course swallowed lake water, so we weren't technically dying of thirst, but we were all thirsting for an ice-cold pop. "To the grain elevator," directed Peachy.

We all sprinted to the changing rooms, and all came out at the same time. We hopped on our bikes and raced for the grain elevator. Poopy, who was in the lead, was standing on his pedals and pumping hard to stay ahead of me. Up ahead of him, a mirage of what looked like a lake shimmered off the pavement on the elevator side of the railroad tracks.

Poopy bumped over the tracks and almost lost control. From where I was at it looked like he was sliding side-ways through the mirage water. He then somehow managed to execute a very sharp turn into the grain elevator parking lot. He jumped off his bike, nonchalantly letting it crash into a concrete curb slab at the entry way. He then jumped over the slab as his bike went down. He slammed through the elevator's office door, and poof, was inside just like that. That son of a gun was first in line for the pop machine, and therefore first to get a seat on the old and beat up couch in the office. I managed to get in right behind him.

It wasn't exactly cool inside. In fact, it was hot and dusty. Old Carl was puttering around the place, big sweat stains under his arms. Why anyone would wear bib overalls in a grain elevator office is beyond me, but he has his ways, ways which seem to work for him. He's been around the elevator for as long as I can remember, and although he's not the sharpest tack in the box, he's never had an accident, or gotten sucked down into the grain like that other guy that got killed a few years back. Well, maybe he did have an accident once upon a time, because he has one eye that looks in the wrong direction. He looks like a Santa Claus in bib overalls with a wandering eye. I went over to check out the old pop machine. It's probably the oldest working pop machine in Minnesota. The pop machine and Old Carl go well together.

Poopy had already pulled back the pop machine's sliding metal lid. I looked down into the metal rows to see what was what. Poopy had snagged an orange pop, but there were some left, along with grape, root beer, cola, and ginger ale. I pulled a root beer down the row and over to where I could pull it out, then fed in the dime. Out she came, and I grabbed the other side of the couch. I took a good long swig and looked out the big window to see where everyone else was.

Old Carl was looking out the window too, while fluffing out his beard. While watching him I went into sort of a trance. When that happens, I just go with it. The guys tell me when I do that it's like I'm looking off into space, seeing something no one else can see. It's sort of like that, I suppose. What I first saw was Old Carl standing there by the window with sparkling dust motes swirling and spinning around his head. Then I tranced into seeing shining galaxies pin-wheeling right out of God's own beard. Then Peachy crashed through the door, and I was suddenly just looking at Old Carl again. Poof!

Peachy snagged a grape pop, like I knew he would. Dingo, right behind him and nearly stepping on Peachy's heels, pulled out a cola. The Beetle, always the sophisticate, helped himself to a ginger ale. Molly, last in, claimed the last root beer, with an audible sigh of relief. Old Carl talked to us using our real first names, which made us smirk and snort.

"Don't drink that cold pop so fast, Larry, you'll get a gut ache. Godfrey, you're nothing but skin and bones! Here's a penny for the peanut machine. And here's a penny for each of your sweaty, stinky friends!"

Most usually always the same thing happens when our teachers call us out by our first names. We smirk and laugh and snort, maybe because we think our real names are so funny. On any account, we laughed, drank our pops, and were hugely entertained by Old Carl. After a while Beetle pointed out that the sun was getting low, so it was time to go.

We left, and once on our bikes we confirmed who was doing what the next day. Beetle peeled off first, heading back across the tracks towards his farm. We took our own sweet time through town, and then Poopy turned off right after passing the drug store, like he always does. The remaining four of us continued through town, riding down the middle of the street as if we owned the place.

After passing the fire station and crossing the old highway Molly and Peachy executed two very acceptable high-speed turns, and raced each other to their house, with Bernard barking and sprinting along with them. Me and Dingo slowed down a bit, because we were still talking about the boat. My driveway came up and I peeled off, waving goodbye as I did so. I was going so slow I lost momentum going up the drive, so I just stopped and watched Dingo chug his way home. I admitted to myself, like I often do, that Dingo is one strong kid. And then I thought about the boat. We were all very excited about the boat.

I got home and read the note Mom had left for me to get busy with the garden, and that there were cold cuts and bread in the fridge for supper. I worked the garden for a while, putting a wooden pole in place in the center of the garden for this year's butzemann. Then I pulled in lettuce and onions to go with the sandwiches. While I was making sandwiches the phone rang, and it made me jump. It was early evening, not quite five, and nobody calls then, at least most of the time, anyway. I had been worrying about a phone call from the vet telling me that they had located Ninja Bob's owner.

It was Poopy. Poopy wanted to talk some more about the boat. I cut him off and told him to just come over tomorrow morning and we could fine-tune things. That shut him up, and Aimee was clueless. She wasn't even listening. After supper was done, we watched Jackie Gleason.

When bedtime rolled around, I had a hard time falling asleep. I finally did fall asleep, but then slept until mid-morning, only waking up when Ninja Bob jumped on my feet in bed. I didn't remember letting him in. I got downstairs and Aimee was already getting out the frosted flakes. Right as we started eating Poopy showed up at the door and let himself in. He called out, "What's up, toots?"

Aimee let fly with a spoon full of frosted flakes and caught Poopy square in the forehead. She scampered off to the bathroom and locked the door. My sister well understands the dynamics of a physical altercation with Poopy. Poopy stuck his head in the sink, ran water over his entire head, and then sat down across from me where Aimee had been sitting. I thought he was going to do something unseemly to Aimee's breakfast. What he did instead was to eat Aimee's breakfast all up. He wiped his mouth, looked at me and said, "Come on, we've got a boat project to get to!"

Then, he dramatically dropped the spoon into the empty bowl, and it rang like a bell. And then a bell kept ringing. I stepped outside and looked across the street, and the bell in the church steeple was just hanging there. Poopy stepped outside and looked at me sideways, and then he said, "Let's go, Eric. Come on, snap out of it. Let's go." The ringing stopped.

It was a perfect Minnesota summer morning. It wasn't too hot, and it wasn't too cool. The sun was shining through the trees along the street, and when we rode down the street the sun felt pleasantly warm. We'd slow down every time we came to a storm grate, to check for any loose change that might be down in the grate. We saw two pennies and made a note to ourselves to come back with a stick and gum to pull those pennies out. Near another grate we came across a dead whippoorwill. It was covered with maggots and maggots were crawling in and out of it. Its eyes were gone.

When we got to Poopy's house his mom was already working on supper. She had a big kettle on the stove and was cooking up ox-tail soup. Poopy told me ox tail was cheap meat, but if you slow cooked it you got good soup. Well, I know it makes good soup. We have it a lot. I just didn't know up till then it was cheap. We checked around to see if the coast was clear. His mom was still busy in the kitchen, his dad was probably just getting back to the dairy after making his milk truck deliveries, and the sisters were out and about somewhere.

We went to the garage where Poopy produced a small metal pail that he said no one would notice was missing. It took him a bit longer, but he finally found a garden spade that he said would do the trick. We took these items and hid them under a lilac bush away from the house, so that we could make a sneaky move out when the time came.

We got back just as the sisters showed up, and Poopy's mom said it was lunch time, and to have a seat. We were watching the clock and knew we would have to finesse this. We each got a big glass of milk (back then there was always a lot of milk at Poopy's) and a big, fat and goopy peanut butter and jelly sandwich. The girls chattered and asked us stupid questions like, "Do you hold your breath under water until you pass out?" and "Are you wearing your underwear today?" while we just ate.

At high noon the town siren went off, and we rushed off, to go 'bike riding'. When we got to the work site we were in luck. The crew was off to lunch. We did have one small problem, in that old Mrs. Jensen was out on her front porch across the street. I told Poopy that I would go over and talk to her while he scooped up the tar. It worked out beautifully, and Poopy headed down the street while I was still talking to her. We got to my house and hid the pail of tar behind the furnace. The tar was starting to get hard. "We'll have to heat it up again to soften it up," opinioned Poopy. "That's what campfires are for, to heat things up," Poopy went on, while taking on an intellectual air.

Having finished our part of the mission, we biked over to Peachy's to learn the status of the boat. All the rest of the guys were there with exciting news. It hadn't rained the night before, and although we had pulled the boat all the way out of the water, there was still water in the bottom of the boat. Peachy stated that this demonstrated scientifically that the hull was sound. We all agreed with him because we really wanted to test out the boat. We were also happy to skip the effort of taring the bottom of the thing. We got to work right then and there to fine-tune our plan.

The plan, such as it was, involved a camp out, when the moon was full. In this way we would be able to make our way through the woods without giving ourselves away with flashlights. We would bring along empty coffee cans to bail out most of the water. We would construct poles to pole the boat out onto the water, because we didn't have oars or oar locks. We wouldn't go out too far, as this was just going to be a test run. It only took us a few more days to gather our materials.

We double checked the calendar to make sure that we had the full moon right. We gathered the required parental permissions (except for The Beetle, of course). I had to do double duty in this regard, because I had to finesse a sleep over for Aimee. I really do try and stay on good terms with Aimee's dorky friend. A few days later and after much ado, we set up camp. What could go wrong?

The Ghost Fish

We went through our normal routine, setting up camp and gathering wood. We checked out our poles, determined as a group that they were fit to use, and then hid them away from prying eyes. Bernard was no help in this regard, as he kept dragging the poles from out of their hiding place on the other side of the barbed wire fence. Poopy finally distracted him by throwing another stick, until Bernard got tired of the game. "*So far, so good,*" I thought to myself.

Peachy had strapped a cast iron Dutch oven to his bike carrier and we were eager to try it out. We had biscuit mix and a big can of beef stew. I contributed little onions from the garden. The thing about a Dutch oven is that you must bury it in the coals, and you can't tell what the temperature is inside the oven. You've got to wing it, which is what we did. The biscuits came out as one great big giant biscuit that was all burned on the bottom. We pried it out, tore it into chunks, and then poured piping-hot beef stew over each of our portions. It was delicious.

Dingo brought along his new transistor radio, which he was eager to show off. I still wish I had a radio, and I looked at it with envy. Dingo saw how I was looking at it, and he handed it over to me and said I could spin the dial. I found a great rock and roll station, and we started listening to great songs, like *La Bamba* and *Stagger Lee*.

Like we expected, Mr. Red Cloud came clinking and clanking along up the old fence lane, just after sunset. We asked him to tell us more stories, so he took a seat on one of our sitting logs by the fire and he rolled a cigarette. He looked around and asked if anyone else would like a cigarette, and Poopy said he would very much like to try one. Mr. Red Cloud rolled him up one, and we sat there in awe as Poopy stuck the cigarette in his mouth. Mr. Red Cloud pulled a burning stick out of the fire and lit his cigarette first, then Poopy's. Poopy took a puff, and then threw up into the fire. It was ghastly.

After Poopy cleaned himself up and rinsed his mouth out with pop, he asked Mr. Red Cloud about why on earth anyone would smoke a cigarette, and who started smoking the stuff in the first place. Mr. Red Cloud settled into his story and told us that Indians had started smoking tobacco a long time ago. He told us tobacco smoke was used to please the spirits, because it rose to the heavens.

Mr. Red Cloud finally left after wishing us good night. We fiddled around for the next few hours, gathering firewood and talking to each other about '*what if*'. What if the boat has a slow leak? What if the hull is sound? Then what? Finally, it was time. The full moon was riding high in the sky. It was about midnight. We changed into our shorts and took off our socks, putting our bare feet into our tennis shoes. We slathered ourselves with bug dope and got our poles. Then, feeling well equipped, the four of set forth into the moon-lit woods.

We took our time, picking our way through the deep shadows and splotches of moonlight. Peachy had insisted there be no flashlights, as this was a secret mission. We had to feel our way along the little, narrow path. We would hit a dark patch in the woods, which seemed to happen quite a bit. Those woods are thick. We had to climb over fallen trees and tangled tree limbs.

It was truly a good thing that we had put on bug dope, because the bugs were out in force. We hadn't been affected too much by bugs near the campfire because of the smoke. The bug dope did some good once we were in the woods, but we could hear the angry swarms of mosquitoes dive-bombing us from all directions. They just refused to land on us, all slathered up as we were with bug dope.

Coming up to the lake seemed almost magical. Dogs or maybe coyotes were howling off in the distance. Bernard started in and we had to tell him to shut up. Loons were crying off the other side of the lake. The moon's reflection shimmered on the lake, sending pieces of moonlight adrift on little ripples that spread out towards us.

We oh, so carefully put our poles and bailing can in the boat, and then all together shoved the boat into the water. I was in the stern with the bailing can. Bernard started to whine on shore, and Peachy told him "Shush," and he quieted down, just sitting there on the mucky shore.

I started bailing, while Poopy, Peachy and Dingo started polling us out, stern first. They had to stand up so they could push on the poles better. They were all kind of wobbly. Laughing, I said "Sit down! Sit down! You're rocking the boat! The Devil will pull you under!"

Peachy told me to quiet down. He then told his crew to just push out a little further, and to then push back to shore. He didn't want to waste any time trying to turn the boat around, he just wanted to see if it was seaworthy.

Once we started moving Peachy rather urgently instructed Poopy and Dingo to immediately come to a full stop if anyone's pole went in too deep. Peachy, looking back at me and my constant bailing, then told them to stop and head back in. I pointed out I was still bailing, and I was bailing fast, and they had better jolly well put their backs into it. The guys pushed for all they were worth, and I continued to bail like crazy. It was when we reversed direction that I saw it.

Moonlight reflected off its scales. It was a big old carp, and it was quite dead. Little bits of it were trailing along around it in the water. Its eyes were gone, and its mouth was open. And, it was moving along behind us, seeming to follow the boat's wake. I stared at it, waiting for the vision to pass. Poopy was nearest to me, his back to me and polling for all he was worth. I bailed and looked back. It was still following us, its body undulating in the water. Its tail was moving back and forth. Its tail was moving back and forth *with purpose*. It was swimming. It was swimming. It was swimming. "Poopy," I whispered, "look, look behind us."

Poopy looked back, almost losing his balance. He stopped polling. We were almost to the shore and the cattails. Poopy kept looking back for a moment, and then he gave out a little, high pitched '*Eeeee*' sound. Then he said, in an odd and screechy high-pitched voice, "There's a dead thing following us!"

Peachy and Dingo caught a glance back at it, and at that point we started going down by the stern. As we went down the fish went down into the dark water behind us. I was shocked and scared, and I was darned if I was going to be in the water with a horrifyingly dead yet swimming fish. I caught a whiff of something very much like lutfisk. I gagged as I flailed my way to shore and took off running. I slipped once into the muck and went down hard on one knee. I heard a big splash behind me as one of the guys went down. I heard Dingo swear, and Peachy yelling "Come on! Come on!"

I charged through the marsh grass and into the woods, missing the trail. I could hear the guys thrashing along behind me, and I just kept on running. I found myself in a particularly dark patch of woods, so I stopped to get my bearings and look around. Something moved in the deep darkness off to my left. I jumped, ran and veered right towards where I could hear the other guys crunching and cracking through the woods, but there were these glowing green lights in that direction, all along in the dark places where there was no moonlight. I was having none of it, as I was truly spooked. I moved to the right.

As I changed course something moved again off to my left and this made me lunge forward at almost full tilt. A branch hit my face, and as I grabbed it the branch broke off and I went down hard. My left arm went straight into what felt like a bunch of thorn bushes, and it hurt bad. I jumped up, hanging onto the branch, and I swung it. It made a whistling sound. I swung it towards whatever was off to my left, and then I started moving forward, holding the branch out in front of me.

I could still hear the guys off to my right, and the green lights were behind me. Up ahead I could see the moonlit clearing, and it looked like I was looking down a dark tunnel, with the opening ahead of me. Whatever it was to my left moved again in the dark, and I ran for it. I hit the clearing at a full run and hit one of the few remaining stretches of barbed wire fence with my belly. I bounced back hard and heard a ripping sound as I landed flat on my back. I heard the guys calling for me and I struggled up and then used the branch to press down on the fence so I could climb over it. Bernard trotted out from somewhere, and I remember thinking, "*Where were you when I needed you?*" Bernard ran off towards the guys and I limped along behind him.

I got to the fire and threw my stick on it, and then another couple of pieces of wood. Poopy was sitting on one of the sitting logs just hugging his knees. I could tell he was badly frightened, just like me. Dingo was standing with his back to the fire with his hands on his hips, looking back towards the woods. Peachy was angry. We were all of us wet and frightened, except Peachy wouldn't admit he was frightened. Peachy turned and looked at me in the firelight and said, "Eric, you're bleeding."

I sure was. I brushed away the blood trickling down my face and then looked down at my belly. My t-shirt was ripped and bloody right where my belly button is. Peachy walked over to his tent, calm as you please, and pulled out his first aid kit and his canteen. He handed me his canteen and told me to take off my shirt. I had two gashes on either side of my belly button. They were deep gashes because you could see the meat. Peachy took the canteen, poured water over my gashes, and then he poured rubbing alcohol right into them. I yowled, and then Peachy growled at me. He told me not to be such a big sissy.

After this admonishment, Peachy put ointment on two gauze pads and taped them to my belly using first aid tape. My head got a band-aide, and then he looked at my arm. He said it looked like stickle thorns (whatever that is) and poured more rubbing alcohol right over my arm. Oh, how it stung! Then he told me that if I didn't already have a tetanus shot that I would have to get one right away. I got out of my wet clothes and changed into my jeans and my old but clean t-shirt. While I did so Peachy tended to Poopy. He asked him if he was alright, and Poopy didn't say anything. He just sat there hugging his knees. Peachy sat down next to him and said "Look, there's an explanation for that fish. I'm sure of it."

Dingo, still with his back to the fire, said that it was probably a tangled line stuck somewhere along the keel of the boat. He said he caught a dead fish when he was fishing in the marsh grass at his grand-pa's place way up north on Leech Lake. He said that's what you call a ghost fish. Dingo explained that it's just a carcass that you accidently snag with your hook.

"Well, we'll go back and find out," said Peachy.

"Not tonight," said Dingo emphatically.

We all agreed with Dingo's sentiment. Dingo and Peachy changed out of their wet clothes, and finally Poopy did too. He said he felt better after our little talk. What Peachy and Dingo said made a lot of sense, but I was still spooked. I rested on top of my sleeping bag, and I kept wood on the fire. Bernard was restless, and he paced back and forth for a long time. At last, he laid down right outside our tent. That made me feel better, and I started thinking about Ninja Bob. I couldn't remember if I had left him in or out. I dozed off still thinking about him. Dreams came, first about Ninja Bob asking to be let in at the basement door, and then about Katrina Hooch giving me a free bag of dry cat food at Swenson's grocery. In that last dream Katrina looked completely lovely. I still remember that dream to this very day.

Morning Fog

I woke up just before dawn. The whippoorwills were going crazy. Fog had drifted in, and Bernard was off somewhere sniffing around. The fire had died down, and I thought about putting more wood on, so we'd have nice coals for breakfast. Then I thought I saw something in the fog over by the witch trees. The fog itself was sort of moving in tendrils over there, and I imagined there was something taking shape. I was in no mood to go through possible hallucinations by myself after last night, so I woke up Poopy. "Hey Poopy, look over there, by the witchy trees. Do you see what I see?"

Poopy struggled out of his bag and wriggled up next to me. We both looked out at the swirling fog. Poopy gasped and grabbed my arm. Then he let out a breath. "Look, Eric, it's just a deer standing there. It's just standing there, looking at us. It is kind of weird, just staring at us like that in the fog. Where's Bernard? It's just the fog, Eric. Dead fish don't swim, and they sure as hell don't swim through the fog."

The buck just stood there, with spirals of fog looping around its antlers. I called for Bernard and the buck took off. As I kept calling for Bernard the birds seemed to calm down and the fog started to lift. Bernard came trotting over from somewhere in the cornfield. There was rustling around in the other tent, and eventually Peachy emerged. I got up and plunked myself down next to the fire pit and threw on some wood.

I scratched my arm and both legs. Both my legs were starting to itch almost as bad as my arm. There were little red bumps all over me. I sat there just scratching away. "Don't scratch," said Peachy. "It will make it worse."

I took a drink out of my canteen and looked up at the sky. The fog was going fast except for bits and pieces still back in the woods. The sun was coming up, but you could still see the moon. I was feeling headachy, and I thought it might be tetanus poisoning. I decided to skip breakfast and just go home.

By then everyone was up and Peachy coached us all on what to tell anyone about how I got so banged up. The story was that I was gathering wood in the dark, and that I tumbled over the fence with a heavy armload of wood. It sounded good enough to us all, and we practiced it a bit before I left.

When I got home, Mom was up already because she didn't sleep well. It was because of Ninja Bob's early morning yowling to get let in. I told her my story, she sighed, and said she would call Doc Glover at nine, and then get more sleep before her shift. She looked at my arm and my belly, and she told me to take a bath and to give myself a good soaking. I fell asleep in the tub. Mom tapped on the door and told me I had a three o'clock appointment to get my shot, and to not forget it. I dried myself off, and the bath towel felt very good on my arm and legs when I rubbed extra hard. I was clean, but I felt all banged up and exhausted.

I climbed into bed, but not before setting my alarm. I dozed off with Ninja Bob plopped down on my feet and purring away almost as loud as Mr. Gutzman's old lawnmower from down the hill. I woke up before the alarm went off because I was hot, sticky, and itchy. I figured the horseflies had really had their way with me out in the woods. I jumped into my jeans and the only clean t-shirt I had left and got downstairs. Mom was waiting.

We got to the doctor's office, and I remember that the sidewalk was almost as hot as a griddle. It was a relief to get into the air-conditioned office. Dr. Glover gave me my tetanus shot, put ointment and a new, big bandage on my belly, and then took a good look at my arm. "Eric, I think you've got a good dose of poison ivy or poison oak. I'm sending you home with a bottle of calamine lotion, on the house." Mom thanked Dr. Glover and settled the bill. I waited in the car and thought about what I knew about poison ivy. I didn't know much.

I got home, and immediately slathered my arm with calamine lotion, and oh, did it feel good. Mom took another look at me and said I was a mess, and she was having thoughts about me going camping with the guys anymore. She saw the look on my face, and then she said what she always says, "Eric, be more careful, please. Just be more careful. Stay home today, no running around, do your chores, the garden needs work, your sister will be home soon, take care of things." Then she was off.

The phone rang, and it was Peachy. He wanted to know if I got my shot. I told him about my poison ivy. I told him I had to stick around for the rest of the day. He just had to tell me about the fish. He and Dingo had gone back just after I left. Poopy didn't want to go back, so they left him at the camp as a lookout. "*Some lookout,*" I thought to myself.

Molly had come peddling up the lane with another batch of her famous blueberry pancake batter just as Peachy and Dingo came back out of the woods. She was sworn to secrecy, both on how I really got hurt and about what they found out about the fish. The boat was sunk, with just its bow sticking up among the cattails. Peachy went on to say he had gone a little way back into the water with one of the pole sticks. He saw the fish down under the water near the sunken stern of the boat.

Peachy set the pole down behind the stern and in front of the fish, and as he pulled the pole up, the fish started to come up. He said then he could make out the fishing line coming from somewhere under the boat. He went on to say that he threw the pole into the lake and got out of the water fast, because he was getting bitten up by horse flies, and the water felt slimy. Then he said, in a taunting way, I missed out on what were probably some of the best blueberry pancakes in the whole world. I didn't care. I told him I had chores to do. Before hanging up I asked him if he had any calamine lotion.

Peachy said he had a huge economy sized bottle of the stuff, and he would bring some over the next time he dropped by, or the next time I came over to his place, whichever came first. I told him he better come by. I told him I didn't think I would be gallivanting around town anytime soon.

An Official Visit

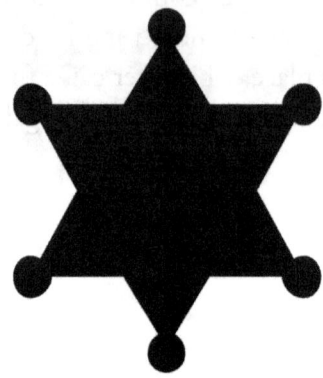

The next day I wasn't feeling very well, so I did my chores, pulled a bunch of carrots and onions and radishes to go along with dinner, and then checked what Mom had left in the fridge. I put more calamine on my arm. A bunch of red bumps had broken out on my chest, and under my chin. I covered these new rashes with more calamine lotion and stretched out on the coach with the fan going and the windows open. Aimee got home and she said, "Yuck! What happened to you?"

I told her my artful blend of truth and lies while making dinner. The phone rang and it was Mom. The first thing she said was, "Eric, honey, you're not in trouble. Constable Benny and Chief Wilcox will be coming over tomorrow morning to talk with you about a little bone you found in the woods. You're not in trouble. I'll be home a little after midnight, and I'll be up in the morning when they come over."

Well, now what? I thought to myself. Maybe it was a human bone. Otherwise, why would a cop and the fire chief want to talk to me?

Maybe it had something to do with our little outing in the boat. I called Peachy's number to give him a heads-up but got no answer.

The next morning, I shook off a dream I was having about a big old dead fish following me wherever I went, including up the stairs, and then through the air of the upstairs hallway. As I woke up, I was scratching myself, with new itchy bumps under my private parts. Ninja Bob was parked on my feet, just watching me. I got up and checked myself. My arm was covered with big fat blisters that were oozing this yellow puss. I had new red itchy bumps all over my body, and my legs were starting to blister up like my arm. I had blisters between my fingers on my right hand.

I stood in my bedroom and covered my arm, my privates, and my legs with what was left of the calamine lotion, and then put on my jeans to cover up. When I put on my jeans, I noticed my waist felt itchy, right where my jeans ride on my hips. As I was coping with this, Mom called from downstairs and said the Chief and the Constable were waiting for me in the kitchen.

Constable Benny and Chief Wilcox were coming into the kitchen as I got downstairs. Chief Wilcox was wearing his fireman's shirt, and Constable Benny was wearing his constable shirt. This was official. Mom asked, "Would either of you gentlemen like coffee?"

"Yes please, Ingrid," said Constable Benny. Chief Wilcox just nodded yes. He was staring at my arm. "Have a seat son," said Constable Benny. "We'll keep this short. Can you tell us where it was in the woods you found that little bone?"

I blurted out that I found it in East Anderson's Woods, where Mr. Red Cloud had his camp before he got hired by Chief Wilcox. Then I realized that maybe I had blabbed too much. I stopped and looked down at my feet. "Go on, son," said Constable Benny.

I told them how me and Mr. Red Cloud had been under a tree talking when the wind blew down part of a nest, and that some of it went down my back. I told them I put the bone in my pocket while Mr. Red Cloud was fiddling with a feather. I also told them you could still see part of the nest, and that it was high up in the tree.

Mom said, "For heaven's sakes, Eric! What on earth could you have been thinking, going up by yourself and talking to some bum living in the woods!"

"Well, I agree with you Ingrid, of course," said Constable Benny. "But in this case Mr. Red Cloud turns out to be OK. As a matter of fact, he's moved into the fire station as our on-site maintenance guy and night-time radio dispatch guy."

"He's still the hired hand at my farm during the day, too," said Chief Wilcox, finally saying something.

Constable Benny, seeing the look on Mom's face, said, "See, that little bone has gone through freeze and thaw cycles, and fallen off the other bones it was connected to, not held together by tendons. It was up there for a good while." Constable Benny thought for a bit, then turned to Chief Wilcox and said, "We'll get Red Cloud to show us the spot, and then send him up a ladder and check out that nest."

"Well, not today we won't," said Chief Wilcox. "Red Cloud's down at County General getting ambulance attendant training."

"I want that nest," said the good constable. "I can take the boy over to wherever this place is located, and you fire department guys can figure out how to get up that tree. Ladders, pole climbers, whatever works. Is that OK with you, Ingrid?"

"Yes, of course," said Mom. "Let me tend to his arm first. It looks so angry."

The men sipped their coffee while Mom wrapped my arm up in gauze. While she was wrapping away Constable Benny looked at me and he said, "Son, have you found anything else interesting or, you know, different or strange out in the woods?"

I looked at him and said, "Well, way off on the other side of the woods, on the other side of West Anderson's Woods, by the railroad tracks, we found a tooth that had been broken in half on a rock."

Constable Benny's eyebrows went up. "You found this on the other side of West Anderson's Woods? Was this by any chance near the trestle over the railroad tracks?"

"Yes sir," I blurted out, not thinking.

"When about was that, do you remember?"

"Umm, that was last summer, right after school let out," I replied.

Constable Benny looked at me real closely. Chief Wilcox had taken over from Mom and was tying off the gauze, wrapping it at the elbow with a clever little knot. "There was a report about boys swinging off a rope dangerously close to a passing freight train, this spring," said Constable Benny.

"Oh, we've been told to stay away from down around there, and we surly do," I equivocated.

Mom looked at me, and then at my arm which was leaking a little bit of yellow gunk into the gauze. She made a clucking sound. Then she got on the phone with Doc Glover as we left. I got to ride with Constable Benny in his old pick-up truck, with Chief Wilcox following behind in his old station wagon. I was feeling itchy and uncomfortable, but I was also excited. We parked in Firefly Field well behind the Hoot Owl Barn where the woods start, and then cut into the trees. We went down the little trail until we got to the site, and I showed them the tree. We could still see part of the nest, way up there.

Chief Wilcox said, "Yep, pole climbing equipment. We'll get on it."

Constable Benny looked down at me and said, "Let's get you home, boy."

That suited me just fine, because I was hot and itchy. We got back in his truck, but just before we got to my house Constable Benny pulled into Lucky Lurky's. "Come on, son," he said.

I walked in with Constable Benny feeling ten feet tall. We sat down at the counter and Constable Benny ordered two big, frosty cold mugs of root beer. Just after we were served our two root beers a loud and obnoxious hot-rod pulled up with Katrina Hooch riding shotgun and that jerk Tommy Docker driving. I've heard him called 'Tommy Knocker' around town, and I don't like the insinuation when it comes to Katrina Hooch. He had his hair all slicked back with greasy kid-stuff. Katrina saw me, and she waved and smiled. I smiled and waved back. Then someone over at the table full of teenagers yelled "Hey Kat!" and Mr. Jerk-face and Katrina went over to sit with them.

Constable Benny looked at me with a little half-smile. "That guy's a jerk," I said under my breath.

Constable Benny, still smiling, gave a little nod of his head. Then he said, "Let's get you home son, you look like a bad county road."

The Creeping Crud

Constable Benny got me home lickety-split. Mom was waiting for me in the kitchen with a pan, a turkey baster, and foul-smelling medical solution in a big brown bottle. She told me that the stuff was special medicine for poison ivy, and that I was supposed to stand in the bathtub and use the turkey baster to squirt it on where I was itchy. The turkey baster was so I wouldn't waste the stuff by just pouring it on. The pan was for squirting the stuff on if I was in my room or downstairs. I ran upstairs to try the stuff out. It didn't work worth a darn. By that, I mean I was still itchy. Also, I was horrified to note I had new patches of little bumps under my chin and up my butt.

I put on my ratty old bathrobe and went downstairs to sit while quietly oozing yellow gunk from all over my body. I decided on our big easy chair in front of the television. Mom looked at my condition and got two dish towels, which she placed on both arms of the easy chair, so I wouldn't get the chair all gunky with yellow ooze. All that was on for afternoon television was soap operas. How anyone, anyone at all, can watch soap operas for even just one hour is beyond me. I just sat there in in hot, sticky, itchy misery.

I waited for Mom to leave for work and then made a few phone calls. I needed more calamine lotion, and I needed it bad. I got through to Poopy and Peachy, and they both said they'd bring some over. I thought to myself that if they didn't make it over by today, then all they'd find of me in the morning would be my lifeless scalp laying in a pool of yellow goo on the easy chair.

They both showed up after what seemed like forever. It was hot, I had the fan on, I was wearing my bathrobe, and I was leaking sweat and gunk. I had put the last of my calamine lotion on my face, chest and arms. Yellow patches of sticky puss were leaking through caked layers of calamine all over my body. It was in this way I greeted them at the door.

"Holy cow, you look a mess," commented Peachy.

"You look like the creeping crud," offered Poopy. "You have crud all over you," he sympathetically observed.

"Gimme the bottles, you guys, just gimme the bottles," I pleaded.

"Here you go, Cruds," said Peachy, smiling.

"I think we should go," said Poopy apprehensively. "This might be like leprosy, and I don't want to catch any of it."

"Well, we better be off then," said Peachy. "See ya, Cruds!"

That's what he called me. Cruds, indeed! That was last summer. That's what kids have been calling me ever since. They've been calling me Cruds. For Ever and Ever, Amen.

That night I slept on a shower curtain draped over my bed because I was oozing so bad. I stayed awake in misery until sometime after Mom got home. Then, I finally drifted off to sleep. And now, I'm really going to tell on myself. I woke up in the easy chair in the living room downstairs next to the encyclopedia set. Birds were singing and Ninja Bob was yowling outside to be let in. So, I guess I was sleepwalking. So yeah, both me and my sister are missing a few marbles out of the bag. But everyone knows that now, don't they?

What Peachy Learned

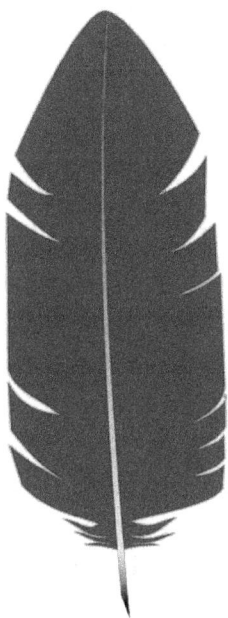

I lost out on the 4th of July because of my situation. Also, no one came to visit me, except for Katrina Hooch. She showed up all bright and shining at the kitchen door. She was wearing short shorts, a halter top, and she had her black hair pulled back in a ponytail. She stood there at the door clutching a bag of dry cat food. There I stood, caked in calamine lotion with yellow bubbles of gunk weeping out of the drying cracks of lotion. I was mortified.

"Good gracious, you look a mess!" she said.

"Uh-huh."

"Well, I haven't seen you around for a-while, and I know you've got this big old stray cat under your wing, so I thought I'd bring this by."

"He's not a stray. He is my cat."

"Of course, he is. I know how well you've been taking care of him. So, here you go. I'll just set it down here by the doorstep. I hope you feel better soon, Crudsie!"

"Thanks."

"You are most welcome. See ya."

The only good out of the situation was that Katrina couldn't see how bad I was blushing. I was humiliated, and I wished to high heaven she hadn't seen me in such a sorry state. Of course, it doesn't matter now.

Katrina skipped down the steps and hopped on her bike. She stood on the bike peddles and flew down the hill like a bat out of hades. After Katrina's visit, I did get a few phone calls. Dingo called and said the guys had saved up a bunch of firecrackers, and that the plan was to use them on the final and last Massacre of New Ulm because his mom said he was getting too old to play with little-boy playsets.

Dingo went on to say that the plastic cowboys, the Wild West Town, the wagons, the teepees, the fort, and the whole darn shebang, was going to the Salvation Army. But not before one last big massacre, with explosions all over the place. Also, he had been forced to go along on a family Fourth of July get-together in Rochester, so he had missed out on the Fourth, too. That statement made no sense to me. I wished that I had a big family with all kinds of relatives to do stuff with, but for some reason Dingo felt short changed.

I got a call from Peachy with alarming news. He said Poopy's house was for sale, and Poopy's dad had quit the dairy because he kept losing customers on his milk route. Peachy also said that he was grounded. That went a long way to explaining why no one had come over. Peachy went on to say he had really fouled things up. He had been thinking about my tree climbing story, and he had decided to do some tree climbing of his own.

Peachy's place has a pine grove along one side of their property. On the other side of the grove are a bunch of smaller lots that people bought up and built homes on when the original farm was divided up and sold off. The back yards of those places look out on the grove, and they all have backyard fences, some small and basic, some large and substantial.

One of the big and tall backyard fences belongs to the Shultz family. One of the most beautiful of the high school varsity cheerleaders is Debbie Shultz.

Peachy had a theory that Miss Shultz sunbathed in a natural state in her backyard. He was of this theory because Debbie didn't have any tan lines when she wore her little polka-dot bikini to Salt Lick Lake. Peachy decided that he needed to do research on the matter. Peachy's Dad was in the Army during the war, and way in the back of the top shelf of his parent's bedroom closet was his father's prized US Army Artillery binoculars.

Peachy organized a roll of green duct tape and patiently waited for the right moment. Peachy reckoned that the right moment would be when everyone but him was out of the house a bit before Miss Shultz's daily backyard sunbathing routine. The moment finally indeed came. Everyone left the house, with his dad taking off last, saying that he had to go to the fire station for a meeting. As soon as his pop drove off Peachy implemented his plan.

He scurried up to his parent's bedroom and removed the prized binoculars from their official US Army leather case, putting the case back exactly where it had been, so if circumstances changed, he could improvise. He then went out on his back porch, and quick as a rabbit smeared his face with charcoal ash from the bottom of the family charcoal grill. With his father's prized binoculars around his neck and the green duct tape in hand Peachy hot-footed it into the pine grove.

Working quickly, Peachy broke off small pine branches and duct-taped those branches about his body so that he looked like a little walking pine tree. Effectively camouflaged and with the coast still clear, Peachy climbed up a pine and selected a perch which provided him with good concealment and a perfect view of the Shultz backyard. While the view from the perch was good, the perch itself was tenuous, with Peachy obliged to wrap his legs around two rather thin and somewhat flexible branches. Then, out she came.

Miss Shultz was wearing everyone's favorite bikini. She was also equipped with a big beach towel, a transistor radio, and baby oil. Peachy very carefully and slyly raised his father's cherished US Army binoculars to his eyes to adjust the focus. Peachy said the view in the binoculars drew his body forward on those somewhat thin and flexible pine branches, and the treacherous pine branches gave way.

Going down Peachy clawed and grabbed at passing pine boughs. He thus slowed his crashing descent, but he made a lot of noise doing so. He heard Miss Shultz give out a shriek just as he hit the ground. He got the wind knocked out of him, he banged up his right knee, both of his hands were scraped and bleeding, he was covered in pine tar and dried-out pine needles from where he landed, and yet he got up and started hobbling away from the crime-scene. His father's prized binoculars were still around his neck, but as he hobbled out of the grove, he noticed they were rattling like a pair of maracas. They were also bent together in an unnatural way.

Peachy's intent was to get into his house, get into the upstairs bathroom, get cleaned up, and figure out what to do next. He didn't notice his father's old woody station wagon, because his pop had parked in the front drive on the other side of the house. Also, apparently, a rather rapid and terse phone call had been made from the Shultz residence to that of the Peterson residence. Peachy knew that the jig was up when Bernard came bounding out through the kitchen screen door. Peachy then played out the scene for me over the phone, changing his voice for effect.

"Are those my Army binoculars, son?"

"Yes, father."

"Were you spying on the Shultz girl?"

"Um, ah, um, yes, sort of."

Then, Peachy told me that he got a whupping right there on the back porch, and that he got grounded, right then and there, and all the way across the Fourth of July weekend. I felt so much better, knowing that I wasn't the only one to miss out on the Fourth. But Peachy had more to tell me.

While everyone else had gone off to see the Fourth of July parade Peachy had flipped through his father's notebook while vacuuming his dad's study. His dad's notes said that they had found turkey buzzard feathers in what was left of the old crow's nest up in the tree, and that it was because turkey buzzards sometimes take over empty crow's nests.

Peachy also said that the little bone I found was a middle phalange, and that his dad's notes said it came from the pinky figure of a child. Peachy also told me that some state guys and some county guys and some of our own fire department guys had been walking through the woods with dogs, but that they didn't find anything gross. I told him if he wanted to see something gross, he should come over and check me out. Peachy never made it back over to my house while I was rotting away, because he was grounded for so long. I was to see him a few days later anyway, but under very unhappy circumstances.

Sirens

I lost out on a couple of beautiful summer days sitting in the living room with the fan on, the windows open, and covered in calamine lotion. To make Mom happy I would make a show of squirting on the nasty smelling medicine out of the brown bottle, but it was the calamine lotion that kept me from going off the deep end. Also, Ninja Bob picked up a strange habit. It was late at night, and I was listening for Dad's voice to come out of his picture on the wall, because I hadn't heard his voice out of the picture for a long time. Suddenly Ninja Bob jumped onto the bed. My big old cat curled around my head, sunk his claws in just a little bit above my ears, and started licking my scalp. Oh, it felt so good! But I worried that he might get poison ivy on his tongue. He didn't.

Finally, after a few of the most horrible days that I've ever spent (up to that time, of course) I started to feel better, sort of.

I still had patches here and there on my body that were still oozing, but a lot of it had simply dried up. I felt better working in the garden, and the sun started to feel good on my face, arms and legs. It was around mid-week when I felt well enough for a swim. Heck, I needed a swim in my cool, clear lake.

I had watched Breezy the Weather Girl the evening before, and she had said that there was a good chance of thunderstorms for the next few days. She was right. I could see big dark clouds rolling in. But it wasn't raining, and the sirens hadn't gone off, so I decided to give it a go. Aimee and Mary were sitting in the living room, and I just poked my head in the kitchen door and announced that I was feeling better, I was going for a quick swim, and I'd be back in plenty of time to make supper. I took off before anyone could say no or ask to come along.

With the clouds coming in I kicked into high gear, peddling for all I was worth. I just wanted to get into that cool, clear water. If I could get in the lake before the lifeguards closed the beach because of a thunderstorm, then I would dash into the water and take my jolly-good time getting back out. Then I would just camp out at the snack stand until the rain let up. It was an acceptable plan, I reckoned.

I was only a few minutes away from the lake when, way up ahead, I saw Katrina Hooch come around the corner from the lake turn-off. She was on her bike and heading my way. It started to get windy. When she came up to me, I was all smiles. She had put on a pair of shorts over her swimsuit. "Lake's closed, Cruds. Come on then, let's get out of here before we get drenched," she called out.

I was delighted. I suddenly didn't care about losing out on my swim. I would get to ride bikes with Katrina Hooch back into town. "Come on," she said. "Let's race those black clouds into town!"

"I think we lost," I said, pointing up.

"Get going, Crudsie! Step on it!" shouted Katrina over the rising wind.

Big black clouds were right over our heads. A gust of wind pushed my bike and I wobbled, nearly going over. Right about then the sirens went off, both the water works one and the higher pitched fire station siren. We were out on the dirt road with nothing but corn fields on either side of us. I got going, standing on my bike peddles and pumping as hard as I could. Katrina could have passed me, but she stayed right behind me. There was another gust of wind and I had to sit back down to keep my balance. Another gust of wind blew chaff from the cornfield into my eyes.

Up ahead, on our left, was a long lane running uphill to the Carver's farm, and I was thinking about that when a spout came winding down from a huge black cloud and started twisting through the cornfield on our right, making a beeline towards us as if it had a mind if its own. From behind me Katrina yelled, "The culvert, dive into the culvert!"

I dropped my bike into the ditch and scuttled towards the culvert that runs under the lane that goes up to the Carver's farm. I heard Katrina's bike crash behind me. I stumbled to the culvert and as I bent over, I felt her push me in. Inside, I wriggled around to try and reach her, to try and grab her hand. With her hand stretched out to me Katrina Hooch was pulled up and away by the wind and tossed into the treetops. I know she was tossed into the treetops because I heard that that's where they found her body, up in the treetops, where the crows and buzzards live.

A Funeral

After the wind stopped, I crawled out to look for Katrina. Both our bikes were gone. This confused me. I just stood there, looking all around for any sign of her. The siren in town was still going off. A car pulled up and it was Mr. Gustavsson. "Get in, son, and right now," he said.

I argued with him. I told him that Katrina Hooch was still around somewhere, and that we had to find her. Mr. Gustavsson got out of the car, dragged me over to it, and threw me in. He then jumped in and slammed the door. I remember crying. I told him Katrina had pushed me into the culvert and then disappeared. He looked at me and said, "We'll find her son, but I need to get you home, and then I need to get over to the fire station. We'll find her."

When Mr. Gustavsson got me home Mom and Aimee were both out front waiting for me. I got out of the car and Mom slapped me on the face, and then hugged me. Aimee was crying. "Thank you, Sven," she called after him.

Mr. Gustavsson waved at her, and then took off towards the fire station. It wasn't long after that that they found poor Katrina's body, way up in one of the trees in the Carver farm's tree grove. I had a hard time accepting that Katrina was gone. Mom told me I would have to go to her funeral, because she saved my life. I didn't want to go, but I knew I had to. Mom said she'd come with me. I dreaded going.

I went upstairs to my room and sat in my closet, underneath the singing shirts. I sat in there for the next few days, coming out only when called to do chores or to come down to the kitchen to eat. I refused to see any of the guys, and when they would try and come over to visit, Mom would just shoo them all away. Mom would come and check on me from time to time, but when I heard her coming up the stairs I'd just come out of the closet and lie on my bed. She told me that I was grieving, and that the funeral would help me with my grieving process. After she would get done talking to me, I would go back to my closet and sit in there with my grief and my guilt. Ninja Bob refused to come into the closet with me, and when I tried to carry him in he would hiss at me. The singing shirts didn't sing, and Dad's picture didn't talk to me or smile at me.

Katrina's funeral at Oak Grove Methodist was a few days later. I felt ill to my stomach that morning, and I threw up in the bathroom. But I knew I had to go to her funeral. I had to go. I put on one of my singing dress shirts and a nice pair of slacks that Mom had bought for the occasion. Aimee got to stay home.

I walked into the church with my head down. I was ashamed of myself. It was my fault that Katrina had died. Before Mom could say otherwise, I darted to the very back pew on the left side, by one of the big windows. I scrunched in tight and hunched down. Mom came along and sat down next to me without saying a word. Grandma Lungren saw me back there and she gave me a little smile, as if she didn't understand that Katrina's death was my fault. The Petersons and the Gustavssons were sitting with Grandma Lundgren, and I ignored them all.

Katrina's casket was up in front of the alter, and the casket was open. I just kept looking out the window. It was sunny out there. I wanted to be out there more than anything else in the world. Out beyond some old oak trees was the church graveyard. I didn't think they were going to bury Katrina there, because the graveyard looked too old, and too little. I just looked at the little graveyard while they sang hymns and prayed and talked about what a fine and brave girl Katrina had been. I just sat there turned away from them, looking out the window with tears rolling down my face.

When it was time to go up and look at the casket I wouldn't go. Mom tried to pull me up, but I wouldn't budge, and she gave up and went up there by herself. Some people turned around and looked at me, but I just kept looking out the window. Finally, it was over, and I scooted right out of there and into our car. Mom came along after a few moments and got in. But she didn't drive home. She drove over to the town cemetery.

We drove on one of the little roads that curl through the cemetery to where there were a bunch of cars, and we got out. I told Mom in no uncertain terms that I was not going over to the grave. She said that that was OK, that I could stand behind the crowd, close to our car. At least I was outside, and I could stand by myself. I realized it felt very good to be outside. There were more prayers and there were more words, and then people started to move towards their cars. I jumped into our car and slunk down in the seat.

Mom got in, looked at me sideways, and then started the engine. I rolled down the window. Somehow, Mom had been right about going to the funeral. I felt a little better. But then, instead of turning back towards the house, Mom drove back towards the church. I looked at her, and she said, "We have to drop off these pies."

I hadn't even noticed, but there were three pies wrapped up in tin foil riding along in the back seat. That seemed OK to me, and I just rode along, enjoying the fresh air with the window rolled down. We got to the church parking lot and the Petersons pulled up next to us. They had brought some stuff, too. Peachy and Molly got out, both carrying covered baskets. Mom asked me to carry in one of the pies. I walked behind all of them, not really wanting to go back into the church, with all those people. Peachy dropped back and walked with me. He gave me a sidelong look but didn't say a word.

We didn't go into the church part of the church, but into this big room that was built on to the back of the church. There were lots of tables and chairs set up, and people were putting all kinds of food on a row of tables by a big kitchen at one end of the room. I set my pie down and turned to go, but Molly took my hand and she said that she wanted to sit next to me. I looked for Mom, and she was busy talking to some blue haired church ladies, and I knew I was stuck. I sat down at a table with Molly on one side of me and Peachy on the other. The Beetle showed up, and he sat across from me. Everyone started asking me if I was 'all right'. I told them I was fine, but I just didn't feel like talking.

Although I didn't feel like talking, everyone else sure was. There were even some people who were laughing. They were laughing at a funeral. I'll never understand the way of it. Peachy seemed almost jolly. I supposed that it was because he was technically still grounded, but here he wasn't. He turned to me and said, "Wait until they bring in the ice cream before you get pie. I'm going after fried chicken!"

As Peachy and The Beetle left to get their plates Grandma Lundgren swung past and said 'hello'. I just nodded. I felt a tap on my shoulder and turned around, and it was Miss Lindquist, with a slice of blueberry pie with a scoop of vanilla ice cream on top. She smiled and set the plate down in front of me. Then she said something completely silly, about me being one of her favorite students. I just gawked at her, not knowing what to say. At last, I said, "Thankyou ma'am." Miss Lindquist excused herself. While this was going on Molly had been quick as a rabbit, and somehow showed back up with a plate full of German potato salad, red cabbage, and a white brat.

I looked around, and Mom was at another table having something to eat. I caught her eye and she just smiled at me. We all of us now had something to eat in front of us, and Molly and Peachy were digging right in. The Beetle had what looked like excellent German style creamed peas with pepper, baked ham, and scalloped potatoes, but he wasn't eating. Instead, he was peering at me in a concerned sort of way. Then he asked, real quiet, "Aren't you hungry?"

They were all looking at me, so I took a bite of pie. It was so very good. I had another bite, then another and another. When I got to the crust Peachy said, "Whew, we were worried about you. At least you're eating."

I pushed my plate away and said, "You guys don't get it. This is all my fault."

The Beetle looked straight at me, and he said, "Cruds, it was a tornado. It was a tornado!"

I didn't want to sit there any longer, so I got up to throw away my paper plate away. There was a big trash can near the kitchen door, and that was my way out. I tossed my plate and there was a hand on my shoulder. I turned around and it was Mrs. Hooch, Katrina's Mom. Mrs. Hooch tried to say something to me. She said, "Katrina thought you were, – Katrina said that you're a good kid."

Then Mrs. Hooch started crying and she hugged me tight, right into her breast. I felt myself tuning beet red, but then Mr. Hooch came along and sort of pried us apart. He turned to me and said, "You take care of yourself, Eric." Then he guided his wife over to a bunch of other people. I made my get-away out the church kitchen door.

I made tracks towards the small oak grove and the little church graveyard. I wanted to be in the trees, and under the trees, and in the summer air. I looked behind me to see if anyone was following. Molly was standing in the kitchen doorway, and I waved her away. She just stood there, but she didn't follow. I got into the trees, and then started walking through the graveyard. I drew towards what looked like the newest gravestone in the place. It stood out because all the other gravestones were old and weathered looking, and it was set well apart from the others. There was a rose bush nearby, and a little honeybee was buzzing around the flowers. I stopped and read the gravestone.

Walter and Lilith Carp
Rest in Peace
1948

The little honeybee's buzzing got louder, and I started watching it. It would stop at one flower and take a little sip, then buzz over to another, walk around on top of the flower, then take another little sip. A hand touched my shoulder, and I jumped a foot into the air. It was Reverend Leverkuehn.

"Are you OK, Eric?"

"Yes sir, I'm fine."

"I was talking with your friends in there."

I sort of tuned him out, and just watched the little honeybee.

He said something about Katrina doing what it was in her nature to do. He said something about car wrecks and tornadoes, and the house fire that killed the people whose gravestone I was looking at. Then he said, "Well. I'll leave you to your thoughts. Remember the gift Katrina gave you and think about what you'll do with that gift. I'll let your mom know that you're out here getting some air."

With that he left me alone and walked back to the church.

I watched the little honeybee for a while and then Mom called me from the parking lot a few minutes later. I was glad to get out of there, but I did feel better. It clouded up that afternoon and rained in the evening. I sat downstairs in the living room and just watched it rain. I hoped that all of this wouldn't set me off to sleep-walking again.

Fort Zindernauf

The day after the funeral Peachy, Molly, Poopy and Dingo dropped by for a visit to make sure I was OK. Peachy had used my distress as an excuse to get off being grounded. He had insisted it was his duty to help a friend. Good for him. It was still raining, and they all had on their raincoats. I was in the living room watching an old Foreign Legion movie called *Beau Gest*. They all trooped in and watched the rest of the movie with me. It was still raining when the movie ended, and Dingo had an idea. "Let's build our own Fort Zindernauf in my haymow," he said. Dingo was obviously delighted with his own idea, and his enthusiasm was contagious.

It was not long before we were all biking to Dingo's farm, keeping well off to the side of the road so that we wouldn't get splashed or squished by passing traffic. We parked our bikes outside Dingo's barn and ran smack-dab into Mr. Red Cloud just as he was coming out. He asked what we were up to, and we told him that since it was a rainy day that we were going to play up in the haymow. He grinned, told us to have fun, but not to bust up any hay bales, or we would have to clean up the whole dang mess by ourselves.

We all climbed up the ladder into the haymow and had a fine afternoon, building what we thought was a pretty good facsimile of Fort Zindernauf. We made a gate, passageways on either side of the gate, and parapets over the passageways. We didn't fully trust the hay bales over the passageways, because Dingo fell through the top of the left wall into a passageway while running along the parapets. We knew we'd have to reinforce the passageways in due course.

A couple of the barn cats joined us up there, and they seemed to have a fine time too. They would take off running pell-mell down our newly constructed passageways with their tails all fluffed out. While I watched them, I thought that maybe I should have brought along Ninja Bob. But then I reflected on the very real possibility that he had been shot on this farm back in the winter, and that maybe he wouldn't appreciate the venue.

Molly turned out to be not much help, preferring to swing back and forth on the rope tied to one of the barn rafters. She was wearing a yellow dress that day, and when she swung back and forth, she looked like a giant yellow bell, with her legs like two clappers. She would most annoyingly sometimes kick over a parapet. We would yell at her, but she would just laugh and keep on swinging.

After we were about done, Mr. Red Cloud called up to tell us Mrs. Wilcox had a snack ready in the kitchen. We climbed down the ladder and ran out of the barn whooping and hollering, all hot, sweaty, and covered with hay dust. It was still drizzling outside, and the rainy mist felt good on our hot and dirty upturned faces.

Before going in for our snack Poopy climbed partway up the windmill. Then he did a pretty good imitation of the little guy who died laughing when he got shot from the watchtower in the movie we had watched before heading over to Dingo's. Falling backwards into the very soggy hay wagon, Poopy even included that odd little death squeal that the little guy made when he hit bottom. We were in a hurry, so we only did a sketchy job of brushing the wet hay off Poopy before running in.

When we got into Dingo's kitchen Mrs. Wilcox made us each wash up at the deep sink right next to the kitchen door. Dingo was wheezing, and Mrs. Wilcox made him stick his head under cold water until he stopped wheezing. Then, she looked at the hand towel we had all used to dry off and she showed it to us. It was really, really dirty. Mrs. Wilcox actually clucked at Poopy, and she made him brush himself off better in the mud room before letting him back into the kitchen.

We were treated to bowls of ice cream with strawberries and ground cherries. Mr. Red Cloud and Mrs. Wilcox joined us at the kitchen table, and we told them about our afternoon. This got us a second helping of berries and ice cream. While serving up the second helping Mrs. Wilcox bent over next to me and asked real quietly if I was doing OK. I smiled and nodded yes. After we were done it was time for me to head home. Molly wanted to leave too, and Mr. Red Cloud offered to drive us home in the farm's old beat-up pickup truck. Me and Molly threw our bikes into the back of the truck, happy to not have to bike home through the rain.

Molly jumped into the middle, and because she was riding the hump and because of the stick shift she leaned against and into me. Leaning into my shoulder she took two long, deep breaths through her nose, and then fell fast asleep. I thought she probably passed out because I reeked of sweat and haydust. However, Mr. Red Cloud decided to drop her off first, and when he pulled into her drive she woke right up and hopped right out. Mr. Red Cloud pulled out one of his pre-rolled cigarettes and lit up as he made a U-turn to drive back to my place. I was impressed by his dexterity. And, I must admit, I enjoyed the smell of the tobacco smoke.

"She's a nice kid. You watch out for her," he said smiling.

"I will, sir," I said in all sincerity.

"You know son, when I filled in my hooch out in the woods, I found something. I think I may have been living in a sacred place, on sacred ground."

"What did you find?" I asked.

"I'll let you know, once I've thought more about it, son," he replied somewhat cryptically.

When we pulled up into my drive Mom was outside puttering around in the garden. I jumped out, pulled out my bike from the back of the truck, and headed around back to put my bike away. I noticed that Mom waved at Mr. Red Cloud as he backed out.

Fort Zindernauf would wait for another day. And what a day our next visit to our haymow fort turned out to be. I realized I was getting over the whole funeral thing. It's sort of funny to me, how fast we can recover from really bad stuff. Well, most of the time, anyway.

Ringo's Last Stand

It was several days later, on a hot, sunny day near the end of August and just before school started, when an opportunity arose out at the Wilcox farm. Dingo called Peachy and me and let us know that everyone would be gone from the farm for a good couple of hours, and it was therefore time to play '*Dry Gulch Saloon Gunfight*'. Dingo didn't invite The Beetle or Poopy. Neither one of them had BB guns. While Poopy wanted a BB gun, his parents refused to let him have one. Beetle, on the other hand, had an unnatural fear of guns, even BB guns. And of course, his parents wouldn't let him have one anyway. This was just as well, because Dingo didn't have enough safety glasses to go around to more than three of us. Besides, Poopy had to help his family with their move.

By then they had sold their house and had put money down on the Chooty-Chew. The plan was to turn it into a pizza joint for the teen-agers. They've done a pretty good job. I especially like the new neon sign the place has, with the two devils holding up a pizza pie by their pitchforks. Alighieri's Pizza is cool.

It must be noted that Peachy was sneaky about not telling Molly, because she would have thrown a fit, and ratted us out.

We'd played '*Dry Gulch Saloon Gunfight*' once before, under similar circumstances. That one time before, we had worked out the rules. Everyone had to wear shop glasses, everyone had to wear hats and gloves, and there was no firing at anyone's face or head. I had the crappiest BB gun, the one that you had to cock a couple of times before it would fire. It was mine because I had won it on a bet in the tack room once when we were playing what we called '*The Massacre of New Ulm*'. I did it by shooting a plastic cowboy right off his plastic horse using that very same BB gun. The gun was rightfully mine, but I kept it well hidden in Dingo's barn out of discretion.

Now, based on the last time we played, Dingo got to be the bad guy named Ringo. He got this honor because it was his barn, after all. Peachy got to be Marshal Dalton, and I got to be Fry Pan Freddie, the mean and crusty old bartender of the Dry Gulch Saloon. Not only did I get the lamest gun and the lamest name, but I got the lamest cowboy hat. My hat was the old straw hat with a hole in it from out of the workshop. At least I had a red hanky that I could tie around my neck.

Me and Peachy closed our eyes and counted to one-hundred, and then we got busy to root Ringo out of the barn, which was now through the magic of imagination, an old, dusty saloon. Just by listening to his footfalls, we knew the dreaded Ringo was on the second floor. We went in carefully, ever ready for an ambush, even though we knew he was up above. With Ringo, you can never be too careful.

As we went in, we heard stealthy movements coming from up above. Peachy was of the mind that we would have to rush him, meaning that I would have to be the first one to go up the ladder to the haymow. Once up and through the opening I was to jump left, and then Peachy would charge up behind me and jump right. Then we would corner Ringo and blast him out. What could go wrong?

I adjusted my shop googles, pulled my straw hat down on my head as far as it would go, and clattered up the ladder with my BB gun. As I pulled myself up through the opening, I caught two stinging BB shots square in the middle of my chest. I dove to the left while wondering how Dingo got off two shots so quick. I rolled behind a hay bale while I heard Peachy yelping as he scuttled off to the right. I raised my head over the hay bale and took aim.

Now, the way we used to play this game, once you got behind cover, you were in pretty good shape, because of our strict prohibition against shooting at somebody's head. That being the case, I was not only able to take aim, but to also look around a little bit and figure out which end was up. Peachy had made all the way to one end of Fort Zindernauf, where he was hunkered down. Once there Peachy started screaming, "He's got a gun! He's got a gun!"

"Of course, he's got a gun, you nitwit," I shouted back. And then I saw it. Peachy's right leg was sticking out a little bit and Dingo popped up with what looked like a real six-shooter. It was black, shiny, and beautiful. Also, it could fire as fast as Dingo could pull the trigger, which was pretty fast. He must have planted it up there ahead of time.

I watched a stream of BBs fly straight and true, making little popping sounds as each one hit Peachy's exposed leg. Peachy yelled, swore, and jumped up and into the fort, but Dingo was ready. "You'll never take me alive, sheriff," he called out. Then he disappeared down one of the tunnels.

"We've gotta smoke him out," said Peachy grimly. "You go in from your side, and I'll go in from mine. Let's get this villain." I didn't much want to go down a tunnel, but then I realized if I crawled in head-first then Dingo couldn't fire at me because of our 'no head-shot' rule. It was a good plan, and I let Dingo know what I was up to.

"I'm coming after you, Ringo! And I'm coming in head-first. No head shots!" I yelled. There was a pause. I heard a lot of bustling and rustling as Peachy closed in on Dingo from the other side. Then, all pandemonium broke loose.

Dingo screamed. "You shot me in the head, you #%&!" Dingo then shouted out a whole string of filthy swear-words, followed with "I'm gonna kill you, you big #%*- head! I'm gonna kill ya!" I heard more bustling and rustling, and then a bunch of light flooded the tunnel as Dingo kicked out several bales in order to get out quick, and to also give Peachy a good thrashing. Unfortunately, this caused a good part of the fort to collapse on top of Dingo. I got buried too, but not so bad as Dingo.

I kicked my way out, coughing and choking on all the hay-dust. Peachy was standing on top of bales grinning like a lunatic. From down below a pile of fallen and busted bales we could hear Dingo coughing and yelling, "Get me out of here! Get me out! Help, help, help me!"

"Come on, you fool!" I yelled, "Help me get him out of there – he's choking!" We started to pull off hay bales and toss them aside all hel-ter-skelter, some starting to come apart as we threw them. Then, to my horror, I heard a car engine. The rest of the Wilcox family had returned home a bit early.

We dug Dingo out and he wasn't looking good. He had a big, red welt in the middle of his forehead, and he was making the kind of high-pitched wheezing sound that I had heard before, but now it was higher and shriller. There was dark looking hay dust all over his mouth and around his nostrils. "We gotta get him out of here," said Peachy, in a matter-of-fact way.

We almost threw Dingo down the loft ladder, nearly breaking his neck, but I went down first so I was able to break his fall. We took him by each arm and ran him, wheezing and coughing, up to the house. Mrs. Wilcox was standing at the mudroom door, and as we got closer, she put her hand over her mouth. Then she ran towards us.

"Oh, my dear Lord!" she wailed. Then she grabbed her wheezing and coughing son around his waist and ran him inside, dragging him through the mud room and in over to the kitchen deep-sink. She started running cold water into the sink, and stuck Dingo's head right under the facet. He started kicking and gurgling, and I swear, a bunch of dirty water and dirtier snot started coming out of his mouth and nose. After a few minutes of this coughing, snorting, and gurgling Dingo got some color back in his face. Me and Peachy just stood there, hoping for the best. Mrs. Wilcox told us to leave.

We said good-by to Dingo, and although he was still coughing, he waved good-by to us. When I got home, the phone was ringing. It was Peachy. Peachy let me know that he was in trouble, and that I would be in trouble, too. Peachy went on to say that we were both banned from the Wilcox farm, forever. I asked about Dingo, and Peachy said that Dingo would survive, but that we tore up the hayloft pretty good, and Mr. Wilcox and Mr. Red Cloud were both pissed off about it. I was relieved about Dingo.

When Mom got home, she was already informed of what happened. I guessed then and there that somebody blabbed to her while she was at work. It turned out to be Grandma Lundgren. After hearing my version of the story Mom made me strip down, and then she checked me all over for BB marks, like when she used to check me for wood ticks. All the while she scolded me, while clucking over the two red welts on my chest. I got grounded. I got grounded good and proper, with added chores to boot. I got grounded for the last few precious days of summer vacation. Plus, no more campouts at the Wilcox place. No more sledding down suicide hill. No more playing in the hay loft.

That night in my bedroom I heard my dad say, "That's alright son, just think about it." I looked over at his picture, but he wasn't grinning like he sometimes did. I looked up at the ceiling and thought about it. I needed to try and keep my friends safer. In thinking over the complexities of that, I decided that caring about the well-being of my friends could be a cumbersome and complex business. Well, no matter. I was going to do a better job of it. I swore to God that I would take better care of my friends. Of course, everyone in town knows what a miserable job I did of that, later.

The next day Poopy came over and helped me with my chores, and because he wanted to hear all about the gunfight. Poopy was full of news. He had started off the morning attempting to visit the Wilcox farm, but Mrs. Wilcox told him to take off, as Dingo was not taking any visitors. Then Poopy went over to the Peterson's, but Peachy was grounded, and doing chores out in the grove. Poopy was, however, able to visit with Molly.

In visiting with Molly, Poopy learned that Peachy had to saw down all the low hanging tree limbs in the grove where he had spied on the lovely Miss Shultz. Then he had to chop all the limbs up, and then stack them on the back porch. There was also talk of the Wilcox family suing the Peterson family, except that Peachy was claiming self-defense, on account of all the red BB pockmarks all along his leg. Also, BB guns had been confiscated all the way around, and Constable Benny was somehow involved. And somehow, Grandma Lundgren was involved, with something to do with getting 'these kids' to church more often. This made me remember something Mom had said to me while I was being scolded the evening before, about Grandma Lundgren maybe taking me and Aimee to church.

Me and Poopy worked all afternoon, and we got a lot done while I told Poopy my exciting version of the gunfight. We brought in sweet corn, radishes, lettuce, tomatoes, carrots, and onions. We washed them all and put them up. Poopy skedaddled before Mom got home, but Aimee ratted both of us out. Mom said there would be no visits during my grounding, period. And then, the topic of going to church came up. At first, I was very sullen about it, and offered up the argument that Sunday was Mom's only real day off, and I didn't want to discommode her. Mom said there was no problem, as Grandma Lundgren had offered to drive both me and Aimee to church. That was that. At least I would get to see Peachy, Beetle, and Molly while there, even if under tight supervision.

That Sunday, just as sure as God made little green apples, Grandma Lundgren showed up. Off we went to church. In going to church I quickly discovered something important – the pot-luck dinner after the service. Sunday's potluck was almost as good as the one they had there for Katrina's funeral.

Grandma Lundgren brought a big white tureen full of creamed peas with black pepper up from the church kitchen. There was pineapple upside down cake. I think it's Mrs. Lindquist who makes this delicious stuff, but she won't say because she's modest. There was roast ham. There was mashed potatoes and gravy. There were freshly made dinner-rolls, and there were big chunks of butter in their own white bowls all along the tables.

After having done this for a while now, I know that it's salad in the summer and pickles in the fall. But summer or fall, there's always baked beans, green beans, and peas. There is always pie, and there is always whipped cream to go with the pie. Sometimes there is chicken pot pie.

I'm not talking about those little frozen chicken pot pies. I am talking about home-made chicken pot pies in nine-inch pie pans. I'm talking about chicken pot pies made with cream and carrots and peas and celery and chicken so fresh it leaves tracks in your mashed potatoes. Also, the powers that be let me, Aimee, Peachy, Beetle and Molly all sit together at the same table. We all behaved.

Back to School

What a shock returning to school was! Our gang was diabolically divided up by the powers that be, with Peachy and Beetle going into Mr. Carlson's room, and me, Poopy and Dingo getting Miss Flieschburger's combined fifth and sixth grade classroom.

I watched the kids file into Mr. Carlson's room. All the girls were very excited, and the whole group was made up of the smarter kids who had all the good grades. Boy Scout Kurt was in there, along with Fred, Olaf, Brad, and all the other kids who were going to be in our new sixth grade band. Both Peachy and Boy Scout Kurt got clarinets. Beetle got the French horn. What was really weird was that Molly, who wouldn't be eligible for band until next year, was started on after school flute lessons given by Miss Flieschburger, who had played piccolo at St. Olaf.

Speaking of Molly, there I was at the start of my sixth-grade year with everybody else from last year's class who didn't get into Mr. Carlson's class, and a bunch of fifth graders, including Molly. Molly was quick to take a seat right next to me. Poopy and Dingo tried to sit next to me, but they got moved, with Poopy right by the door, and Dingo right up front next to Miss Flieschburger's desk. You could still see a little bit of the red welt in the middle of his forehead. It was funny.

We got handed out our textbooks, and we realized that we were getting the same math and science textbooks from last year. Miss Flieschburger explained that the year before we had only got part-way through the math and science books, and after a review, we would move on to new material. I envied Poopy, because he was able to see part of what happened in Mr. Carlson's room, including what happened in there with Mr. Carlson and Peachy. That cocky Mr. Carlson learned a thing or two about classroom management from good old Peachy.

What happened was a few days later after all the textbooks had been handed out. Mr. Carlson was giving blackboard instruction, and while he was writing on the blackboard Peachy took out a penny and flicked it at the board. Mr. Carlson turned around and said with a smile that if people wanted to throw him money, he would appreciate larger denominations. Everyone laughed. Peachy, not wanting to be up staged, pulled out a dime and flipped it in Mr. Carlson's direction. The dime sailed through the air and landed flat on Mr. Carlson's forehead, then rolled right off his nose. Everyone in the classroom broke out in really loud laughter, but Mr. Carlson didn't laugh. He lost his marbles instead.

Mr. Carlson grabbed the classroom phone hanging next to the door and called the office, yelling into the phone that he needed the principal to come down to his room right away. Then looking out over his room, Mr. Carlson realized that everyone was watching and laughing at him. Angry as all get out, he stepped out into the hallway, still yelling into the phone, and slammed the door shut. In doing so, he cut the phone cord.

Peachy had to stay after school in the principal's office. That afternoon when school let out me and Molly went over to Swenson's and got a double root beer Popsicle to slobber over. We sat together on the bench outside Swenson's and laughed our fool heads off. After finishing our popsicles, we walked back to our bikes, and Molly held my hand.

I must say that I really hated being back in school. I'm just being truthful. It was so very boring. Molly insisted on helping me with my multiplication tables, and she did show me how to understand fractions, because fractions are just simple division problems. I didn't turn in any writing assignments like book reports or Geography reports, because writing is so boring (This is different, because I'm getting five cents a page!). So, I'm sorry to say this, Miss Flieschburger, but September and October were just so painfully boring except for a few highlights.

One September highlight that I remember well was when I got Boy Scout Kurt into trouble. Our class was in the library when in trooped Mr. Carlson's class. I was minding my own business, sitting by myself at a little table. I had preemptively waived off my fellow troublemakers so I would theoretically stay out of trouble. Molly had acted like she was going to sit with me, but then she went over to talk with Miss Flieschburger.

I was reading a book about Egyptian mythology by a famous Greek historian named Plutarch when Boy Scout Kurt came over and asked about what I was looking at. He is such a goody two shoes, and he had never, ever got into trouble up to that point, so I let him sit with me. As it so happens, I had just got to the part in the book about the legend of Osiris, where Osiris had been killed by Set, who then cut Osiris into pieces and spread the pieces all over Egypt. Mr. Carlson sauntered into the library and eyeballed me and Boy Scout Kurt, but saw that we were being appropriate, so he went over to talk with Molly and Miss Flieschburger. I didn't notice the librarian lurking on the other side of the bookshelf.

Then, low and behold, me and Boy Scout Kurt got to the part of the legend where Isis, the wife of Osiris, looked all over Egypt for the bits of her unfortunate husband. We read together about how Isis found all the bits except for her husband's thingy. Boy Scout Kurt made this odd little snuffling sound, his face turned red, and his shoulders started shaking. This was not what I needed, but I started to giggle too, holding my giggles inside as best I could. It was then that the librarian pounced.

"What's going on here boys?"

"It's, it's the book!" stammered Boy Scout Kurt with tears running down his face.

"Osiris lost his little willy," I helpfully explained.

That did it. We both busted out laughing and laughing real hard. Mr. Carlson came swooping over and had both of us stand in a corner with our faces turned to the wall, until we could regain our composure. Boy Scout Kurt blew snot all over the corner of the wall, with snot hanging off his nose. I nearly wet my pants I was laughing so hard. We were then removed from the library and had to stand outside in the hallway until our classes came back out.

The only other real highlight as far as I'm concerned was in October when I got to read a passage from *The Arabian Nights* in front of the class. We had this activity where we had to read something from a favorite book in front of the rest of the class. I remember Molly read something from a new book one of her aunties sent her from England, called *The Incredible Journey*. The book was from England, but it was about two dogs and a cat in Canada. Canada, as far as I know, is just one big forest, so it seemed very unlikely to me that two dogs and a cat could make it hundreds of miles across Canada, so I tuned her out. But, thinking about it did make me start wondering again about where the devil Ninja Bob came from.

Then, while staring out the window and thinking about Ninja Bob, I got called on. Like I said, I read from the 1932 version of *The Arabian Nights,* translated by Sir Richard Burton. I checked it out from the town library. I read the story *How Abu Hasan Brake Wind.* Miss Flieschburger got really flustered when I got to the part about where Abu Hasan let fly a great and terrible fart during his wedding feast. Afterwards, I pointed out to Miss Flieschburger that *The Arabian Nights* was great literature, and that I had checked out the book from our very own public library. When I talked about it being great literature some of the kids laughed.

Poopy got up and read something very boring from one of the *Little House on the Prairie* books. Peachy had tried to talk him into reading the part in *Huckleberry Finn* about two boys getting shot dead along the river, but Poopy demurred. Dingo, however, did us all real proud, by reading *The Face on the Barroom Floor*.

The next day I got in trouble with the Art teacher, because I tried to copy Picasso nudes that were in a book about Picasso that I found in the school library in the Art section, which is one of my favorite sections. All this tells me something about the serious study of fine art and great literature in elementary school.

But September and October weren't all bad, don't get me wrong. While school was very boring, me and Aimee were still going to church, and I was getting used to the Methodist Hymnal. I memorized The Lord's Prayer and the Blessed Trinity song too. But even now I still don't understand how the Blessed Trinity works in theory.

We got to go to the Octoberfest. There were big tents set up, there were brats, and a big beer garden for the adults. There was a big merry-go-round with a very loud organ right in the middle of the thing. Me and Poopy went into the side show but none of the other kids were allowed to go in, because all their parents said that it wasn't appropriate. Me and Poopy saw a fat lady, a bearded lady, and an alligator lady. When we got back out, we joined the others on the grass and listened to a polka band.

While we were sitting there Aimee and Mary joined us. Right after they joined us some strange looking folks started to walk towards us. They all had on full head masks that made them look like old men and women, and they walked towards us as a group in a weird slow gait. Aimee raised her hands in the air and shouted at them to go away. As a group they turned away and headed off to the beer garden. I looked at Aimee and suddenly she had changed gears. She was all smiles and clapping along to the polka music. No one else seemed to notice.

I really, really got used to the potluck dinners after church services were over. I remember towards Halloween I heard music coming from the church office down the hallway. I was helping to clean up after one especially good potluck. It was something by a guy named Liszt called *Totentanz*. I liked it, and still do.

Finally, Halloween rolled around, and a little bit of fun to go with it. We got to make paper ghosts and pumpkins and witches and put them up all over the classroom. While we were cutting out pumpkins from orange construction paper Molly mentioned that she and Grandma Lundgren had taken Bernard over to the vet because Bernard had cut his paw on something. A little alarm bell went off in my head, but I ignored it. I told myself that the missing cat notice had probably been taken off the vet's bulletin board a long time ago.

That afternoon me and Poopy hauled down my scarecrow from his cross in the garden. The scarecrow's job was done, so we decided to tie it on to my bike and give it a ride down the hill. It went great, and we laughed and laughed, until the darn thing veered into the Gutzman driveway and crashed there, scaring the pee right out of the two little Gutzman kids who were playing in their front yard. We had to run down the hill and get my bike and scarecrow while Mrs. Gutzman yelled at us. After that Poopy rode his bike home, lickety-split, but there were no phone calls, and our parents were none the wiser. At least Mrs. Gutzman knows the difference between joyfully creative play, and outright malice.

That night me and Aimee went trick or treating with Poopy and his sisters. Aimee had thought ahead and made a witch hat in school using felt and construction paper. Before sunset I rode my bike over to the five and dime where I bought one of those cheap little black face masks with one hard earned dime. I borrowed the black knit hat from Ninja Bob's sleeping mat in the basement and made myself out to be a burglar. Me and Aimee told Mom we'd be careful, and that we would be going around with Poopy and his sisters.

Poopy showed up as a devil. His sisters appeared as a ballerina, a fairy princess, and a pixie, in that order, but as far as I was concerned, they all looked like little ballerinas wearing winter coats. Outside the Lutheran Church we ran into The Beetle, and Peachy and Molly. Peachy and Molly were traditional ghosts wearing white sheets with eyeholes. I told them they looked lame. Molly lifted her sheet. She had on her snow pants on underneath, so I guess they were being warm, and practical, because this was one of the coldest Halloweens I can remember. The Beetle was wearing a Superman outfit over his union-suit, which did indeed make him look a bit bulkier. But he looked ridiculous neverthe-less, because he's scrawny and he wears glasses. But he did go flying over the handlebars of his bike like Superman, so I guess there's some kind of connection, somehow.

After we spent time laughing at each other we had to split back up, because Grandma Lundgren was driving The Beetle, Peachy and Molly around, I don't know why. After we all got tired of lugging around our bulging candy bags, we went back to Poopy's, where he and his sisters showed us their new living accommodations at Alighieri's Pizza.

The whole family was, and is, crammed into three small rooms upstairs with just one little bathroom. On my first visit there they did at least have a table and chairs next to two big windows overlooking Main Street. In the spirit of Halloween, me, Poopy and Aimee played with a Ouija board while Poopy's sisters pretended they were all ballerinas and put on a dance show. The words and letters we got out of the Ouija board didn't make any sense.

"Who are you?"

"*ECI*"

"Are you a ghost?"

"*ON*"

"Why are you here?"

"*DAD*"

"What do you want?"

"*TAC*"

Me and Aimee got bored, and it was time to leave, anyway. On the way home Aimee told me that playing on the Ouija board had felt weird to her because her fingers had moved by themselves without her consciously moving them herself. I just rolled my eyes.

We got back home with our stash of loot and then sat on the living room floor and traded candy. When it was time for bed I went down to the basement and replaced Ninja Bob's hat on his sleeping mat. I called for him from the basement door, and Ninja Bob came bounding right in. I'm sure he was feeling cold. I thought about reading up about Ouija boards in the encyclopedia, but I was feeling bushed, so I said 'good night' to Ninja Bob and hit the hay.

Probation

About two weeks later I got home from school and was surprised and concerned to see Constable Benny's truck in our driveway. I tried to think really hard about any trouble that I might have gotten into that was worth a visit from Constable Benny and came up with a big fat zero. Then, I remembered the little alarm bell that had gone off in my head when Molly had told me that she and her Grandma Lundgren had gone to the vet.

I went in through the kitchen door and Constable Benny and Mom were both sitting at the kitchen table smoking cigarettes. Mom looked up at me and said, "Constable Benny wants to talk to you about your cat." I felt sick to my stomach.

"I didn't steal him! He just showed up one night," I said, almost sobbing.

"Son, I just want to take a look at him," replied Constable Benny.

"I don't know if he's in or not, but we can go down and check," I said, not remembering the last time I had let Ninja Bob in or out. We went down to the basement and Ninja Bob was nowhere around.

Constable Benny went over to Ninja Bob's sleeping mat and picked up the black knit hat. "Where did this come from, son?" asked Constable Benny.

"I got it over by the new highway. The Peterson's dog found it, and I took it because my ears were cold."

"Mind if I borrow it son? It may have belonged to someone else, along with your cat. Her name is Ivy Carp, that girl who went missing last year," said Constable Benny, with a sad look on his face.

"It's OK with me. But I honestly don't know where Ninja Bob is. But if we can't find this Ivy Carp girl then I should be Ninja Bob's foster parent, because I've been taking care of him, and I've got him shots and medical treatment and everything," I blurted out.

Constable Benny left with the hat, and I ran up to my room and bawled my eyes out. But then I calmed myself down and remembered that Constable Benny didn't say anything about me *not* being a foster parent to my cat. I went down to the basement and called out for Ninja Bob. He wasn't around, but his food bowl was almost empty, so he had been around sometime earlier, and I started to sort of remember letting him out the day before. It was cold out there, so I started to worry a bit. I called for him again, but he didn't show up.

To take my mind off my worries I decided to hit the encyclopedias and read up about Ouija boards. When I opened to the page and started reading Dad's voice came out all high-pitched and squeaky. Then, suddenly, this horrible rotten egg smell came right out of the volume. I snapped the book shut and shoved it back into the bookcase. I was in no mood for hallucinations. No, not at all, not at all.

I went to bed after thinking I could handle any old hallucination, even a smelly one. I also, remembered that Ninja Bob often stayed gone for a few days at a time. I reckoned I knew where he probably was, and that I'd go looking for him after school over at Firefly Field and the Hoot Owl Barn.

After school I peddled my bike over to Firefly Field. It was darn cold for mid-November. The sky was cold gray and there was a wind. I could see my breath. I got a way towards the field but then quickly turned around. Constable Benny's truck was parked in front of the Hoot Owl Barn, and right next to Constable Benny's truck was Mr. Red Cloud's new, old fire department dispatch jeep. The jeep was Army surplus, and it had been painted fire engine red. I thought it was cool that a guy named Red Cloud was now driving around town in a bright red jeep.

Constable Benny was leaning against his truck, smoking a cigarette and looking up into the air. He didn't notice me, and I got home as fast as I could. I went downstairs and called for Ninja Bob, but he wasn't around. Now I was worried. I put a small cardboard box with a towel in it outside the basement door, just in case he came around in the middle of the night and needed it.

The next day before school I checked again, and Ninja Bob was nowhere around. After school I rode over to Firefly Field, and nobody was there so I poked around the field and the barn and came up with nothing. I called and called. Not really wanting to give up, I biked up past Firefly Field towards the Wilcox farm on the old highway. Out of habit I checked along the side of the road for pop bottles. That's when I found Ninja Bob, way off in the ditch in some weeds.

Ninja Bob was as dead as a doornail, and frozen stiff. I didn't cry or anything. I just stood there looking at my poor old dead cat and thinking about what to do. I remember thinking, "*Well, at least he's not lost and hungry.*"

I just didn't know what to do. But for sure, I wasn't just going to leave him there in the ditch. I biked home, just as calm as you please. I got my pillowcase and biked back to the ditch. I picked him up, and he was so damn heavy it surprised me. But at least he wasn't floppy, because he was so frozen stiff.

There was no way that I was going to just throw him in the garbage, but the ground was so hard I thought I'd have a hard time burying him. I thought of our garden, because that dirt was all dug up, but that seemed wrong, too. Peddling along and thinking about Constable

Benny wanting to see my cat, I turned and started towards town. The lights were on at the fire department.

I parked my bike and knocked on the door. Mr. Red Cloud came to the door and let me in. He looked at my sack. I didn't like Mr. Red Cloud seeing me like that, but I couldn't keep my eyes from starting to tear up. I talked to Mr. Red Cloud while he sat there at his dispatch desk. While I was talking to him I noticed a little stone owl sitting there on his desk. "Do old tom cats go to Heaven?" I asked Mr. Red Cloud.

"There is a spirit in all things. I'll take care of old Jinx here in a respectful and dignified way. I liked him too, son."

"His name is Ninja Bob."

"Yes."

Then he gave me the little stone owl and told me I needed it more than he did. He took Ninja Bob while I was looking at the owl, and then came back with the empty pillowcase. "Keep the little owl for luck," he said.

Mr. Red Cloud told me he would call Constable Benny and tell him about Ninja Bob. Then he told me to come back in a few days and he would explain more about my cat's funeral. I went back home. The house was cold when I got home, and Mom told me there was a problem with the furnace, and that we would be using an electric heater for a few days until she could afford to get the furnace fixed. She didn't even notice my pillowcase.

I went down to the basement, and it was cold down there. I picked up Ninja Bob's mat and threw it into the washing machine. I threw my pillowcase into the washing machine, too. I took the box that was outside the door, took out the towel, threw the towel into the washing machine, and used the box to carry Ninja Bob's food and water bowls to the trash burn-barrel and threw it all in. I dumped Ninja Bob's litter box onto the ground and threw the little box into the burn-barrel. I went back upstairs and told Mom I wasn't feeling well, and that I was going to bed. Mom said there was an extra blanket on my bed, and that she'd try to get back home early from work.

A few days later I went to the fire station after school. Constable Benny's International Harvester was there. I knocked on the door and

Mr. Red Cloud let me in. Constable Benny was sitting at the dispatch desk smoking a cigarette. There was a cigar box sitting on the desk. Mr. Red Cloud told me that Ninja Bob's ashes were in the cigar box. Mr. Red Cloud told me to scatter the ashes at any place I thought was appropriate. I told Mr. Red Cloud I would have to think about it, but I would take the ashes home with me for the time being. Constable Benny just sat there looking at me and smoking. He didn't say a word. I went back home with Ninja Bob's ashes. It was only then that I told Mom and Aimee about Ninja Bob.

The next day I talked to Poopy about the ashes when he came over to the house. I asked him if he wanted to come with me to scatter Ninja Bob's ashes across Firefly Field. Poopy looked at me in a funny way, and then asked if he could borrow my old red wagon, the one that I had used to take Ninja Bob to the vet with. I asked him why, and he said that it was a surprise, but to wait about the ashes until he could return with the wagon.

On Saturday Poopy and Dingo showed up at the house. Dingo wasn't really supposed to be hanging out with me, but he had lied to his folks, telling them that he was just going to hang out with Poopy. What they had in the wagon was this big rock they had lifted off of the little hill with the Witch Trees next to our old camping spot. They asked me to look at it. They said that if I looked at it in just the right way, that it looked like a big, fat, sleeping cat. They called it Cat Rock.

With the cigar box under my arm, we three went to Firefly Field. We all three of us kicked a dent into the frozen ground with our boot heels, and then dumped the ashes out of the cigar box into the dent. We then gently placed Cat Rock over the ashes. While we were placing the rock Constable Benny pulled up in his old International Harvester. "What you boys up to?" He called out. Poopy ran over to the truck and started blabbing his mouth off. Constable Benny got out of his truck.

"Eric, you're not supposed to be here," he said. I looked at him thunderstruck. "Technically, this is Wilcox property," Constable Benny said. "You're not supposed to be on Wilcox property." I stood there with the cigar box under my arm, thinking about Firefly Field and the Hoot Owl Barn, thinking about the falling stars, the swooping bats, and the darting whippoorwills. Tears started to roll down my cheeks.

Dingo walked over to the truck. My short tempered, asthmatic buddy, who is not the sharpest tack in the box, walked right up to Constable Benny. With his shoulders back and his chin up he said, "This is hallowed ground. I always thought someone could come and visit a grave no matter what. If I promise not to hang around with Cruds, that should be enough. He should be able to come over here and pay his respects whenever he wants."

Constable Benny looked at me, and then at the cigar box under my arm. "OK, I'll give you boys some space for now, for your service or your ritual or whatever it is you want to call it," he said. Then he got into his truck and drove off.

That night I lay in bed on my freshly washed pillowcase, laying there and thinking about my cat. I remembered the day he laid that dead bird on my pillow. I remembered about how he started grooming my head on that very pillow when I got poison ivy so bad at Nightcrawler Lake. Even my scalp had got crusty, and Ninja Bob had started grooming my head. Then I started thinking about Ivy Carp before falling fast asleep. Where had I seen something about Carp?

The next day, feeling very glum indeed, I rode my bike over to the Methodist Church to look at the church graveyard again. I found the Carp gravestone and looked at it for a while. There weren't any Carps that I knew of in town, and I wondered what had become of them.

On the way back from the graveyard I noticed one of the church basement windows was just slightly open. There weren't any cars in the parking lot, so I decided sneak into the church through the window. I knew there were canned sweat potatoes in the basement pantry, I knew we were due for a rather slim Thanksgiving at home because of the furnace, and I reckoned that nobody would miss a few cans of sweat potatoes. I got caught down there in the church basement red handed, by Mr. Portman, who had a key and had walked to church that morning to do something or the other.

I was held in the church my Mr. Portman until Constable Benny showed up. He had put on his official Constable shirt, so I knew I was in bad trouble. At least he had the heater on in his truck. Constable Benny didn't say a word to me. He just rolled down his window a bit and smoked a cigarette while he drove me home. I was very ashamed of myself.

Me and Mom had to go down to the fire station a few days later where a juvenile court was held by a juvenile judge up from the Arrowhead County Courthouse. Some fire department guys had set these hard and uncomfortable folding chairs in a few rows, and they all hung around, too. I recognized some of them from church.

A table was set up front with the American Flag and the Minnesota Flag on either side. The judge was sitting at the table. I had to sit next to Mom. Mr. Wilcox was there, and so was Mr. Red Cloud. Both Mr. Wilcox and Mr. Red Cloud just stared at me. Constable Benny and Reverend Leverkuehn were there, too, and Mr. Portman, the guy who caught me. Grandma Lundgren showed up just before the judge started things and sat next to Constable Benny and started whispering in his ear to beat the band. She was whispering so fast that she made this little hissing sound.

I just sat there, so very ashamed. I didn't say anything until the judge asked me if I did it, and I told him yes. When the judge asked me why I did it, I told him that I'm just a kid who gets into trouble, and that I saw the window was part open, and that I just wanted to explore around while the church was empty. Mom sat there and stared straight ahead, without looking at me.

The judge gave me probation, which meant I had to start doing chores at the church after school and on weekends. I would have to shovel snow, once the snow started, and in the meantime, I had to pick up branches and twigs from the side yard, vacuum the whole big common room, change out the vacuum bag, empty all the wastepaper baskets in the whole place, take out the trash, and put the hymnals back in place in all the pews after services. The chores went on and on, and I wasn't even a real Methodist.

Blood on the Ice

It was Sunday and Mom's day off. She was sitting at the kitchen table smoking Lucky Strikes and listening to the radio. She told me she didn't know how many more Sunday's she would have off, because she was quitting the Old Kountry Kitchen and going to work at Alighieri's Pizza. I wasn't really listening to her talk about changing jobs because I had my own misery.

I was pretty much off limits for everybody, because I was getting into so much trouble. I was still in school with the guys, and I was still in church with some of them, but I wasn't allowed to sit with them, not even during church potluck dinners anymore. That being said, I still lived above the Swamp, and that's where we play hockey. I heard a bunch of yelling, went out, looked down, and there they all were, sweeping away the hoar frost on the Swamp with a mismatched collection of brooms. I asked Mom if I could go down and join them. Absentmindedly, Mom told me to be careful, and to report when I came back in, with no tricks. She always says that now because of what I did a couple of years ago.

One winter day back then I came in after playing hockey and Mom was in the kitchen making meat loaf. I grabbed raw hamburger out of the bowl and stuck some under my bottom lip. When she asked me how the hockey game went, I told her that I got hit in the mouth, and when she turned around, I pulled out my lower lip and the hamburger dropped out of my mouth and went splat on the linoleum floor. Mom fainted dead away and hit her head on the edge of the stove on her way down. From that day forward I always had to give an accurate report, with no kidding allowed, after coming off the ice. Anyway, she seemed to forget my off-limits status, so I hot footed out of the kitchen and down to the basement.

I got on my skates and kind of skated down the hill to the Swamp. I asked the guys if it was OK for me to play. Peachy said that they weren't supposed to hang out with me, but that if I played goalie, they wouldn't really be playing that close to me, at least most of the time. This seemed to be a suitable compromise. I set myself up, and we all had fun until I caught a hockey puck in the forehead, along with a skate blade. That really rang my bells, I'll tell you what.

I went all black for a moment, and the next thing I knew I was laying on the ice. I pushed myself up on my elbows, but I was still looking down. There was blood on the ice, and I could see down into the ice. I was right over the spot where an old raft that we had made years ago had gone under.

We had built the thing with a mast and sail made from a pole and white canvas we stole from a construction site. When the wind hit the sail just right, the whole thing would turn over. After getting good and waterlogged, our badly made raft finally sunk, and we had all swum to shore. Staring down into the ice I could make out the raft just barely down there, just dimly down there. I could make out the mast, with the canvas wrapped around it. It looked like a shroud around a body down there. There was ringing in my ears.

The guys all rushed around me. I remember Peachy saying that I was bleeding a lot, and that they better get me to a doctor. I put my mitten up to my head and it came away all bloody. But I wasn't so much worried about the blood. I was trying to tell them what I had just realized. It was like some sort of vision.

"She's down there under the ice," I stammered. "The Booger Lady is down there under the ice!"

"We gotta get him to a doctor," exclaimed Poopy. "He's been knocked coo-coo."

My friends half carried, half drug me off the ice and up the hill to the kitchen door of my house. They didn't even knock, they just dragged me in. Mom was sitting at the kitchen table smoking a cigarette and thinking about changing jobs. She looked at what the boys had drug in and fainted right there at the table. She put another good knot on her head, almost as big as the one she got a few years before.

A Reckoning

Having friends is just as important as having children, I think. And you can start having friends a lot earlier in your life then when you can start having children. Just before Christmas Vacation my friends and I all had a breathless huddle on the school playground. Some of us were not supposed to be hanging out with others of us, but during recess what are they going to do?

I explained the different threads of my thoughts and suspicions about the whereabouts of Ivy Carp. I explained why I thought she was somewhere in Night Crawler Lake. Both Dingo and Poopy thought I was as crazy as a ****house rat, but Peachy saw the opportunity for a nice, risky and naughty adventure, and so he glommed onto the idea.

On 21 December, just a few days before Christmas, Molly, Peachy and I headed out for our last trip to Night Crawler Lake. December 21st is the darkest day of the year, and it always will be. Nothing can change that, not now, not ever

Beetle and Dingo played at Dingo's house as a distraction, because me and Peachy were not allowed anywhere on Wilcox property. Poopy, who was supposed to be the lookout at the start of the trail to the lake, was sicker than a dog with a sore throat, so he stayed home.

Peachy and Molly showed up wearing their white sheets from Halloween, but with head-holes so that they both looked like they were wearing white capes. "It's for camouflage," asserted Peachy. Me, I was dressed all in dark winter clothes, and I felt so very stupid. We were going out on a frost covered lake, after all.

We got a late start on the trail because we spent so much time ducking into the woods every time we heard a car approaching on our way down the road to the Wilcox farm. We had to be extra careful because Chief Wilcox, Constable Benny, and Mr. Red Cloud were all driving around delivering food baskets and checking on old folks who lived alone in town. We then used up even more time when we stumbled through the woods rather than walking up the farm lane to the Witch Trees, and our old camping spot. I was getting nervous, because the light was starting to go. It seemed to me that Peachy was just sort of playing and wasn't serious about sweeping at least part of the lake. But, of course, we did get out there.

We got over the fence. No longer worried about being seen, we trooped down the trail like a team of soldiers, carrying our brooms on our shoulders like rifles. The naked tree branches overhead looked like clutching claws. There wasn't any wind to speak of, but every time a little breeze skittered past us the trees would creak and groan. We got to the lake, and it was indeed covered by hoar frost. The bow of the old boat was sticking up out of the ice, with a bunch of frozen cattails just in front of it. We all gave it a wide birth, especially me. I didn't want to spy a dead carp under the ice. Peachy started to nonchalantly sweep the frozen lake a few steps out past the boat, and I was having none of it. He was just playing. I headed out towards the middle of the lake without saying a word.

Molly trotted along, just behind me. It was starting to get dusky. Peachy called out, "Hey, guys, we don't know how thick the ice is out there!" I got mad, spun around, and gave him the 'shush' sign, and continued to trot out, with Molly catching up with me.

Peachy decided that the ice must be good enough, because we weren't dropping through, and he became more enthusiastic. He eventually got ahead of us and started sweeping away. I asked Molly to start sweeping next to him, with me next to her.

"We are gonna have to leave pretty soon," said Peachy.

"But we just got here," protested Molly.

Me, I just got on with it, sweeping and looking down, sweeping and looking down. It was me who called it off, because I stopped being able to see the bottom. At first, I could still see weeds, but then after a few more yards, nothing but gray ice, with little frozen bubbles. Besides, it had become twilight. After I told them I was done and I had turned around, that's when we heard the truck engine.

When the old International Harvester came bumping over the hill with its headlights on, at first, I thought it was Constable Benny's truck, and I just stood there. Peachy on the other hand yelled "Scatter!" and him and Molly took off to my right. Still staring at the damned truck, I realized it was Old Man Durr's, and I started running for the woods. Light beams from the truck headlights seemed to follow me, then something burning hot hit my back as I heard the shot.

I kept running, but my chest hurt, and black salty gunk was coming up my throat and making me cough. It was thick and sticky, and it smelled like iron. It was blood. I slipped and fell down hard on the ice. The headlights swung away from me, and then I heard a load crashing sound, and screaming.

I struggled to my feet and kept running, not looking back. The headlight beams suddenly went straight up into the sky like searchlights. I hit the woods. I was coughing up blood, phlegm, and snot all over the front of my jacket. I stumbled along. Further down the darkening trail

I hung on to a tree. I stumbled forward some more. Up ahead I saw lights. I needed help bad, so I ran for the lights. I hit the ever present and malignant fence and twirled right over it. I landed on my back, and I've never been hurt so bad. The headlights were there at the old fence lane, and I panicked. What if it was Old Man Durr? But I couldn't get up. I just laid there and looked up.

Mr. Red Cloud was there with his fire department jeep, and he had both The Beetle and Dingo with him. Mr. Red Cloud, as it turned out, had become suspicious, and he thought that something fishy was going on. I looked at them all just standing there looking at me, and then I passed out.

Arrowhead County Hospital

I woke up in the hospital with my back all bandaged up. The first thing I noticed was my hospital bed smelled like freshly ironed sheets. My back hurt bad. I would have never believed one BB could do so much harm and damage.

My bed was next to the wall, so at least I didn't have anyone on that side of me. But I was next to two big double doors with an overhead exit light that stayed on all night. All the way at the other end of the ward was a nurse's desk. There was a little Christmas tree on the desk with little sparkling lights, next to one of those green-shaded library desk lamps. The nurses took turns sitting at the desk, even in the middle of the night. They all wore little white nurse hats, and I imagined them as Dutch girls.

Across from me were big high windows, with long green curtains that the nurse on duty would close, sometimes during the day, but most of the time at night. Further down across the aisle were more beds and nightstands, but there were no beds across from me, just a clicking and clanking radiator underneath the window and curtains. The radiator would tick and clunk all night long. One night the nurse on duty didn't pull the curtains all the way shut, and the moon shown through. I was awake and just looking at the moonbeams when Dad stepped out from behind the curtain.

The nurse on duty just kept reading her book by the little desk light. Dad didn't say anything to me. He just stood there smiling. He was wearing the same gray suit as in his picture in my bedroom. Moonbeams slanted right through him. He smiled, I nodded my head, and then he just turned into sparkling moonbeams.

The next day I was really sick with a bad sore throat they called the strep. Mom came to see me, and she held my hand and cried. She said Aimee couldn't come to see me because I had the strep. I tried to tell her that that was OK, but I couldn't talk, because my throat hurt so much. A doctor and nurse came by, and they changed my bandage while Mom was sitting there, and they told her that back was looking better, and my lung was doing well, but the strep was something they were watching very closely.

After Mom left a nurse pulled the curtains shut even though it was still daytime outside, I suppose to help with my nappy-bye time. She gave me some nasty tasting and smelling medicine. I got some kind of shot, too, because I was running a fever again. I slept and then woke up, and Molly was standing in one of the half-open exit doors. Sometimes they would leave one of the doors half open to push the meal cart through.

Molly had on a blue dress, and she was wearing her black church shoes with white socks. Her legs were smooth and shiny. She had her hair pulled back in pigtails, with a blue ribbon on one side and a red ribbon on the other, I guess because it was Christmas. She didn't walk in or say anything, I supposed because of my strep. I gave her a little wave, and she gave me a little wave back, and then she turned and left.

Mom came by for the next few days. When Aimee came along, I knew I must be getting better, and I was right. I was eating ice cream and drinking broth, and I could talk. I asked Mom how everyone else was doing, and Mom said we could talk all about everything when I got home. It was when I got home the next day that Mom told me about Molly's funeral. She sat there by my bed when she told me, and I didn't say anything. Mom kept looking at me and I just looked back at her. Finally, I told her that I felt really tired and that I just wanted to sleep. Mom left the room, and I fell asleep thinking that Mom must be confused.

Later that day Poopy came to visit. Mom came back to my room and told me I had a visitor, and it was Poopy. I told Mom I was very happy to see him, and Mom said she would come back if I needed her. Poopy told me about how the truck had crashed through the ice, about how Peachy and Molly had both gone in, and Old Man Durr too. Molly had gone under the ice and drowned. Poopy told me about how Constable Benny had the fire department pulled the truck out of the water, and about how it was then they found the body of poor Ivy Carp near where they pulled out the truck. Poor Ivy had been wrapped in canvas and weighted down with chains. I think what happened to Old Man Durr might be called irony, except I'm not sure what irony really means.

Poopy told me that they had arrested both Old Man Durr and his brother. Poopy also said that the cops were looking for the tramp we called Hobo Joe. I told Poopy about Molly's visit to me in the hospital, and Poopy said, "Oh, fiddlesticks. Ghosts are no more real than dreams are real. Molly's dead. I feel bad about it, Cruds, but she's dead."

It was then that it sunk in, and I started crying. Poopy cried, too. The day after Poopy's visit Reverend Leverkuehn dropped by. I had just finished having that awful green stuff squirted down my throat so I could actually talk a little. That was when the good Reverend told me he had worked out the deal with Constable Benny and Mrs. Flieshburger with this writing assignment. So here I am now, just about done with writing all this down. It has taken me well past Spring Vacation, but that's alright, because it's kept change in my pocket.

Aimee came to see me a couple of times while I was in my room, mostly to bring me soup, but also to try and cheer me up.

She told me about how the Peterson's were leaving town because Peachy had a nervous breakdown. The news did not cheer me up. She saw the look on my face, so she rattled on about how my other friends were still getting into trouble even without me and Peachy around to help.

She told me about Dingo's Bomber (the old toboggan, now all souped up), and how Dingo, The Beetle and Poopy had a huge wreck. The Bomber went farther than any sled, flying saucer or other toboggan in all of known history. It hit the bump just right and was still in the air when it flew through the gate opening. It tore up right to the edge of the gully and didn't stop there. Aimee said that it was going so fast that it sailed over the gully, almost. The Beetle knocked out a front tooth, and Dingo's right thumb got bent all the way back, so it looked extremely gross when it happened, and that Poopy broke his right arm. She said this really pissed off Poopy's special teacher because he writes with his right hand.

This all did make me laugh a little bit. Then Aimee held my hand and said I shouldn't be sad about Molly, because Molly was in Heaven along with Ninja Bob. I told Aimee not to be ridiculous, because Molly never hung out with Ninja Bob. Aimee said that she dreamed of them both in Heaven together. I asked her what Heaven looked like, and she said it looked like Firefly Field, except with a lot more flowers. I've thought about Aimee's dream, and I reckon that everything is something else, besides.

When I finally got back into Miss Flieschburger's class, Poopy and Dingo were both in casts. They both ran up and hugged me, which was very un-manly. Miss Flieshburger's eyes got wet, and I don't think it was because she was glad to see me. In class Poopy told me and Dingo that some old guys eating pizza at Poopy's pizza joint said whoever killed poor Ivy just dumped her body through a hole in the ice. I don't reckon I'll know about that anytime soon.

I'm taking pills now for both my heart and because of the voices and visions and stuff. I know the medicine is working. The last time I looked up anything in the encyclopedia I just heard my very own voice in my head, not my father's voice.

A Shared Popsicle

I was having a dream. I knew I was dreaming. It wasn't one of those Booger Lady nightmares, but Ivy Carp was there, just the same. She looked like a full color version of her black and white missing poster self, the one I saw in the store last year. I realized she looked a lot like Aimee, only older.

She was half sitting, half laying there in Firefly Field. It was sunny, in a late afternoon sort of way. It wasn't the real Firefly Field, because the Hoot Owl Barn behind her wasn't as dilapidated looking as it really is, and there were a lot more flowers than there really are. She was wearing a long dress, and she had wildflowers in her brown hair. She was smiling at me. She said, "Nice work, little brother. Well done."

Then something moved off to her side. Ninja Bob's big head parted the long grass, just like he used to do. He had both his eyes, and the sunlight made his green eyes look beautiful. I woke up.

Aimee had told me about her stupid dream, and now I just had a stupid dream because of her stupid suggestion, and how it worked on my mind. But my dream didn't have Molly in it, just poor Ivy Carp and my good old cat. The foot of my bed felt warm. I called out for Ninja Bob. Of course, he wasn't there.

I carefully eased back my covers and put my hand on the part of the blanket where he used to sleep. It felt the same temperature as the rest of the covers, but I caught a whiff of dry leaves and hay. I looked under my bed. There were only dust bunnies under there. I sat back down on my bed and pulled in the memory of the dream and held it tight so it would never go away.

It was ten o'clock in the morning. I had really slept in. My mouth was all chewed up inside for some reason. After holding on to my dream I needed to get out of my room and into the sunshine. Mom was waiting for me in the kitchen. She was sitting at the table smoking.

"The police called, Eric. Constable Benny is coming over to see you."

"Yes ma'am."

"I'll get you breakfast," said Mom, getting up.

"I'm not hungry. I just want to sit outside in the sun," I told her.

I excused myself and went outside. Once I got outside, I didn't feel all that much down. It was so nice and warm and sunny. I sat down outside on the back steps to soak up some sun, and then my stomach just dropped. I was expecting Constable Benny, but a cop car was pulling into the driveway.

Then I realized it was an Arrowhead County sheriff's car. It was an older model, with one of those bubblegum machines on the roof. Out stepped Constable Benny. He had on a new County Mountie hat, and he was wearing aviator sunglasses. His full uniform was pressed, with creases in the shirt and the trousers. His shoes were black and glossy. I noticed his pot belly wasn't as big as I remembered it during the winter. They had sent the new, improved Constable Benny to interrogate me some more, I guessed. I looked down at my shoes. He sat down on the steps next to me. I didn't look at him.

"I've had a busy day, so far," said Constable Benny.

"Sorry, sir," was all I could muster.

"Eric, I thought you should know they think they've got the guy that killed the little girl we found in Klammer Lake."

"Was it old man Durr?"

"Nope, it wasn't him that killed *her*. But he's in pickle too, you betcha. Since he was arrested, we've found another body in the lake. This thing's quite a mess for these parts, so I'm not going to say any more about it, but I thought I should let you know about the girl."

"Thank you, sir."

"You know, Eric, you're one good bad boy, or visa-versa."

"Latin," I said.

"That's right," agreed Constable Benny. "I'm going in to talk with your mom in private for a few minutes, Eric, but first I have to ask you for something else."

"OK," I said.

"I need that little stone owl you wrote about," said Constable Benny.

Constable Benny stood up and knocked on the kitchen door and then we both went in. While Constable Benny and Mom talked some more, I went upstairs and got the owl. I looked at it for one last time, and then carried it downstairs in my right hand. All the while walking down the stairs, I stroked its face and chest with my thumb. When I got downstairs, I just set it on the kitchen table without saying a word. I then went back outside so they could talk some more in private.

After a few minutes Constable Benny came back out. I stood up out of respect. Constable Benny patted me on the shoulder, and then walked down the steps to his old, new cop car. Before getting in he turned to me and said, "Eric, try very hard to stay out of trouble, will you do that for me please?"

"Yes sir." I replied.

"Me and the Reverend Leverkuehn have had a little talk, and your probation is done with. But we both want you to finish up that little bit of work you've been doing. Do you think you could agree to that?"

"Well, I'm not sure. I've started bussing tables over at Alighieri's Pizza," I said, without even thinking about it. "They've got a jukebox there now, and everything!"

Constable Benny gave me a little smile, then just got into his car and started backing out of the drive. It dawned on me that I was completely out of trouble. I ran up to his cop car before he got all the way out of the driveway. His window was down, and he looked at me with his eyebrows up. "I went to look at Ivy's grave," I said. What does the W stand for?"

"The W stands for Whippoorwill." he said. "Pretty name, isn't it?"

"Yes sir, it is," I replied.

Then without another word he looked over his shoulder and backed the rest of the way out of the driveway. He waved as he left, and I waved back. The wave was genuine.

The door opened behind me, and Mom stuck her head out. "Please stay out of trouble. Just allow me a bit of peace, OK?" Then she popped her head back inside. I'm no fool. I knew I had better make my escape while the getting was good. Besides, I was feeling better. My main money stash was in my bedroom, but I had a dime in my pocket. I decided to treat myself by riding down to Swenson's and breaking that dime for a jawbreaker. Not to chomp down on, just to suck on. Of course, this wasn't normal. Like I said before, I don't often spend money on a splurge.

I got there and parked my bike up against the bench. Then I sat on the bench. I just couldn't bring myself to break that dime. Besides, it felt good sitting there with the sun on my face. Then I thought about how me and Molly used to sit on that bench. I changed my mind about the jawbreaker and went in and got a root-beer flavored double Popsicle instead.

I closed my eyes real tight and pretended as hard as I could that Molly was sitting next to me. With my eyes closed I pulled off the wrapper of the Popsicle, threw the wrapper into the garbage can next to the bench, broke the Popsicle in half, and with my eyes still closed tight, handed half the Popsicle over with my right hand. There was a little puff of wind, and I felt the Popsicle stick in my right hand give a little tug, like when you get a nibble while fishing.

I kept my eyes closed tight until suddenly, I got what felt like a big, cold kiss smack on my right cheek. My eyes popped open, but for a second, I didn't dare look over to my right. I just sat there frozen. Then, my eyes clicked to the right. The Popsicle was only about half an inch from my cheek. I used my pinky finger to touch my cheek. When I looked at my pinky there was Popsicle juice on it. It was just me trying so hard to conjure Molly up that I popped myself in the face with my own Popsicle. That's it. The medicine was, and is, working just fine. I don't hear or see things that aren't there very often, anymore.

But funny as it seems, I could feel myself blushing. I looked down. My tennis shoes cycled back and forth, as if they had a mind of their own. Then I saw a shadow, and I looked up. It was The Beetle. He said that he saw me sitting on the bench and acting strange. I told him what I had been doing, as there was nothing else for it. He grinned at me with his missing tooth, and then stated that since the Popsicle wasn't licked, that he could take it off my hands. We both sat there slobbering away and laughing our fool heads off.

Beetle was around for a few days from the fancy private school he's now in. The reason The Beetle was in town was because Grandma Lundgren had laid down the law to her tight lipped and tightly wrapped church lady of a daughter. Beetle would not only get to spend unsupervised time with his old friends, but also some adult chaperoned outings (If you're reading this Mrs. Gustavsson, I'm sorry for offending you ma'am. But honestly, you shouldn't get in the way of an honest and decent friendship).

Conclusion

Writing this all down was more work than I ever thought it was going to be, but I'm done. I'm feeling pretty good, and there's only a few weeks left until summer vacation. What I mean is, I spent just about the whole darn spring doing this. But it's a nice day, and now I'm off the hook. I've got a bunch of money for the State Fair, and for the rest of the coming school year for that matter. I've pretty much managed to do all this writing on the sly without anyone really knowing except for one slip, which wasn't my fault.

The Beetle caught me a day after the Popsicle incident, before Grandma Lundgren took him back up to Mankato. He and his grandma came by the church to do something or the other, and The Beetle noticed my bike outside. I had told him that my probation was over, so he was curious. At first, he looked around outside because everybody knows I've been doing errands around the church. After he couldn't find me, he came around inside, and he spied me writing at the table in Reverend Leverkuehn's study.

He didn't do or say anything at the time, but he sure did take note of my untypical behavior. He asked me about what was going on later the same day. I told him what I was doing. It was just easier to tell him the truth rather than to lie. I also swore him to secrecy. It felt wrong to swear The Beetle to secrecy, but there was nothing else for it.

The Beetle's back up in Mankato now, and he kept his mouth shut like I knew he would. But because I'm done writing this, I'm sure Constable Benny will use it to talk about certain things with other folks. That means word will start trickling out about some of what I've written. This is only to be expected. However, I'm going to stay mum until Constable Benny tells me otherwise. I also ask none of this be shared with any kids at all, please.

In any event, I'll see The Beetle soon enough at the State Fair. We'll be getting together for the State Fair because Grandma Lundgren is going to drive me and Poopy up there for the day. She's going up there anyway, to meet some old-folk friends of hers. While we're up there we're all going to meet up with The Beetle. Then it will be corn dogs, french-fries, all washed down with ice-cold root beer. Then, God willing, we'll take rides on the rollercoaster, tilt o' whirl, and of course the Ferris wheel.

After that, when we're low on cash, we'll walk over to the Hippodrome to paw around for free stuff and watch all the pretty girls stroll by in their shorts and tennis shoes. I'm hoping that somehow Peachy shows up, but I just don't know, because no one is talking about his nervous breakdown. Dingo is out of the picture as the Wilcox family is moving to Florida, and the Wilcox farm is being sold. Mr. Wilcox says he can better enjoy his Navy retirement and his new-found wealth in Florida. I shall miss Dingo.

People say that Mr. Wilcox made a lot of money because the farm is going to be turned into some kind of new housing development. People say that Mr. Wilcox used some of that money to pay for numerous medical bills. I'm sure of that. People also say that a new housing development will be good for the town. I'm not so sure of that.

Before the State Fair trip, I'm supposed to go to the Mayo Clinic so they can run more tests. Mom and Grandma Lundgren and Reverend Leverkuehn say it's about my ear and my heart, and it's also about making sure the medicine is working so I don't hear bells when no bells are ringing and see things that aren't really there. They're going to get my heart checked, because sometimes I still run out of breath in ways that I didn't used to. It doesn't matter to me, if the tests and stuff don't take too much time.

To tell the truth I would like to get my ear fixed, as sounds are still muffled in my left ear. I notice it most when I watch TV. If I watch straight ahead, things sound fine. But if I turn my head to the right, the sound comes in muffled. As far as my heart goes, I'm here to tell you that my heart works just fine.

Now that I'm done with everything, I can go anywhere I want today. I could go over to Alighieri's Pizza and make money. Mom's started to help in the kitchen, besides waiting tables. She can spin pizza dough over her head! I could go and hang out at the fire station and talk to Mr. Red Cloud. Mr. Red Cloud has become something of a local celebrity ever since they figured out that his little hooch in the woods had been dug out right next to an old Indian burial mound.

I'll get around to talking with him sometime today, I'm sure. But I've decided that what I'm really going to do first thing today is to take a sunny bike ride over to Firefly Field. I'm going to go over there, sit in the shade on some soft grass near Cat Rock, and spend time with my cat.

The End

www.ingramcontent.com/pod-product-compliance
Lightning Source LLC
Chambersburg PA
CBHW051642260626
47170CB00004B/1287